THE MESSENGER

May this be a pleasant journey!

Louees Broer

THE MESSENGER

A Challenge of Faith

DONALD BROCK

iUniverse, Inc.
New York Lincoln Shanghai

THE MESSENGER
A Challenge of Faith

All Rights Reserved © 2004 by Donald Brock

No part of this book may be reproduced or transmitted in any form or by any means, graphic, electronic, or mechanical, including photocopying, recording, taping, or by any information storage retrieval system, without the written permission of the publisher.

iUniverse, Inc.

For information address:
iUniverse, Inc.
2021 Pine Lake Road, Suite 100
Lincoln, NE 68512
www.iuniverse.com

ISBN: 0-595-30731-0

Printed in the United States of America

Contents

Chapter 1	ROME, JULY	1
Chapter 2		8
Chapter 3	DETROIT, JULY	12
Chapter 4		22
Chapter 5		31
Chapter 6		33
Chapter 7		38
Chapter 8	ROME	40
Chapter 9		43
Chapter 10	DETROIT	53
Chapter 11		57
Chapter 12		65
Chapter 13		74
Chapter 14		83
Chapter 15	ROME	87
Chapter 16		95
Chapter 17	DETROIT	98
Chapter 18		108
Chapter 19	SOMEWHERE IN TURKEY	114
Chapter 20	DETROIT	118
Chapter 21		125
Chapter 22		139

Chapter 23 145
Chapter 24 156
Chapter 25 160
Chapter 26 170
Chapter 27 176
Chapter 28 183

CHAPTER 1

ROME, JULY

Pope John Alexander wearily responded to the knock on his door, "No one today. Please, I will be alone."

From beyond the door in Hungarian, his native language, "It is I, Janos. We must talk."

"Not today, my friend."

"It's about the Prefect of Police, Inspector Stella. He is here. He wishes to interview about Marie, about her death from your window."

John Alexander placed a bookmark in the small book of Hungarian poetry he was reading, thoughtfully recalling the face of the poet he had known when they were both young men. This poet had sought refuge from the turmoil had sought forgiveness for forsaking the barricades of Budapest during the revolution in 1956 and fleeing to Oslo.

Now he, the Pope of Rome, like the Hungarian poet Sulyok, sought both refuge for the moment and forgiveness for his failure in the tragic affair of the young housekeeper, Marie.

He placed the book on the light stand and slowly raised his six feet frame from the reading chair.

With a sigh of resignation, he opened the door slightly and continuing in Hungarian affirmed, "Of course," gesturing with an open right hand extended. "Are they waiting?"

Monsignor Janos Majee filled the space of the slightly opened door. His face did not show his full dismay at viewing the unnaturally unkempt appearance of Pope John Alexander. The usually well groomed gray speckled black hair of the pope was in need of combing. A black stubble beard of two days marred his swarthy face and surrounded his dark lifeless eyes. The death of Marie had stolen the bright adventure from his eyes. He thought, his personal pride would not have allowed this condition unless he were ill, at least not in the fifty years he had known this friend, now pope.

"You have not shaved. That is not like you."

Pope John Alexander dismissed his friend's observation with a 'so what' motion of his hand. "I am preoccupied."

"Commandant Raymond has called. They await your answer in his office, at your convenience."

He took a deep tired breath. I'm afraid that I do not have much more to tell him." Pointing to his wrinkled shirt, he continued, "I will wash and dress. Have Raymond escort him here in twenty, no, thirty minutes."

Rome, this Wednesday morning of July, was unusually warm. Large groups of visitors gathered at the gate of the convention hall adjacent to St. Peter's Cathedral. The heat radiated from the cement of the square as a moist clinging vapor. No breeze wafted in the square. Men in shirtsleeves, carrying their suit coats, wiped their sweaty foreheads. The crowd slowly increased in numbers as the tourist buses sequentially emptied their eager passengers at the end of Via della Conciliazione. This was the day they were to reach the high point of their visit, of their pilgrimage, to Rome. This would be a memorable day in their life because this was their delayed celebration of the millennium, a year of the rebirth of the church, a continued celebration of the Jubilee, the Holy Year. They were here to visit the home of their faith culminating in a general audience, to see the personage and hear the message of their pope, the new Pope John Alexander.

The hum and murmurs grew within the crowd. Those closest to the entrance gate had read the notice posted on the gate in several languages. The news spread quickly throughout the milling crowd.

The audience with the pope had been canceled.

The word passed from one to the other with utterances of disappointment and frequent comments of discontent. "He must be ill" was commonly heard or "some emergency" had occurred. The crowd grew to fill the corner of St. Peter's square as a large milling beehive of conversation. Their unhappiness was accentuated by their personal discomfort produced by the heat, humidity and crush of the bodies of the crowd.

The great celebration of the millennium had been disrupted by the declining health of the previous pope. The ravages of the culmination of the assassination attempt twenty years previously, the multiple abdominal surgeries and the progressive assault of Parkinson's disease first on his physical well-being and finally attacking his mental agility had finally immobilized this giant of a man.

During the latter years, his shuffling gait, his apparent lack of strength had presented a declining physical appearance. His spirit, heart and determination however, were dominant as his public appearances persisted to thrill the masses. His travels continued to amaze his associates and the world as he completed over a hundred national and international ecclesiastic and evangelical visits spreading his commitment to social justice and peace fostering national and political attitudes of human dignity.

This indomitable spirit and determination had ground to a crawl during the great celebration year of the millennium. His public appearances before the public throngs at St. Peter's square continued at his insistence. With assistance, clasping his cross as support before him, he had appeared at the podium and at his window, and silently blessed the cheering one and a quarter million pilgrims that had crowded Rome during that year. He had insisted on appearing personally at the opening, the breaking through and disassembly, of the sacred doors on the seven cathedrals at the beginning of the great holy year. His dream of traversing the path of Abraham, the city of the conversion of Paul and the path of the life, death and resurrection of Jesus during the holy year of the millennium had been only partially fulfilled because of this physical decline. Neither his physical decline nor the political turmoil of Israel, however, could deny his triumphant visit to this holy place during the first year of the millennium.

Even now, the celebration of the year of the millennium continued. The world came to see the new pope, to pass through each of the seven sacred portals, to renew their faith in the marble evidence of the history of their religion.

The murmurs and discussion of the cancellation of the pope's audience were everywhere.

"You never know about these popes. Half of them seem too old to do the job. The old pope wouldn't have canceled the audience. He'd have seen us come hell or high water. Wish I had been here then."

"Well, this new pope, Pope John Alexander is only sixty eight. They don't come much younger generally. Must be some emergency. He looked well Sunday afternoon."

The gathering crowd was one of the numerous over-subscribed audiences this year. Even this year, years after the millennium, the Great Jubilee, the year declared to be the celebration of the rebirth of the church the numbers were large. The number of general audiences had been increased to accommodate even as the previous years had been the greatest tourist crush in history. The vitality of the church was proclaimed as evidenced by the great numbers making this historical pilgrimage to Rome, the home of the church. Despite such proclamations, the dissension within the church, the divisions within the church at all levels threatened to tear the basic fabric of the church structure. The great economic depression in the world only accentuated the pressures on the church.

Around the corner from St. Peters and up the hill in the Vatican, Pope John Alexander, the now vestige of Peter of our time, sat again before the open window reading a book. The prefect of Vatican police had left having fulfilled the obligation of his office. A delicate warm breeze passed across the new screen in the window. His sallow eyes looked up from the book to the trees in the courtyard outside the sitting room. With a deep sigh of fatigue, he turned to the coffee service and poured another cup of the strong pungent coffee that reminded him of his home, Hungary, that reminded him of the city of his birth, Gyongyos. This moment offered a fragment of refuge from this entrapped world in which he found himself. He returned to the book. The poems in the book of Tibor Tollas of his beloved and traumatic youth matched his troubled mind and soul that tottered on the brink of despair.

He, himself, had avoided being sent to the prisons at Vac or Tatabanya during the occupation and revolution. The poets, however were imprisoned for what they thought, occasionally for what they did or what they wrote, like Tibor Tollas, imprisoned for what he thought and wrote. "Twenty Cherries" he had written leading to the words "when God's richness breaks in the face of man" to "as if dreams were waiting for man." John Alexander reproached himself as a long felt guilt that he had never been imprisoned in those terrible days of the revolution but today he felt as tragically entrapped, not in his body but in his soul.

He lay the book on his lap and stared out the window, the actual and symbolically tragic window, with it's newly replaced screen. He had declared a day of privacy.

He was not to be bothered further. There was to be no business to attend to. The calendar was to be cleared. He was sorry. The ambassador from Germany could be rescheduled. Someone else could receive the officer from the Bank of Geneva. Such a visit usually meant a generous disposition to the church of a will of a deceased account. Someone else could receive this generosity.

This was one of the few days in the clerical life of Pope John Alexander of 54 years that he had denied himself sharing in his daily orders.

The occurrence had not been with intent but one of omission.

His fast had now lasted three days. It was a fast of liquids only. On learning of the fast at the end of the second day, Cardinal Vittorio had summoned Dr. Marcus to visit the pope.

In their privacy, the doctor had listened to his friend and patient as he took his blood pressure, "your blood pressure is good" and listened to his heart and lungs, "and your lungs are clear."

"Why must you do this, Daniel?" He called him by his given name as he had all the years of their life. The new pope had come to Rome the previous fall when the College of Cardinals had selected him over his protest to follow the beloved Polish pope.

Marcus was one of the few Hungarians to accompany the new pope to Rome. There were the two priests to assist him who had come with him and, of course, there had been Anna the long time housekeeper who had begged to continue in his service.

"I grieve, Marcus. I have failed Him. I am alone."

"But, how long? You are healthy and strong but no longer young. Do not bear this more than a few days, my friend." He rolled down the shirt sleeve after taking the blood pressure cuff off. "You better take care," he had continued with a forced smile, "or I'll have your nose at racquetball next Monday."

"In your ear, Marcus," John Alexander quipped in a halfhearted attempt to match his friend's challenge.

"Well, I'll be sending up an order of vitamins and supplement. Surely, you'll take them? And don't forget your daily medication," he had concluded.

"We'll see. We'll see. Now leave me. I don't feel like chatter or backgammon tonight."

He had felt a moment of refreshment in the relaxed discourse in his own familiar language with his long life friend and physician. His isolation in his difficult Italian and among the many Polish speaking Vaticans was accentuated in these moments. His fluency in French, Spanish and English were not much refuge. His adequacy in German, Russian and Slavic exceeded his Italian, although his clerical Latin had improved. His native Hungarian was always a quiet refuge.

In this, he had been grateful that Anna had insisted on continuing in his service. She was very insistent in her own way in many ways and her company was always appreciated as they conversed in their native Hungarian, much to the unspoken displeasure of others in attendance who knew not of what they spoke.

As he sat there slumped in the chair, a tear formed at each eye and ran down each cheek to disappear in the gray-black stubble of beard of three days. He was a tall man and a well developed physical individual in good health. He had always believed in the old tale of sound body, sound mind. He had no paunch. At six feet even, his 192 pounds presented a pleasing appearance. He stood before the window in his stocking feet. The newly adorned white collarless shirt contrasted with the wrinkled trousers. He raised his hands to the light of the sky and the trees. "Oh, Father. How could I have failed You."

He turned and approached the small altar at the end of the room. He lit a candle at the side. There were three now, one for each day of the fast. He kneeled before the altar. The shadow of the polished wooden cross above flickered from the light of the candles. He clasped his hands at the rail as his head slowly cushioned on his hands. No one was there to hear the sobbing of Pope John Alexander. No words were spoken. No prayers were heard. A light sweat, with small beads of perspiration, formed on the bald crown area of his head. Finally, he rose from the altar. He wiped each reddened cheek with his shirtsleeves.

His body felt wilted. Fatigue replaced the usual vigor he felt. His mind raced as he sought the couch. "Words have failed me to my God. I have forsaken him. Where may I turn? Oh, my soul." He sought refuge as his long body curled up on the couch with knees drawn close to his chest. As this moment of fatigue closed into sleep his thought faded, 'Poor Marie. Why did Anna insist on bringing her into this house? God, give me strength where I have fallen.'

Across the street, sixty feet from the great columns of Michelangelo that formed the periphery of St. Peter's square, in the shade of a branch of the Banco Italia, a small audience formed and reformed watching the exhortations of one of the many street preachers that had descended upon the world during the early years of this third millennium. They watched his demonstrative declarations, not understanding his urging their need for repentance of their grievous sins at this moment in time, in Italian. His message was lost upon the ears of these pilgrims whose grasp of Italian was primarily concerned with the preservation of their lira and finding their way to the ancient wonders of the city. They might have been more attentive to this olive skinned orator if they had understood that the proclamation that he himself was the new Peter and that he alone, in this momentous time of the millennium, would lead them to salvation as the earth disappeared into some dark hole of the universe. Of course, if they had understood him, they may have believed he was a prophet who had wandered in from the desert. Instead, they shook their heads and moved on, believing a shave with a bath and a clean drape cloth to cover his body was obviously his greatest need.

CHAPTER 2

Cardinal Vittorio's frown and severe countenance reflected the discussion. "The press is becoming very restless. His Holiness has had the mysterious so-called virus for too long. The story is becoming tiresome and they are beginning to ask questions."

"It has been four days now and I am concerned for his health," countered Monsignor Janos Majee. "He refuses to see even me. I have spent most of my years with him. I am one he chose to accompany him from Hungary."

"He has not taken the power given to him. His plan is not understood yet. We still fill his office. He has no schedule."

Majee responded, "He has never been a man of power. He felt the office spoke for him. He has always been a man of the people.

"He has written continually these six months the message of humility and profound desire for unity, reconciliation in the early years of the millennium, reconciliation with God and with the neighbor, on the part of both individuals and communities.

"The millennium is the time of learning and understanding, resolution of prejudices, he has written. Surely you who have chosen him recognized this in the process of his selection.

"He is not the recluse. If the six hundred here cannot come forth and rally and give life to the diverse but common church in example, how can you expect the eight hundred million Catholic faithful in the world to rally forth?

"He has received your response to the formation of the Pontifical Council of the Third Millennium and awaits your recommendation for appointments to the committees. He has established the pilgrimage that John Paul was not able to completely fulfill the last year of the millennium to visit the holy land in

September, to walk the path of St. Paul, to Damascus the place of his conversion, Mt. Sinai, to recall the journey of Moses out of Egypt and the holy places of Jerusalem."

In spite of Majee's elaboration, a voice from the end of the table barely audible protested, "He is a pigeon resting in his nest, waiting to be served. He does not wish to be one of us."

Majee could feel the undercurrent of resentment that an Italian had once again not been elected pope. He reflected on the process that had failed to again place an Italian at the head of the church. John Paul had indirectly chosen his successor. The one hundred nineteen voting cardinals were primarily people he had selected. He had selected all but eleven of the consistatory. The conclave had lasted eight days, twice as long as the four days of the longest session to elect pope and under the new rules set down by John Paul, the Italians would have had to wait out the twelfth day when only a simple majority would have been necessary to elect their choice instead of the traditional two-thirds of the voting cardinals.

Majee bristled at this overt disdain of his beloved pope and friend. "It is you who have elected him." He looked to the three cardinals who sat at the table, indicating these three of the eight in conference at the table. "It is you who have abandoned him in these early days. You have failed his writings and directives because of your attitude."

"You forget your place here," he was remanded starkly.

Monsignor Majee was forthright in his response. "I do not forget my duty to my pope. He knows that his election was the end of a long and difficult decision. He knows that he is not a favorite within this house. He knows that the Italian and Polish did not hold him as a favorite. I can assure you that his Italian has improved and that he has understood some of your derisive comments. But, he will not respond in kind to you." There was a long pause. Such a chastisement direct or indirect had seldom occurred. He continued, "And, as you can see, my Italian is more than sufficient. You seem to forget his last New Years Eve message. His message of joy of the year, the year of jubilation. A Jubilee Year of reconciliation and social justice concepts to the whole of humanity was seen and heard by radio and television by over a hundred million people throughout the world.

"As I have said, already the plans for September are well under way to fulfill Pope John Paul's dream to walk the path of Abraham, Moses of Egypt and Mount Sinai and revisit Damascus, the city of the conversion of St. Paul.

"It is his ecumenism and vitality that you have not embraced. You are the ones sitting in the pigeon's nest. He has spoken over the delays in achieving agreement with the Patriarch to accompany him. He still awaits the arrangement of the Rabbis and members of the Knesset to meet in Jerusalem. I assure you, he may pick up the phone himself."

"To be sure, I can be, will be, his eyes and his ears." He paused again as he felt he was going further than need be.

The silence at the table was now interrupted by words and utterances of agreement that indeed his Italian was proficient. As he seemed to be the center of attraction at that moment, he continued in a more supplicant manner.

"My friend and teacher is greatly disturbed at these times. He is not at rest. We have not shared an evening cigar and brandy in many days as we had previously. His only relief has been his weekly racquetball with Dr. Marcus. As you know from his last letter to the council of Bishops of the United States, he is very disturbed by the affairs in North America. The increased acceptance of euthanasia, the sins against the children, and the resurgence of abortion there even by many of the professed trouble him greatly. And now the death here of the housekeeper Marie has distressed him very personally."

"Yes, it is true. Is he to deal with those of the bishops there who have signed the non-position paper on the question of euthanasia?"

"He feels the loss of faith in America is greater than these signs.

"He has recently expressed great concern for the general conditions brought about by the prolonged world wide economic recession. He feels this has accentuated the moral problems in North America, France and even in this country."

Cardinal Vittorio asserted, "Bringing the woman Marie into this house was a mistake. Security has asked many questions regarding his relationship with this Marie. It has been many years that the nonreligious have been responsible for the personal care of the pope. It was his personal decision and this is what has become of it."

Monsignor Majee again felt assaulted in the name of his friend. He remanded his response. "It has all been so unfortunate. I, of course, was there serving as his holiness' interpreter in the discussions with the security. They examined the second story window from where she had fallen." He did not relate that Pope John Alexander had not been forthcoming about the events of that moment during that investigation except to the fact that he was the one who had notified the secretary to call the security and physicians because there had been an accident. This had all been duly recorded in the police report. But the monsignor was deeply disturbed. He had commonly been his friend's confessor. He had not been called to see him for this or any other reason since several days before Marie's death. He feared not only for his friend's health but for his very soul.

The priests finished the last of the wine and coffee and left the room.

Monsignor Majee sat in contemplation. He was in great conflict. What he knew and what he did not know about his friend and teacher's personal problem at this moment left great doubt and left many questions unanswered. He had not had further conversation with John Alexander since the papal police had visited. Only Anna had been to see John Alexander daily, except for Dr. Marcus as his physician, to relate news as to his well being.

Anna was allowed to spend a few moments each day to arrange the affairs of the pope's personal rooms. She only would relate that he had not shaved in this week's time except to receive the prefect of police and appeared to wear the same trousers and white collarless shirt each day. Sobbingly she related, he had cried, as she did, when Marie's name was mentioned and that he did not desire to carry on any conversation even in his beloved native Hungarian. Dr. Marcus was only allowed in to see him because he demanded to see after his health. But he would not discuss their mutual friend except that Majee press him to cease this fast.

He made his way to the pope's quarters and knocked firmly on the door.

"Yes?" eventually came the query in Hungarian from behind the door.

"It is Janos, my friend. Let us talk."

After a few moments the answer returned. "No, perhaps tomorrow."

CHAPTER 3

DETROIT, JULY

The solitary bicycle rider left his new residence behind and headed toward Forest Avenue.

He avoided the youngsters playing rollerblade hockey on the asphalt residential street enjoying their summer vacation from school. He pedaled slowly. A slight sweat moistened his brow and ran down his small gray speckled black beard. The warmth of the July morning accumulated on the nape of his neck below his shoulder length hair.

Two blocks to the south was Forest Avenue and then two blocks to the left was Bush Park.

In all his travels, each city, large or small, had its variety of parks where local residents could find nature's quiet and friendly conversation.

He would seek this quiet and hopefully friendly conversation for this was the essence of his life. Only among people could his mission be fulfilled.

The park on the south side of Forest Avenue was a series of intertwining asphalt walks coursing between a wooded area of maple and oak trees. The green foliage provided a cool shading of the partially grassy areas. Several park picnic benches were interspersed. This July was already warm at mid morning.

Daniel Adams sought the shade of the trees as he toured his new neighborhood on his bicycle. Beyond the trees, the neighborhood boys were already busy with their form of baseball where nine or ten boys could make up their own rules of play.

Nearby, two mothers were busy with their infant and preschool children setting up their things on a shaded picnic table.

The trees on the sides of the sidewalk formed an arch at the top over the sidewalk as their branches met at the top.

Adjacent to the sidewalk, under this umbrella, three small tables had been set up and seven or eight men were sitting about.

The men were mostly elderly, appearing to be retired. Four were paired off, busy at some endeavor at two of the tables.

Daniel redirected his wandering toward this area. Where people were was the place of his work. He stopped his bicycle at the paired players. They were playing checkers.

"You're new here, I guess," one of the older men in jeans and a blue striped shirt asserted. "My name is Charles. Play chess?" he continued, leaning back in the gray kitchen chair that needed painting.

"Why, yes. Just moved here. Call me Daniel," he replied. He rested his bike against a tree and extended his hand in greeting to Charles. "I'm no expert at chess but I would be pleased to play a match with you."

"Have a seat," Charles agreed pointing to the upright canvas backed folding type picnic chair on the opposite side of the table.

"It's been a while."

"Never mind. We don't play for money, just to pass the time. Anyone with a beard like yours looks like they might play chess."

Daniel stroked his short beard, black with a touch of gray streaking, as he sat down. "Do you have any time limits on moving?"

"Naw. We got all day. Till it's time to eat, that is. Don't mind talking generally while we play, either," he continued as he arranged the chess pieces on the checkered board.

Daniel contemplated the chess board. It had been many years since he had played chess. It seemed like a lifetime or more, another lifetime, another place.

"Your move, Daniel. You're white."

Daniel moved the white queen's pawn two spaces forward. "Do you fellows play here every day?"

"Most every," Charles responded watching the pawn move. "We're most retired. Don't look like you are. Laid off from work like a lot of others? This recession is hitting everybody. Everybody's looking for work."

"No. I've just begun looking for work. Are you the only one playing chess?"

"Most play checkers," Charles continued as one of the men standing by pulled up a chair to watch. "Now, Amos here, he plays backgammon. But, nobody will play with him much. He plays too fast and makes too much noise when he plays. Scares you half to death. Course, he's played since he was a kid.

These Lebanese play backgammon like our kids play checkers, even better. Eh, Amos?"

"Whatever you say, Charlie," Amos affirmed with a grin. "Just like your chess. I'd look out for him, kid. He's what you call a sleeper."

"Don't call me Charlie, Amos. You know better than that. You know my name is Charles. Charlie's my cousin and a drunk. Call me Charles. This here is Daniel."

"How do you do, Amos?"

"Pretty well, Daniel. Looks like you're doing pretty good, too. Already, you got Charles thinkin' before he moves. Not many get to him that soon," Amos continued with a big grin knowing he could rile Charles a bit.

"Never you mind how long I take. This Daniel ain't no amateur at this game, even if he ain't played in a while."

"Maybe he can just think faster than an old man, Charles," with his grin getting bigger. "You gotta good play there, Charles. Look at your bishop."

"Where do you get something cool to drink here? Do they sell beverages at the store across the street?" Daniel inquired motioning to the stores on the north side of Forest Avenue.

"Not there, Daniel. Maybe early in the morning would be okay or at the bakery next door. Nobody crosses the street to buy anything at the cafe. Besides, they only have machines for soda now and that costs too much. We generally bring our own thermos and maybe a sandwich for lunch." Charles pointed to his lunch bucket, the same one he had carried to work each day when he worked at Dodge Main. "Like leave them alone and they leave us along, generally."

"What do you mean?"

"I forgot you're new around here. It's the kids over there, the bikers. If we bother them over there, we're just asking for trouble. You might be okay, being younger, but we would just be asking for trouble."

Daniel saw most everyone had a lunch bucket or a paper bag. Across the street, Daniel noted the lunch counter. The Star Cafe had opened for lunch. The sign hanging in the door had been turned over to indicate, "OPEN".

As Charles ceremoniously sat back in his chair and announced, "Check," a motorcycle came to a halt in front of the Star Cafe.

The roar of passage of the Harley made everyone look-up. As they watched, the young woman passenger got off. As she stood talking to the driver, she arranged her black sleeveless leather jacket and straightened her leather skirt.

Daniel observed the driver grab at the back of her skirt as she turned to enter the cafe. This was followed by a turn of the head and a smile by the woman.

"It gets pretty noisy now and then," Amos stated as a second motorcycle roared up to park in front of the cafe.

Daniel returned his attention for a moment to the chess board to respond to what Charles thought was a moment of triumph. He responded to the expected check by taking the offending bishop with a knight and quietly proclaiming, 'check'. His glance noted the slender biker had taken his cap and goggles off and had placed them on the seat of the bike. The biker's black leather jacket glistened in the sunlight and was accentuated by the silver embroidery and the star shaped epaulets on each shoulder.

Daniel was fascinated by the physique of the man that was evident through the black undershirt when he took his leather jacket off. He could see the rippling muscles gyrate the tattoos on his upper arm as he diligently polished the chrome parts of the Harley with a maroon cloth. Finally, the biker strutted into the cafe.

Charles had extricated himself from the check move and commented, "No sir, Daniel, no sense taken a chance on going over there. Your move, sonny."

Daniel surveyed the chessboard and decided a move or two would conclude the game. He could recall a similar chessboard arranged many many years ago where he had won the tournament. He could see that Charles was an accomplished, shrewd, player. In order to allow Charles to win, Daniel determined several debatable moves that would allow Charles to proceed to win. As a new comer, he did not wish to offend Charles.

"Damn, sonny. You had me on the run for a while there. Didn't think you knew how to make a mistake. Check!" he declared again.

This time Daniel did not resist losing even though the opportunity was there.

"Another match, Daniel?"

"Looks like he threw the game to you, Charles," Amos said goading Charles.

"How would you know, old man? Do they play chess at your mosque? You never play chess here. Just your noisy backgammon."

"Just never wanted to show you up, Charlie," Amos went on. "Where did you move to sonny?"

"Another game? Why, sure, Charles. I moved into a house two blocks over on Ivanhoe just the other side of Forest."

As they continued to set up the chess pieces, Daniel related, "Lucky. Got a nice room. Mrs. Erdhiem and her not too well husband were looking for a roomer. I answered their 'for rent' sign."

"That's that Jewish couple, Amos. Not many of them around here. No synagogue for them around her," Charles explained. "Sort of like you, Amos. A long way from your mosque."

"That's why we hold service at a store on East Grand Boulevard. We have over twenty families and our own Iman."

"Your own what, Amos?"

"Our own Iman. Like your priest, Charles."

"Your move, sonny."

Daniel moved his black pawn to begin his defense against Charles' attack.

"What are you, Daniel? A Jew, too, living with that Jew family?" Charles began.

Daniel paused from surveying the chessmen as his mind rapidly rattled through the history before responding thoughtfully. "I'm just a Christian, Charles."

"Are you Catholic?" Charles inquired.

"Not exactly."

"Then you must be one of those Protestants," Charles persisted with some disdain.

"Not really."

"Well, you must be something."

Daniel could see that Charles was getting a little agitated as each question was asked with increasing curtness and his questions became louder such that the other men nearby stopped to watch as the conversation began to sound like an argument, one sided to be sure. No one ever talked religion at the part. They talked of politics, maybe, but not religion.

Amos felt the rising moment of irritation and interjected, "We're just a fine economical group here," smiling and holding his hands out in supplication.

"Ecumenical, not economical, old man. What would you know about it anyway?" Turning back to Daniel, "You're probably some Jew and don't want to admit it, sonny, with that beard. Probably have a skull cap in your pocket, too," Charles persisted now standing behind his chair.

A crowd had now gathered about the group of three engaged in the rising conversation.

Amos again interjected, "Now we're all too old to be getting into this, getting worked up like this. We've never had such disagreements before."

"Not before sonny showed up here. There's something funny about him. Isn't there, Jew boy?"

Slowly, Daniel rose from his chair and addressed the gathering that now had reached over twenty men who frequented the north end of the park. "I'm very sorry to be the cause of such a conflict of words. My new friend, Charles, a superb chess player,"

This was interrupted by a growling "humph" from Charles.

Daniel continued, "feels everyone must be exactly something. Well, I am something exactly. I am a follower, a messenger, of the living Christ. I practice and am a messenger of the word of Christ and his kingdom." He raised his hands before him toward the crowd.

There was silence. They waited for his next words.

The next words were clear to all as he continued, "We are all people of the Christ, the God of all. I bring the message of peace and love from the God of the Catholic, of the Protestant, of the Jew and of the Moslem," as his gaze fell first on Charles and finally on Amos. There was a smile on his face that embraced the small gathering crowd, which now had grown to include the several women and their children.

"Peace to you, Charles," he said looking directly to Charles as he placed the tips of his fingers briefly to his forehead. "Peace to you, Amos," he repeated again and again placed the tips of his fingers briefly to his forehead. Repeating the gesture, he said to one of the women who had gathered near, "Peace to you, young lady."

"What's this thing to the forehead?" Charles inquired with a small inflection of questionable curiosity.

"That is a sign of the mense, the mind, a sign of pure thought, a mind free of thoughts of distrust, or of animosity. It is a sign used by many people through the ages, by the friends in Babylon I recall and used by some tribes who were followers of the fisherman, Jesus."

"Why do you say you bring a message?" began one of the men in the crowd.

At that moment, a series of sharp sounds came from the opposite side of the street. The head of each person in the crowd turned toward the cafe across the street.

"Gunshots," several voices uttered almost simultaneously.

"Those rotten, rowdy, no-goods," said one man from the crowd.

At that moment the two bikers ran from the store and soon were astride the maroon and silver Harley. The remaining biker appeared, backing out of the cafe, and soon was upon his bike. Following a short animated conversation between the bikers, the air was filled with the noise of the two cycles roaring off in opposite directions leaving a plume of acrid exhaust smoke at the curbside.

As the lone biker sped west, he looked toward the crowd of people now peering as a chorus of one toward the cafe and shook his left arm and fist in defiance toward them.

Daniel Adams immediately separated himself from the crowd and hurriedly crossed the street toward the cafe.

"Stay here, Daniel," shouted Charles. "There's only trouble over there."

Others called restraining comments to him as he continued on.

Daniel approached the door of the cafe rapidly as he heard the screaming and sobbing sounds of a woman. He could not see through the grimy windows. He stopped momentarily at the doorway.

The waiter or proprietor was peering around the passageway from the rear of the store.

The woman who was at one corner of the room was alternately wailing and calling out "Jeremy" as she kneeled over a prone unmoving body with her short black hair flailing the air as head shook in a 'no' 'no' fashion. Her long black skirt was blood soaked where her knees rested adjacent to Jeremy. The air was filled by the pungent irritant sharp odor of gunpowder like a prelude to the fireworks of the fourth of July.

Listening closely, the wailing almost imitated praying. Daniel approached the woman, passing by the three round tables and their sets of wire-backed chairs. "May I help?" Daniel quietly asked as he kneeled next to the woman.

The injured young man laid on his side beside the legs of the pinball machine. Blood covered the back of his denim shirtsleeve and continued to slowly pool behind him reaching the woman's skirt. His bare right arm clutched his chest.

"He's dying," she cried. "My Jeremy is dying." She held her arms up in despair. "Oh mother, Mary," her wailing continued almost to a whimper.

Daniel leaned forward, moving the boy's long blond hair now filled with blood to one side. He placed his hand at the side of Jeremy's neck and noted, "His pulse is still there. Very fast. Have faith." He gently turned Jeremy on his back to reveal at least two wounds. "Oh," Daniel began as he noted a wound near the elbow of the left upper arm that was bleeding freely, "this one we can do something about." He firmly grasped Jeremy's upper arm at first with both hands. Jeremy's arm was large and as well developed as his shoulders and required two hands to firmly compress the blood supply. This stemmed the flow of blood. At that moment the waiter appeared beside them. "Get me a kitchen towel," he instructed the waiter. "Hurry." The second wound was in the upper chest where the blood slowly oozed as though the denim shirt was a dark red sponge. Jeremy's hand, covered with blood, grasped the chain at his neck. His glazed eyes, half open, stared nowhere into the space. His lips quivered and mumbled, "Holy Mother," then drifted off as his hand fell from the blood stained cross it had held. His head fell to one side with finality.

Daniel placed his hand for a moment at the side of Jeremy's neck. There no longer was a pulse to be felt.

Valentine, with her piercing black, frightened eyes, looked to the ceiling and beyond and whispered, "Oh, Mother of God. Don't let Jeremy die."

Outside, the noise of police arriving filled the air as the sound of their piercing siren subsided. The two policemen entered through the cafe door in a rush.

The waiter, with towel in hand, motioned to the group in the corner stating, "The guy on the floor's been shot. He's probably dead."

One of the policemen stopped by the waiter to begin his report. The second policeman crossed to the corner of the room and addressed the attending pair. "How is he?" He observed Daniel's grip obstructing the flow of blood from Jeremy's arm as he placed his hand on Jeremy's neck. He then looked into one of his eyes pulling the lid fully open. "You can tell EMS to be on their way. Nothing to do here for this one. This is a homicide," he called out to his partner.

Daniel, still on his knees and still grasping the precious spot to control the bleeding of Jeremy's left arm, took Valentine's hand with his free left hand and said softly, "Let us pray." A moment of silence followed. Daniel quietly invoked, "Lord, let thy will be done. Let His will be done."

Valentine looked to Daniel as to ask, "is that all?" and began, "Hail Mary, full of grace,"

Jeremy blinked his eyes and the sallow skin of his cheeks began to pink. He remained unresponsive.

Daniel called to the waiter, "You can bring that towel here. Please tear it lengthwise."

"I thought," the waiter began.

"The towel, please. I believe the officer was mistaken."

As Daniel released his grip on Jeremy's arm, the blood began to ooze again on the slightly crusted blood. As the officer watched, Daniel quickly applied a tourniquet of the towel segment again quenching the flow of blood. The flow of blood from the chest wound had ebbed.

"You better call the EMS back. This young man needs their help."

Officer Blake looked to Daniel and Jeremy with eyes wide open in amazement. Jeremy, once thought dead, now lived.

Daniel rose in response to the policeman's request for information. Before turning to the policeman, said to Valentine, "Remember, the Christ God moves in wondrous ways." Approaching the policeman, he commented, "You must have been mistaken. He appears to be holding his own now that his arm is not bleeding."

"Oh, he was dead all right. I don't know how this happened. Well, lucky you came by," he commented as he began filling out more forms. "What's your name?"

"Daniel. Daniel Adams."

"Address?"

"6701 Ivanhoe."

"Telephone?"

"Don't have one."

"Where were you when all this happened?"

"Across the street playing chess."

"Well, we'll talk to the rest of them over there, too. What did you see?"

"I only heard the shots. When I looked up, the two motorcycles were driving away."

"Who was driving the bikes?"

"I wouldn't know. I'm new here."

"Well, the girl will know. Maybe some of your friends across the street will know something."

"I am afraid they are too frightened to admit that they saw anything of use. They are very afraid of such people."

"Same old story," the policeman related.

Daniel observed the EMS were there and were attending the injured Jeremy.

Valentine was being questioned by the second policeman.

"Jeremy. Jeremy Plodsky. We're talking about getting married."

"How did this happen?"

"The guy wanted to play the pinball machine while Jeremy was playing it. Jeremy said to wait. He was almost through with the game. The guy didn't like that so he kicked the machine, put it into tilt. Jeremy said something he didn't like so the guy shot at him. Four, five times. Hit him twice. I thought he would die."

"My partner said he was dead when he looked at him."

"Well, he was wrong, wasn't he?"

"Must have had a cardiac arrest that restarted."

"I think Mr. Adams had something to do with it," Valentine replied and glanced toward Daniel.

"Tell me about the shooter."

"He was a biker. Wore a short sleeve denim shirt. Had a brush-cut, not long hair like the others, and carried a green scratched helmet. I think the gun was in his boot. Didn't pay much attention until he became nasty."

"A few too many beers by the looks of the place here," as he pointed at the two littered tables each with a number of empty beer cans and scattered food wrappers. "Well, none of them paid their bill. They were in a big hurry to get out of here."

Valentine clung to Daniel as he began to leave. "Don't leave, Mr. Adams. What if he turns bad again? What can I do, alone?"

"The EMS will take care of him very well now."

"Where can I find you after this?"

"Ask the others across the street if I'm not there. You will do very well by yourself, Valentine. Just have faith. Peace be with you," he finally said.

Daniel left the cafe and slowly walked across the street to his new found friends who were buzzing with conjecture.

Daniel was the center of attention back at the park.

"How many were shot? Who was shot?" and various descriptive expletives. "Just those thug kids," or "What will happen next?"

"It was some unfortunate argument. One young man was shot in the chest and arm. The EMS has him stabilized. They have started an I.V. on him."

"We saw that as they carried him out."

"Who was in there?"

"Just the waiter and the young man's woman friend."

"And those two bikers and that woman," one of the checker players interjected. "Bet it was them what did it," he declared.

"Probably the one with the beard," Amos surmised. "He looked real ugly."

Daniel, although the center of attention, did not engage in the controversy. He knew who the culprit was but didn't wish to confirm Amos' observation. "Perhaps," he said. "We'll let the authorities deal with that."

Daniel motioned Amos to one side for a private conversation.

CHAPTER 4

"Thought you weren't comin' by anymore," Charles commented when Daniel showed up at the park. "It's been three days since that shootin'. Thought it might have scared you away. I'm sorry about making such a fuss with you. I can see you're a religious type fellow. You're some sort of a hero, savin' that fellow's life and all."

"No apology needed, Charles. I haven't been around because I've been working."

"You're a lucky fellow, Daniel. So many out of work now. Things are really tough. The papers call it a recession, even talk about a depression. What kind of work?"

"I had a part-time carpentry job. Built a set of built-in bookcases for a family. Mrs. Erdhiem put a notice up at her synagogue for me looking for carpentry jobs. Am to see about another job tonight. Very lucky." Daniel smiled feeling at ease among his new friends.

"Charlie's probably not really too happy to see you," Amos grinned winking at Daniel "He says you give him quite a fit at chess."

"Nonsense," countered Charles. "Nothing like good competition for a fella to keep his edge. Right, Daniel?" He nodded to Daniel to sit at the table. "I'm really glad to see you. I'm really sorry for getting after you, arguing last time. Just meeting you and everything. Arpad here was saying he was interested in what you were saying before the ruckus started across the street. You had a message or something."

"I am Arpad." The short man with thick black hair and a shock of black hair over each eye stepped forward and extended his hand. "I am the baker across the street."

Daniel received his new acquaintance with a warm extended handshake and sat down at the chess table. "Hello, Arpad."

"Yes. I would like to hear more of what you have to say. We have many discussions, really arguments, at the center about religion, politics and the border war at home."

"The center, the Hungarian Cultural Center, the other side of the river in old Delray," Amos chimed in.

"You are Hungarian?" Daniel queried.

"From Baja, a beautiful town on the Danube. Came here when I was eleven. My cousins and nephews have had to join the army back home. They are close to the border and the fighting is not far away."

"Why do they fight?"

"No one knows anymore. It's been going on for over ten years now. Some say it's the religion. Others say it's the farmland or the bauxite. It's all so crazy."

"Your move," Charles interjected.

Daniel looked up from the chess game as the late afternoon conversations of the park players were interrupted by the screaming and shouting of a woman and the cursing of a man. All eyes turned to the Star Cafe as the blond woman in leather skirt and jacket rolled on the ground just outside the front door. "Stop. Don't," could be heard shouted between screams. The biker in the black jacket appeared at the door.

The men from the game tables were now on their feet watching the events unfolding across the street.

"There they go again," proclaimed Amos. "She gets it every week or so that way."

"It happens often?" Daniel inquired.

"Every once in a while she gets a good whippin' from him."

"That's not right," Daniel stated as he moved to the curb line in front of the spectator group.

"No. Don't get involved, Daniel. This is no ones job to do 'bout it," Charles interjected.

The two women at the play area had begun gathering their children and belongings preparing to leave to avoid the disturbance.

The biker started toward the woman again. She scrambled to her feet screaming, "No more, you bastard," and ran across the street toward Daniel and the group of men.

The biker was half way across the street shouting, "Come back here, Naomi."

Daniel took a step from the curb and the woman called Naomi took refuge behind him as she protested again, "No more, Tom. No more."

The biker stopped suddenly in the middle of the street in front of Daniel, exclaiming, "Out of my way, old man."

Daniel surveyed the man who was demanding passage to reclaim his prey. He remembered the rippling muscles and physique he had seen before. He knew that physically this would be a losing cause to fight. He could hear the sobbing Naomi shielded behind him. He could feel the quiver of her fear from her closeness. It was not reasonable to attempt to fight this man. Besides, this wasn't Daniel's way.

Attempting to reason with the biker, he began, "I know I'm barely old enough to be your father, so I'm not really an old man, Thomas. Even so, I do not care to fight with you. What has this woman done to offend you?"

"None of your business."

"It's everyone's business to help each other."

"Well, you're not this sister's keeper. So, out of the way."

"Leave this be Tom and I'll come."

"You'll come, anyway, bitch," the biker replied and struck Daniel across the face with the back of his hand.

Daniel was stunned by the blow and his vision became blurry as tears began to well in his eyes. Through the slightly hazed thinking, Daniel gathered the strength to respond. "Please leave us now. I don't intend to fight you."

"That's your problem, little man. All I want is the woman," Tom stated. As Naomi was shrieking, "No, No", Tom struck Daniel again with his fist to the side of his head.

Daniel fell to his knees with the thought that this man actually did wish to hurt him. With his strength he could have easily thrown Daniel aside to reach the woman. Daniel had been beaten before. Being beaten, physically injured or humiliated was not new to him. He gathered all his will and strength together and slowly regained his feet. His vision was blurred because his brain and thoughts were hurt and blurred. Tom, standing before him, was a hazy vision. His brush cut blond hair formed a fuzzy out cropping above crooked eyes and mustache. Naomi's voice was distantly heard to say, "now, see what you've done?"

Tom was responding, "Look what he done to my hand. I think he broke a bone in my hand." With this he stepped forward and threw Daniel to the ground. He was surprised as the crowd of men moved forward as a group to surround the fallen Daniel on the curb."

Daniel's limp form lay at the curbside. Red welts had begun to appear on his left cheek and temple. There was a small pool of blood forming that spread from his head adjacent to the curb next to his head. He did not respond to Charles who was pleading for him to, "Say something, Daniel. Say something."

Naomi looked up as the roar of the motorcycle leaving momentarily broke her concern for Daniel.

"Better not move him none. He may have hurt his neck," Amos asserted. "Someone better call 911."

The commotion must have already alerted someone. At that moment, a police car arrived. The officers made their way through the crowd that had gathered about Daniel.

The officer kneeled beside Daniel who was still unresponsive. He obviously was alive because from the movement of his chest it was evident that he was breathing. As the officer took Daniel's wrist to feel his pulse, Daniel began to pull his arm away.

"What happened here?"

"The biker beat him up," voices from the crowd replied. "The one with stars on his leather jacket," someone said.

"Well, trouble seems to follow this fellow around. Isn't he the one who was at the shooting across the street the other day? Daniel something, Isn't it? Better call EMS."

"Better lay still, fella. The EMS wagon will be here in a few minutes." The officer began to make out his report. "The injured man's name is Daniel? Daniel what?"

"Daniel Adams," Charles said.

"Who did this to him? Anyone know?"

The crowd was quieter now. They had retreated from fear of involvement, fear of retaliation.

"Damn fool," Amos said. "He shouldn't have gotten in the way of that biker."

"Well, he wasn't going to let him beat up that woman," Charles informed Amos.

"Anyone know the name of the biker?"

"Tom," Naomi said. She was still kneeling beside Daniel who was still not moving. "Tom White," she continued and stood up to face the officer.

"You must be the biker's friend the way you're dressed. Looks like you could use some ice on that cheek of yours. He hit you? This Tom White fellow or did the fellow on the ground, this Daniel Adams fellow, hit you?"

"Well, it wasn't Daniel Adams."

"You're sort of little to be knockin around. This biker your old man?"

"He isn't anymore. I'm old enough. I can take care of myself."

"Officer Blake will be taking down names, addresses, and statements, as you can see," nodding to his officer partner.

The ambulance van proceeded in measured haste. The siren blared to the sky as the van moved rapidly through and around the Friday homebound rush traffic. The weaving and turning of the van caused Naomi to hold tightly to the side seat of the van. She wasn't sure whether the excitement of the encounter or the ship like weaving and turning of the enclosed van was causing her nausea. She was sure she would throw-up. She held the ice pack to her bruised face. She held tight to the seat with her other hand, as the black leather skirt was slippery on the van seat. Daniel lay strapped to the cart in the van. She could not see his head as his neck and head were encased in a plastic restraint system to prevent any damage to the neck and spinal cord. The technician had begun an intravenous and was taking Daniel's blood pressure again. A green blanket covered him. His feet could be seen to move with irregular twitching under the blanket. After recording the blood pressure, the technician examined Daniel's head and eyes with a small flashlight. Shaking his head, he called through the window to the driver, "He's in bad shape, Elmer. His pupils are dilated and don't respond. He's a bad head injury."

"Call his vitals in to St. John so they know what to expect," Elmer called back.

"It's all my fault. Hurry," Naomi pleaded.

"It may be too late, lady."

"It can't be."

"He may never wake up by the looks of it."

"No. It wasn't his fault. He has to be better."

The emergency van backed into the emergency room entrance of St. John Hospital. Daniel was wheeled into the emergency room on the gurney.

"Another one for you," the technician told the ER triage nurse. "Only a head. Was in a fight. Struck his head on the curb." He handed the transit papers to the nurse.

An aide placed an identification bracelet on Daniel's wrist as he was transferred to a hospital cart.

"Sign for that neck brace," the technician asked. "We'll pick it up next run."

"Take him to critical care. Watch his breathing. May have to tube him," the triage nurse instructed. "Stop at x-ray and get a head and neck scan. Neurosurgery consult will meet him there."

Naomi sat in the corner of the room in intensive care. Daniel was the center of an array of tethers that extended from his body. There were tethers to the electrocardiogram recorder at one corner adjacent to the head of the bed. There were tethers to two intravenous containers hanging at the opposite side of the head of the bed with their regulating boxes dispensing fluids at a predetermined regular rate. Each box blinked a red flashing number indicating the rate of flow. The head restraint had been removed as no cervical damage had been detected by x-ray. Daniel's head seemed fixed in position by the tubing that led from his mouth to the respirator that now breathed for him. The rhythmic pulsing of the respirator haunted the silence of the room and the light. The dancing lines of the electrocardiogram tracing decorated the dimmed light of the room.

"Too bad," the nurse said to Naomi. "Are you his wife?"

"Just a friend," she replied. She looked away from the nurse who was staring at her. She felt uncomfortable in the leather skirt and vest top. She turned her right shoulder out of view of the nurse to hide the butterfly tattoo.

"Too bad. Dr. Solari didn't think it would do any good to operate," she continued. "Such a nice looking young man. Did the doctor talk to you?"

"Yes. He said it appeared hopeless. Said he could relieve some pressure from the bleeding if he operated, but there was too much brain damage where he couldn't operate. He would see him again in the morning."

"Are you going to stay all night?"

"I think so."

"Some friend to do that."

"It was my fault. He kept me from being beat up. He has to get better."

"You can stay on a couch in the lounge or,"

"I'll stay here, OK?"

"I'll get you a blanket."

Naomi stared at Daniel lying quietly in bed. The sound of the respirator, a monotonous mechanical repetition, lulled her to sleep. It was after eleven when her own sobbing awakened her. The sudden realization emerged that everyone, the doctors and nurses, were convinced that Daniel would not get better. That Daniel would die! A subconscious realization. She was surprised by a commotion at the nurses' station. The conversation was accompanied by directions toward Daniel's room. Finally a nurse ushered an elderly man in a gray waistcoat to the room. Leaving him there she said, "Just a few minutes."

"Hello," he said holding his cap nervously in front of him in his hand. "I'm Amos. I was at the park. How is Daniel?"

Naomi began to sob. "It's all my fault. I don't want him to die."

Amos stood in disbelief. His face became red with the blush extending to his balding head. Tears welled in his eyes as his hands grasped his ears. "I don't want to hear that. I didn't know it could be that bad." He approached Daniel. Tears flowed freely down his cheeks. "He was such a quiet, nice man. No hope?" he asked looking at Naomi.

She shook her head with the blond curls flouncing about and raised her hands indicating her despair.

Amos' shoulders slumped as he stood at the bedside. He turned to leave the room slowly shaking his head on the way out.

Naomi stared after him in numb despair. It seemed rather automatic for Naomi to think of Tom White. Her association had been so close for so long that the relationship and conflict were difficult to subconsciously separate. Consciously, she knew he was responsible for Daniel's injuries. Subconsciously, she knew Tom would be blamed for Daniel's condition. Accordingly, she automatically sought a telephone to call him.

"Tom."

"Where are you, bitch?"

"At the hospital."

"What are you doing there? You're not hurt."

"Not this time. And never again, Tom. It's not me. It's that man you hurt. He's going to die. The police have already been here twice to check on him. They're looking for you. They talk about possible murder if he dies and they're looking for you."

"Who told them? You?"

"Oh, everybody knows. Everybody saw you."

"I didn't hit him that hard. I just threw him down. It was his fault. It was your fault. He's a strange one."

"And he hit his head on the curb," she finished his sentence and began to sob.

"What are you crying about?"

"I don't know. I don't want him to die. I don't want you to go to jail. I don't know," she finished with a weak sobbing cry of despair. She hung up the phone. She sat in the phone booth with her head leaning against the wall and clutched her purse bag to her stomach. She felt like curling up in a ball, to be far away from all this. She had nowhere to go. She could only return to the flat she shared with Tom White. But she had no way but the bus to get there.

Saturday morning, six a.m., Dr. Solari appeared at the intensive care department. On looking at Daniel, it was startling apparent that improvement had occurred. The respirator was no longer attached to support his breathing. Although still apparently unconscious, regular movements of his arms were present and appeared purposeful as he rearranged the blanket himself. "How can this be?" Solari asked quietly to himself. "How can this be?" Solari repeated aloud. "This can't be. I examined the scan myself."

He approached Daniel. He examined his eyes. "Impossible," he exclaimed. "His pupils are down and react." He examined his reflexes. Where the reflexes of the extremities had been clonic and tight now they were in normal range.

"Were you here all night?" He addressed Naomi.

"She nodded her head.

"Who took the intubation out?"

"He did, himself, a little while ago."

Solari shook his head in slow amazement. "Well. Can't deny the improvement. I've never seen anything like this. We should repeat the scan. The edema should be less at least. I just don't understand this. I want Dr. Packwood to take a look at him. Doesn't make sense."

The three doctors gathered around the sets of scans placed on the viewing screen. Each set was a series of x-ray images of the scans of Daniel Adams' head and brain setting silently with the fluorescent light shining through telling their story in shades of gray, black and white. To the left was the set of scans taken Friday night. To the right was the set taken Saturday morning, fourteen hours later. The radiologist was pointing from one set to the other comparing the findings. "The area of hemorrhage at the base and left parietal area are clear here with the adjacent haziness of brain damage yesterday. The same areas here today are free of hemorrhage. There is still considerable edema but no demonstrable brain damage evident today."

"This doesn't make sense. Are you sure these are the correct films?"

"No question, Charles. Didn't you say he was improved today?"

"Sure. But hematomas don't clear up overnight. Let's go back and take a look at him."

Dr. Solari led Dr. Packwood, the senior neurologist, to intensive care. Each was silent in contemplation of this serious conflict in their knowledge and experience in such cases as Daniel Adams represented and the recognition of the reality of what was really happening in this case.

Naomi was standing at the bedside clasping Daniel's hand. "He says he's hungry and would like something to wash his face," she announced to the two doctors as they entered the cubicle.

The two stopped, looked quizzically at each other. "The truth is hard to believe sometimes, Charles," Packwood said quietly. "Doesn't look like you need me here. I've got a few other patients to see and teaching rounds to make with the residents. When you figure this out, you can tell me all about it."

The nurse appeared along side Dr. Solari. "He says he would like to sit up and wash," she said as she set a wash basin on the table next to the bed.

"Looks like you're feeling better," he said to Daniel. "Let's see how everything is before we go ahead with this." He began his routine neurologic examination. The lower limb reflexes, strength and range of motion were tested. The same examination continued to the upper extremities. "Let's take a look at the eyes," he countered as he peered into the pupils and retina with the ophthalmoscope. "Everything looks fine, Mr. Adams. Now let's set up here," as he finished his examination. "No reason you can't wash up. Order this man a soft diet for starters. Make a tracing of the EKG and then disconnect the permanent leads. I'd like an electroencephalogram this afternoon, even though it's Saturday. We'll repeat the scans tonight if you can get it scheduled between the ER cases. I'm very pleased that you have shown such improvement, Mr. Adams, although I don't understand it all. We'll be moving you out of this room soon to a regular room."

Daniel had begun to wash his face and beard. "Is there any reason I can't get up? I'd like to shave and shower. No reason I can't go home as far as I can see."

"Let's repeat the test and I'll be by to see you later."

CHAPTER 5

Daniel was home again, home to the rooms that he called home. He sat on the bed in his sparse bedroom. He had been here on this new mission only a short time. His vision was still narrow. But his experience had already been daunted by very simple events. His faith had been called upon. A faith which was in no need of testing for he was here in another time and place to again bring his message.

He fell upon his knees and held his hands forward in supplication. The rain splattering against the window dulled his quiet plaint. "I'm lost here. I have called upon you and you have answered. You have been there even in my pain. Many will not understand when I return to them. I know not what to say." His voice was agitated. His body was tense. His shirt was wet with sweat.

He now remained silent. There was no voice. There was no sign. Daniel now was prostrate in prayer in silence. A calm set in. Daniel became relaxed.

He now was on his knees again.

"I fear not for I know you are with me. The throng will call for you. I will answer for you, my father.

"I know not why you have sent me in your name, but I do not walk alone."

Whereupon he fell into a deep sleep on the floor. The fatigue of the ordeal of mind, body and soul of the past several days had taken its toll.

Mrs. Erdhiem appeared at the partly opened door announcing with a light knock, "I made some black bean soup, if you would like some. It will make you feel better." There being no reply, she peeked around the door. "Mien Gott, Daniel. You should be sleeping on a bed," she announced in her pronounced syllabic accent. "And you just from the hospital," she continued. She approached Daniel to assist him to the bed. He groggily assisted her efforts to the bed. She tucked the comforter about him and stroked his head as he fell back to sleep. "How do you get into such a business?" she queried with a concerned look.

CHAPTER 6

❀

The police cruiser stopped quietly in front of a brick two flat home. The two officers approached the front doors within the brick front porch area. It was already a warm July morning at ten a.m. The sweat under the officer's arm was evident as he rang the doorbell of the door to the lower flat. The shrill bell sound filled the porch area from a partially opened porch window with each of several rings. Finally, the head of an elderly gray hired woman appeared behind the window that formed the upper half of the wooden door. As she pushed the window curtain to one side, she frowned as she glanced first to one and then the second officer. She opened the door the four or five inches that the safety chain would allow. Her head reappeared there.

"What d'ya want?" the woman's deep voice inquired.
"We're looking for a Tom White at this address, ma'am."
"He lives upstairs, rear. Him and that woman," she rasped.
"Thank you, ma'am." They turned to leave.
"Won't do you no good. He ain't there. Ain't no one up there. Heard him come stomping down those steps with those boots this morning. Saw him ride out the garage down the alley on that red motor bike."
"We need to look for ourselves."
"Don't know as that's right, him not being home."
"Well, we have to see for ourselves." The two officers turned retreating down the porch steps. They made their way along the narrow cement walkway between the side of the house and the rusted fencing of the yard. At the back of the house the walk extended to the back of the yard to a rusted metal fencing gate that led to the unpaved alleyway.

"I'll check the garage." The older officer walked through the weeds of the small back yard to look into the window of the garage. On seeing a motorcycle within the garage, he turned toward his partner with a thumbs up sign and returned to follow him up the outside stairway to the upstairs landing of the second floor. "The old lady must have been mistaken," he quietly noted.

They knocked on the door. The man in a white undershirt, beer in hand, peered out the window of the door, then opened the door part way.

"Are you Tom White?"

"He's not here."

The police officers looked at each other. The man at the door matched the description with short blond hair and mustache.

"Will you step outside, please?"

"Sure," he replied. With a rush he opened the door, brushed between the officers, vaulted over the railing of the porch, hung on the railing a brief moment, and dropped to the yard below in a rolling landing. As he scrambled to his feet running to reach the garage, the officers raced down the stairway in pursuit.

The young officer reached him with a flying tackle as he attempted to enter the side door of the garage.

Theodore White was a big man, over six foot four with a chest to match. Of course, his self importance exceeded his size. He approached the front desk of the police station with an unlit black cigar in hand that contrasted with the white dinner jacket and bow tie that he wore. "I'm T.C. White. Theodore White," he announced to the desk sergeant. "I understand my son is being held here."

Theodore White was a well-known local business and political figure in local affairs whose name opened doors. Immediate and proper attention was expected and usually received when he was involved with city affairs.

The desk sergeant rattled some papers about, looked up, informing the party clad inquirer, "Sorry to disturb your evening, Mister White. He's here again. Young Tom seems to keep you hopping, doesn't he?"

"Well, this is more serious than any of the others. There's no fixing this one, sergeant."

"Don't look like it."

"This will take some attorney work to get straightened out. Can I see him now?"

Theodore White sat in the interview room awaiting the delivery of his son. The room, in dark gray was in need of a paint job as were most of the city properties. Routine business kept the daily police world in revolving door activity that scarce attention was given to appearance. At least, daily maintenance kept the dust and debris from accumulating. He pushed aside the over flowing ashtray and lit up his cigar. He sat back in the wooden chair as he completed the cell phone call.

"Norbert," he declared to the party answering.

"I don't care if he is busy. Whatever he's doing can wait. This is T.C. White and I want to talk to him, now."

He puffed the cigar and snapped the ashes off the end onto the floor. He tapped he fingers on the soiled green table awaiting Norbert. Norbert Schmitt was a local attorney well versed in criminal activities and was not known for plea-bargaining.

"No, it's not me, Norbert, even though you wish it were. It's Thomas. He's injured some fellow in a fight and it doesn't appear the fellow will live."

"Yeah, probably a charge of manslaughter. Just a minute, they're bringing him in now. Hold on."

"What are you doing here? I didn't send for you. I don't need your help in this or anything else. Just leave me alone," Tom declared. He stood square footed and ran his hand through the brush cut. He knew the brush cut was out dated for his age group but wore it as a statement of his personal independence. "Take me out of here," he instructed the officer.

"Sit down, Thomas. This is more serious than you think," he said with a glare as he held his hand over the cell phone. "He's here now," he continued to Norbert. "Who did he hit?" He looked to the son now seated across the table. "Who did you hit? The attorney wants to know."

"Some preacher guy at the park. He was getting in my face so I pushed him down. I didn't really hit him or anything. He hit his head when he fell. Everybody could see that," he answered.

"Did you hear that, Norbert? Said it was an accident."

"Yes. He doesn't sound too apologetic."

"That's the way he is. He thinks he's always right."

"Go back to your party and leave me alone. I can take care of myself."

"Hear that? He's been that way ever since his mother left. The preacher? The one Crawford's been writing about in the *Press*?" He looked to the son who had gotten up to leave. "If this was the preacher who's been in the paper you better let me help you. This could be manslaughter and Norbert Schmitt is a pretty good lawyer."

"I don't need any Mafia lawyer."

"You will come in and represent him, Norbert?"

"Oh, he'll settle down. Of course he'll want you. He needs you."

"Thanks. We'll be waiting."

He looked to the son who was still standing prepared to leave. He looked around the room, the unkempt room in disrepair. Just like Tom, he thought, neglected by himself and neglected by his mother who had walked out on both of them. He had spent his life taking care of business, taking care all the other things that seemed important to him. He had given Thomas all that money could buy. That's what he always called him instead of Tom because Thomas was more formal and represented more of what he had expected or had hoped he would become. Two more years of college and he would come into the business with him. But college wasn't for Tom. Even a new Corvette wouldn't replace the Harley that he drove. College wasn't for Tom. The business wasn't for Tom. No place constricted in a business suit was for Tom. Of course, that was what his friends said, too. Seemed like the boy didn't have a positive view of anything. As far as he was concerned every institution in the world was corrupt and abusing taking advantage of the common people and he wanted to be considered the common people, like he felt guilty for having anything money could buy, a three floor house in Rosedale, a country club. So here he was, the rejecting son with nothing but trouble and a part time job. Couldn't remember when he saw him smile.

"Does it have to be this way, Tom?"

"It seems to be the way you want it. It's never my way."

"How would you like it to be?"

"I'd just like you to be off my back."

"I was at a wedding when I was called about this. That was nothing important compared to this, to you."

"Afraid I'd wreck your reputation?"

"Not really. Nothing like that. Look, for a lot of reasons neither of us understand, we haven't been able to see things in the same light for a long time. I have no intention of telling you how to run your life but strangers treat each other better than we do. When this problem is taken care of, and please let Schmitt see it through, let's just sit down, you and me, and have a beer together, sort of start over. Like I said, strangers treat each other better than we do."

"I'll talk to this Schmitt. About the beer, we'll see."
"Fair enough. It's your call. You have my number."

CHAPTER 7

The park was subdued. Monday afternoon was usually not too busy. A small group of men sat about the game tables. Amos had brought the disturbing news of Daniel's irreversible condition. Charles was playing a quiet game of checkers as Amos looked on.

"He was just a dumb kid," Charles allowed. "Should have known better than to be mixed up with that kind."

"He didn't deserve to die over such a thing," Amos countered.

"Never know what's going to happen anymore. I remember when such things never happened."

They were interrupted by a young woman who approached crossing the street from the Hungarian bakery that was next to the Star Cafe.

She stood uncomfortably before them. The bright eyes complimented her short black hair that hung down to her shoulders.

Charles looked up as to inquire but said nothing.

Amos spoke first. "Hello, missy. Aren't you the one was in the cafe the day of the shooting?"

The girl gathered her flowered skirt close to her. "Yes. I'm Valentine. Val Boden. I'm looking for Mr. Adams."

Amos looked at Charles and then to the ground. The other men looked away. "I'm afraid we have bad news."

"I'm looking for Mr. Adams because he saved my Jeremy's life in the shooting last week. It is a miracle and now he is all better. He's even back at work parking cars at the hotel," she related excitedly. Her face flashed a large smile of satisfaction.

"I don't think you'll ever be able to thank him personal like. He's in the hospital. Unconscious. From a fight."

Valentine Boden was not yet convinced. "But when he's better—"

"He ain't goin' to get better. Doctors figure he ain't goin' to make it, lady. Just ask Amos here."

"Fraid so," agreed Amos. "Saw him last night."

Valentine quivered as tears began to appear at her eyes. "Where is he at? What hospital? He can't die. I prayed for him at mass yesterday. I thanked God for sending him to save Jeremy's life. Arpad said, 'he was a holy man,' he thought. He said he wasn't surprised that Jeremy has gotten better. He wants him to talk, to preach, at the Hungarian Cultural Center."

"You don't understand," Amos again said as he took her gently by the arm. "I saw him last night at the hospital. Holy man or just any man, the man isn't expected to live."

Valentine broke into tears. "My prayers will be answered."

CHAPTER 8

ROME

Monsignor Majee was unaccustomed to seeing Pope John Alexander in the disarray of the moment. He was distressed at his sallow complexion behind the unshaven face. Sleep deprived gray eye sockets hung below his disheveled hair. He noted four candles now flickering at one side of the altar. "What are you doing to yourself, my friend? How can I help you?"

"I'm afraid no one can help me. I have failed my God in my weakness, in what I have failed to do and in what I have done. I have no where to turn."

Janos Majee listened to the hollow distant voice of Pope John Alexander.

"It is not possible. You must be mistaken. Are you speaking of the death of Marie?"

"Of that and more my friend."

"Surely, you don't feel responsible?"

"We will not speak of her death, Janos. But, you will attend her funeral tomorrow for me. Take Anna. See the family. See the mother."

"I will do that. The newspapers are asking questions as to why she would commit suicide as the *L'Observatore* has said."

"I know. Some how they know it was from my apartment window too."

"Probably from the family."

"Perhaps. I understand there was a note."

"Security has not delivered it to me," Majee affirmed. "They may not have had it translated yet," he added. His thoughts continued. He wasn't going to discover the cause of his friend's depressive seclusion directly from him. He would have to pursue the matter with security. "I will pursue the matter. How long are you going to continue this seclusion, this fast? Marcus is very concerned with your health."

"My physical health is the least of my concern. A little deprivation may help my soul."

"There are important matters to attend to."

"I know."

"You have not been yourself since returning from the visit home six weeks ago and now this."

"I know. That is why I commissioned the new council on a dialogue of faith and hope to the professed Christians of the world."

"And they are prepared with the first draft of the proposition for you to review and discuss before delegating the council committees."

"I know it is urgent. It is also important to create a document of truth and of the times with great care and with the right timing. The church is asleep in the new nations. The reforms of the Second Vatican Council have never been understood by the people in many parts of the world. Perhaps in Poland. But other countries, like our beloved Hungary, have been left behind. Even after 1989-1990 and the fall of the Berlin Wall, the people of the new nations have been most concerned with bread and their physical survival. Their soul longs for the mother, the church, for the word. The world longs for the words of joy and hope."

Majee smiled inside as the energies of John Alexander sparked with concern for the church.

This was short lived as he continued, "But enough of that. I will continue my fast." Pope John Alexander rose wearily from his seat. "I will schedule a meeting with the council after the funeral of Marie."

He turned toward the altar. "I will meet with you tomorrow night. Put the Oratorio on the computer as you leave, softly," he concluded.

Monsignor Majee stood momentarily before the computerized stereo which was on pause pattern, typed in Liszt, brought up number 26, modulated the sound and left the room with the penetrating sounds of the Christus Oratorio in the background. On leaving he observed his friend at the altar.

His mind flashed back almost fifty years before.

Janos Majee's thoughts returned to the terrible days, October of 1956, when as a student at the University of Budapest he went out onto the streets with his classmates to take up the cause against the occupying Russian Army and government. He had become acquainted with John Alexander, then Father Daniel

Merse, who as a newly ordained priest had received the wounded partisans into his church in suburban Budapest. They had worked side by side ministering to the dozens of wounded secreted in the basement of the church.

Their paths hadn't crossed again until the priest had returned to Budapest after two years at Rome's Angelicum and had been appointed as lecturer in ethics and philosophy at the University. John Alexander had always been a decisive person with the subtle ability to weave his way among the people avoiding political retribution from the Communist regime. His ministering to the ill, the hungry and the homeless was tireless. Majee had followed the teacher as his mentor and entered the underground seminary patterning his action and life after this model.

In return, Father Daniel had recognized the devotion and had arranged for his clerical studies.

CHAPTER 9

The morning rain and the overcast skies accentuated the mood of Msgr. Majee and Anna on the trip to the small Hungarian community on the north side of Rome. Anna was not especially pleased, "I am not comfortable this way."

"You said that before. Papa would have it no other way. He would have insisted even if I weren't going."

"I am not used to big black limousines and a chauffeur. A bus would have gotten me there all right," she persisted. It always has before. Why didn't he come?"

"He thought it best," Janos Majee answered as though there had been some discussion. "He didn't want to interfere with the priest of St. Stephen. They would have wanted him, expected him, to officiate. and under the circumstances."

She interrupted. "What is he to do? The poor man. After all these years. I never thought, never expected something like this." A tear had appeared at each eye like a rain droplet on the car window. She stopped midthought to dab her eyes with her crumpled handkerchief.

Monsignor Majee was immediately aware that Anna knew something important about John Alexander's state of depression following Marie's death. "Go on Anna. What is it?" he urged.

Anna began to sob. "All these years. He was a saint," she murmured.

Janos had difficulty hearing her over the noise of the rain and the traffic. "What?" he queried.

"You should ask him," she replied in her sobbing whisper.

"About what?"

"Marie."

"What about Marie?"
"She told me."
"Told you? What?"
"About him and her."

Majee sat in amazed silence and despair. He must know. What he was being led to believe could not possibly be true. "What did she tell you? I must know. What are you saying?"

"She came to him."

"What do you mean, 'she came to him'?"

"She told me. You know how fond she was of him."

"But she was just a girl not even twenty-five. He's almost seventy."

"But 'how handsome' she would often say. I would agree and just laugh at her."

"I know she was fond of him. Everybody knew how she would do anything for him. Just like you or I would."

"But not like that."

Majee had no response to the statement because it had no specific meaning. The intended meaning was what he awaited with great anticipation and even fear.

"She told me that in the morning she was returning with ironing and things and there he was coming out of the shower, wet with only the towel, 'so tall and strong', she said. She was surprised. He was never around when she had things to do and she was always finished in his quarters by ten in the morning."

"So, then she left," Janos Majee urged.

"She said he turned away with the towel around him expecting her to leave. But, she said, she just stood there. He looked back and was surprised that she was still there and was undoing her blouse. He told her she must leave. She said she continued to remove her blouse and then one thing led to another. She said she could tell all the time that he wanted her to stay." Her sobbing was continuous. Her story was told in halting sobbing spurts.

"What do you mean 'she could tell he wanted her to stay'?"

"She said he was different then. He stared right at her and his mouth made strange movements like kissing motions."

Janos Majee sat silent. He could not, would not, believe this story. His friend of fifty years was too strong, too dedicated, yes, too holy to allow this to happen. But then, he is a man; indeed, a physical man, a man who enjoyed a cigar, a brandy and physical exercise, but in a private way. He is a man who enjoys the senses for personal relaxation, even personal pleasure, like his beloved Liszt. He had heard criticism of his personal habits compared to other popes. "She told you all this?"

Anna was now silent. She had retreated.

"And you believe this story?"

"What am I to believe?" she asked.

"You can not believe he would fall to this! I will have to ask him."

"You can ask her mother, today."

"She told this story to her mother?"

"That's what she told me and her mother told her to apologize to him. In fact, she said her mother was going to telephone him and apologize herself."

Majee sat in silence. There seemed nothing more to discuss. The story was full circle. Majee now knew the story. He doubted the story was entirely true. He wouldn't believe. The problem was that the way John Alexander had reacted there was an essence of fact in the story. The problem was further complicated by the fact that Anna and Marie's mother were privy to the story. As the limousine turned into the driveway of the church, Janos was more uncomfortable and perplexed than any time in his life. What had Marie's mother told John Alexander? How had Marie accidentally fallen from the window? How did the press know which window, which apartment? Why did security call this accident a suicide? Her local church didn't believe this was a suicide. What was in the note that security still held?

It would take all his strength and prayer to meet with Marie's parents, as he certainly would. John Alexander told him to do so and to arrange a meeting during the next week where he could express his personal condolence.

The funeral of a young person is always filled with the fatiguing emotions of total pain and grief freely expressed.

Majee's meeting with Marie's mother was tempered by the undercurrent conversations of the congregation concerning the *Gazetteer* report of the 'Pope's Girl' as the story was being entitled and the mother's continual apology for her daughter's conduct.

Majee was most interested in exploring the conversation the mother had had with her daughter and what she had then conveyed to John Alexander subsequently in her telephone call of apology.

"His Holiness sends his deepest sympathy to you on your loss," he began. "He prays daily for your Marie." He felt the vibration of the small tape recorder in his shirt pocket.

"She has died in sin. There is no hope."

"Why must you say that?" he urged.

"She told me everything. Even after confession, I fear for her. Her sin is so great. She has sinned against the pope."

"Can you tell me what happened? What did she tell you happened?"

"How can I forget? It was all so fearful," she began shaking her head, her face wet with tears.

"Yes, of course. Please, go on."

"It was in the morning, she said. She was putting away some ironing," she began slowly while staring at the wall of the rectory where they met. "And there he suddenly appeared. He had come out of the shower. There he was only with his towel. She said he looked so tall and strong."

Majee listened to words almost identical to those of Anna's story. He placed his hand to his chest. He could feel the soft vibration again of the tape recorder. This vibration was dwarfed by the stressing heartbeat that he also felt.

"He turned away with the towel now around him. He turned again toward her and stared at her. She could tell he wanted her. Oh, mercy, must I go on?"

"Please, it would be well to know the whole story."

"She began to remove her blouse. He continued to stare at her. He just stood there."

"He didn't say anything?"

"He just stared at her while she took her blouse off."

"And what else?"

"What do you mean, what else? She doesn't wear anything more, she is so small."

"No. I mean what else happened?" How could she say, 'she could tell he wanted her'?

"She said he stood there with his eyes blinking or winking and his lips smacking or kissing-like. She could tell. Then he turned and went into his bedroom and she followed him."

Msgr. Majee and the mother stood silently for a moment.

"Then what did she say happened?"

"She just said, 'one thing led to another', that's all."

"And you think what?"

"What else would one think? A mother knows what a daughter means."

"Anna said you telephoned Pope John Alexander."

"To apologize. I told Marie to do so. She said she would just go to work like nothing happened. So I called him."

"What did he say?"

"He asked me what I was talking about."

"He didn't know?"

"He pretended not to know but I explained it to him."

"You told him this story."

"Most of it, but he didn't need to hear it. He knew," she said with the finality of conviction. "He was there wasn't he? It wouldn't have happened if Marie hadn't thrown herself at him. I said I understood and apologized to him. What more could I do?"

Msgr. Majee was overwhelmed. What was to become of all this? What was to become of his friend? "And you told this story to the papers? *The Gazetteer*?"

"Oh, mercy, no. They were on my back asking questions after the accident, her working for him and everything, but I didn't say nothing. They were asking questions of neighbors and Marie's friends. One reporter is at the church today taking pictures outside and everything."

Majee could see the picture. The over zealous reporters eager for scandal had scoured the area for any tidbit. *The Gazetteer* had become overly zealous in recent years and over these years the unspoken wall of courtesy to the papacy had been broken slowly but surely. The readers were eager for such news. Circulation increased and profits rose. Rome may be the home of the church but the people of Rome had drifted as much as the rest of the world from the church. Of course, anything appearing in *The Gazetteer* with it's home in Rome was copied throughout the world. If they reported it, it must be authentic, so it seemed. These facts only compounded the problem. "I appreciate you telling me this story. I will keep it in complete confidence, as you must want it to be. You must know that Marie knows the grace of God. If her priest has heard her confession and the sorrow of sin from her heart, God knows. Come, let us pray."

In the center of the room, Monsignor Majee knelt and she joined him.

However, in private conversation with Father Franz, Majee received an entirely different disconcerting line of comment. "These are serious times for the church. We look to his holiness for leadership in all areas. He took the name Alexander to give new meaning to the name, in the name of morality. And now this and by one of us."

"I'm sure there is some good explanation for all this," Majee responded. "We must all stand firm with him." His thoughts quickly reflected to the priest's comment regarding part of the choice of John Alexander's name in title. In the choice of a name, he had stated he wanted to give new meaning to the name Alexander as pope. He had referred to Pope Alexander VI who in the years of Columbus had soiled the imagery of the papacy. Not only had he been one of the last popes elected by bribery but, in addition to simony, his eleven years in office were considered synonymous with personal immorality, ecclesiastic immorality. "I am affronted at this relative comparison," Majee bristled.

The priest quietly responded, "He has no problem with us. He has his own personal problem. He is too much 'man' to be pope, it is said. How does be intend to address other problems, the dissidents in America and France for example; if his own person is in disarray? How is he going to represent the Church facing declining attendance, the decreased numbers of those in vocation?"

"He is a remarkable man."

"I know. You forget where I have come from. I would never let my countryman or my pope down, but I fear for him and the church in these troubled times. And, his strength is needed in this continued great celebration of the Jubilee.

"Pray for him. He needs all our strength."

Anna was no less disconsolate on the return trip to the Vatican.

"Perhaps, I should never have come to Rome. Maybe, I should just go home. If I hadn't been here, I wouldn't have brought Marie in to work. The nuns would have taken care of his things. Then, he wouldn't have been involved in this."

"It was not your fault. I still do not believe the whole story. He depends on you. He needs you. He needs all of us."

Her sobbing still punctuated his mind as he entered the Vatican security forces offices.

Inspector Stella promptly responded to the presence of Monsignor Majee. Their discussion was a continuation of the prefect's recent inquiry of the pope. "The file? The file. It's right here," he indicated as he produced the thick manila folder.

"How do you discern that this unfortunate event was a suicide, my inspector?"

"Without a witness, or a witness who will say anything?" He began gesturing.

"Slow. Slowly, please," he remanded to the inspector's excited rapid explanation or excuse for and explanation as he perused the file.

"His holiness has nothing to say. So, accident, suicide, what else? Surely not some type of assault?"

"Of course not," Janos affirmed precluding the inference that the pope may have been implicated in the young woman's death, her fall from the window. "Do you feel your investigation is complete?"

Inspector Stella shrugged his shoulders, "But, what else? I see no reason to probe further."

"Would you have the results on the blood tests? The drug tests?"

"But why? We did none."

"I understand that there was a note. It does not appear to be here in the file."

The inspector opened his desk top-drawer and extracted a wrinkled envelope and held it up.

"You did not open it?"

With a shrug, he replied as he handed the partially crumpled envelope to Majee, "But what for? From the writing on the outside, it is in Hungarian. Would I have some stranger translate it? I wish this to all go quietly away. I find great embarrassment in this case."

"So you probably didn't speak to the reporters?" Majee suggested confirming his impression that the information of the pope's relationship to this case did not come from this office.

Majee gladly took possession of the unopened letter. Closing the file folder he noted, "I see the autopsy revealed only the head injury."

"Most unfortunate. The only kind of an injury that would have dispatched her from a fall of only eighteen feet."

"And this doctor, the pathologist. Do you trust him?"

"He knew nothing of the circumstances of the girls death, just that she fell. He does now, of course, after the papers reported their stories."

Returning to the residence, Monsignor Majee perused the file after the dinner hour, page by page. There was not an inkling within the file to soothe his feeling of a mystery in this situation, a mystery, the answer to which, was probably lost with the death of Marie. The note from Marie certainly did not shed any light on the situation. He opened the envelope and extracted the folded note. As he unfolded the message a fifty thousand lira paper note fell to the floor. Mysterious, he thought. A large sum of money for such a person as Marie. He perused the note anticipating some explanation.

"My priest and very precious friend," the note began in Hungarian. "Words can not express how sorry I am for my actions. I know there will be dreadful stories told. Forgive me for my sin and accept my apology. I could pretend that I needed the money but that would not be true. The money is a donation to the church. It is only right. I should resign my job but I couldn't bear not to be where you are. It will be your decision. Your servant, Marie."

There is no explanation in this note Majee concluded. Why would the money be an issue? It is only right, she had written. The letter would have gone into greater detail he discerned if she had any intention of a suicide. Since the letter was written before her death and the notorious stories how did she know it would come to this? Therefore the answer was some kind of an accident. Perhaps, the reporter at the *Gazetteer* would be able, if willing, to provide a glimpse into the truth that he was seeking.

It was 8:45. The Monsignor was greeted graciously almost as a long expected visitor. "Monsignor Majee, please come in. Please. Please be seated. Would you like a morning coffee? We expected you or someone to come by here, sooner or later."

"Yes. I would like a coffee. Cream. One sugar. Why would you be eager to see us, see me? You have not been much of a friend during recent years. And now, with this story."

"Ah, yes. But news is news, eh? It is not that we are eager, shall we say, but you must have your side to the story, eh?" he said assuredly with a confirming hunch of the shoulders and a smile. "There is only one side to the story, so far."

He continued, "Of course, of course. Now, Roberto here has put the story together so far. He is ready to hear your side of the story."

"I have no side to give to you, as you put it. I only search the truth. I seriously question that you have the truth."

Roberto's face presented a broad smile as he chuckled, "Oh, but we do. We do have the truth and, I might say, we have been most kind to your pope."

"He's not just my pope, he is pope to all of us, to millions all over the globe."

"To your pope," Roberto reaffirmed, interrupting. "He is not my pope. I have had my baptismal record stricken, erased. I am no longer Catholic, like many others in the world."

Majee was not surprised. Such a practice had become more than an occasional embarrassment since 1995 when the French bishop Jacques Gaillot had been removed as head of his diocese and the practice had spread from France to the United States and elsewhere. It was a problem John Alexander wished to deal with in a positive way during the celebration of these early years of the millennium. He felt this Roberto was then truly an enemy of the church. "You do this out of anger, out of revenge or hate, then?"

"No. I am just a reporter. The truth is the news. The news is the truth."

"How would you know that this is the truth?"

"The little girl was a braggart. She was in love with this pope of yours, this man of flesh."

"Do not speak unkindly of the dead."

"I do not wish to or mean to. The words are hers. The words of her best friend. She said she would get him. She bet her best friend she would. Fifty thousand lira. Fifty thousand lira for the body of the pope."

Monsignor Majee was crestfallen. The game, the gamble, the throw of the dice to bring down the pope for fifty thousand lira. Now he knew the significance of the fifty thousand lira note in Marie's note, the donation to the church, the winning of this unholy wager. 'It was only right' she had said. There was nothing right about this tragedy.

"And her friend paid the fifty thousand?"

"On the word of Marie? The word of such a deed was proof enough to pay off such a dastardly wager?"

"Oh, no. The evidence. The evidence is here in this envelope." Roberto gleamed as he withdrew a pair of jockey shorts from the large manila envelope. "Cost me fifty-five thousand lira to buy these from the girl. These are the underpants of his holiness, slightly wrinkled, with his laundry mark. This is the evidence."

Majee bristled. "How dare you consider this evidence, evidence sufficient to besmirch the good name, the holy presence, of the pope? Everyone knows she took care of his laundry and others in the residence. This means nothing." His face was red with rage as he waved his hands in the air with a motion of dismissal.

Roberto, his editor and Majee were the only conversants in the large office area. The surrounding reporters, secretaries and others all stood in rapt attention to the conversation. There was a bevy of twitters that blossomed from the smiles and partial sneers of the bystanders.

Roberto was not subdued by this response, "We have not mentioned this in the paper. The whole story fits together. Besides, we are still trying to find her diary."

Majee felt the sharp jab of final defeat. A diary with this story and what more in words, descriptions, feelings spoken, betrayal, a girl's imagination let loose upon the world. "The mother. She would know."

"She knows of the diary, of course. But, she says she has no idea where it is now. It is lost or stolen," Roberto concluded.

"If found, it would clear the name of your, our pope. Would you print that also, if the case?"

"Of course, the truth would be refreshing or more damning," Roberto agreed in the contradictory affirmative. His smile struck a note of defiance to Janos Majee.

"What could be more damning than your demeaning title of 'Popes Girl'?" Janos flamed in return.

"Well, don't be too upset, monsignor. We could expand our story with perhaps a picture or a caricature of this Marie woman with one of the Borgia woman." He laughed. "Side by side. You know, a history lesson. The life of Alexander the sixth."

"You are evil," Majee concluded, turned and walked out of the office.

CHAPTER 10

DETROIT

Sam Crawford slowly drank his coffee, dunked the donut and pondered the story he had just heard. He reviewed his notes. He had been a reporter for the *Press* for many years. He had a gut feeling when there was a story worth pursuing.

"So, you say he's not going to press charges against this biker who decked him."

"Naw. He's out on the street now."

"You say the docs didn't think he would live? That his head bleed was so bad they couldn't operate? And, the next day he goes home?"

Crawford continued, "Doesn't sound right. What about the kid who was shot? You were there, too?"

Officer Charles Blake nodded his head. "I saw him myself. This woman's hysterical beside him with this Adams fellow. I look at the kid. He's in a pool of blood. He's not bleeding anymore. His eyes are gone. No pulse. He ain't breathin'. I tell the EMS to go home, nothin they can do. He's dead."

"Yeah, then what?"

"Then, the kid's alive and I have to call EMS back right away. Spooky, that's what it is."

"Some fluke. That's all," Crawford stated. "Where's the kid now? What hospital?"

"No hospital. Over night and he's out. He's jockeying cars at the Hotel Ponch right now. Doesn't make sense."

"Nothin to it," Crawford said. He left a tip at the lunch counter and turned to leave. "I'm getting too old for these wild goose chases, Charlie. Thanks for the info lead, though. Always good to talk to you." Sam Crawford put his hat down over his forehead to cover his face from the drizzle and got in his new Ford Contour. He sat a moment to make a few notes. Jeremy Brodsky, Val Bod, Val Boden, that's what their names were. When things don't add up, there's a problem. A problem sounds like a story, he told himself. The rain turned into a steady afternoon drizzle as he turned his car towards the Ponchartrain hotel. Less than five minutes later he had pulled under the protected drive-through entrance of the hotel. He parked his car the first spot from the curb entrance off Randolph Street. He jumped out of the car and placed the cardboard sign *Press* under the windshield wiper. This would give him at least twenty minutes before anyone got excited even though the hotel was at one of it's busy congested moments of cars coming and going, people in a hurry and baggage appearing and disappearing from the curbside entrance area with porters scurrying.

Crawford watched as the carhops also disappeared and reappeared as they moved cars into and out of the parking structure, as they gave parking stubs and exchanged bills and coins as they delivered cars to the entrance of the hotel, occasionally helping with baggage. There were three carhops and were black except for one. He assumed that the white kid was his quest, the white well built kid with the blond hair that reached his shoulders. That would be Jeremy. His thoughts rambled. Didn't seem possible. A shot in the arm and a hole in the chest with all that blood loss less than a week ago. Doesn't look like that today. Can't be him. Well, he had to find out. Fat chance of much conversation, he thought, as busy as they were.

"You Jeremy Brodsky?"

"Yeah. You the cops? I already told them all I know."

"Naw. I'm from the *Press*. I'm here about the guy who helped you. This Adams fellow."

"Yeah. Too bad about him. My girl told me how he got his ticket punched. Too bad."

"He's not dead."

"That's not what she said. Look, I gotta go. I'm on the next park."

"I'll be waiting, over here by the door. Talk to me when you have a chance, would you?" he asked as he retreated toward the hotel entrance doors. He lit a cigarette and watched as Jeremy jumped into a car and drove off into the parking garage. As he reappeared from the lift area, he jumped off ready for his next car. Crawford mumbled to himself, "Sure doesn't seem to have any trouble getting around. Looks pretty healthy, not like he had lost a lot of blood."

As soon as all three carhops were waiting for the next flurry of action, Jeremy came to Sam Crawford, bummed a cigarette and inquired, "What do you mean, he's not dead?"

"He's as alive as you are. Seems like two miracles to me."

"I talked to my girl, Val, just an hour ago and she said the doctor's didn't expect him to make it."

As he scratched notes in his note pad he corrected Jeremy. "Like I said. I hear he's better, too. Healed. Back on the street like you. Tell me about you. Tell me about the day you were shot."

"Nothin' much," Jeremy began. "I sort of remember the ambulance ride. It was all real fuzzy. I woke up for real in the hospital. I remember the doctors talking about the x-rays and checking for bleeding in my chest and locating the bullet in my back next to the ribs."

"How much blood did they give you?"

"None. They said my blood was o.k."

"You know, you left a barrel of blood on the floor of the cafe and your shirt was a red sponge. Where'd they take the bullet out?"

"My back," Jeremy said as he raised the shirt up his back.

Sam examined the red, slightly bulging area the size of a silver dollar. A line ran through the middle, the line of surgery that was embroidered by seven black knotted sutures. The scar line was healed pink and smooth. "Sure look smooth," he noted. "Just like the entry wound?" he asked.

Jeremy turned to show his chest. The bronze cross on the chain dangled out. He suddenly became aware that by now several bystanders had gathered and were watching and quietly, with a blush, pulled his shirt down. "None of their business," he said. "None of yours, either, mister."

Sam ignored the remark and said, "Let's walk down here for a minute," heading for the car. "And your arm's better? All healed up like your chest and back?" Sam could see the red depressed areas on his arm.

"Yeah. The doctors said I was lucky the bullet missed the bone and everything."

Sam Crawford was silent for a few moments. He knew this was a story. A real story. A story beyond belief, beyond reality. There was a serious mystery about the two events.

"How lucky do you think you are, or were, Jeremy?"

"Lucky, I could have been hurt bad," he agreed.

"You're lucky to be alive."

"That's what Val said."

"Do you think the stranger, this Daniel Adams, had anything to do about it?"

"That's what Val says. She says I was lucky he showed up."

"Do you believe in prayer, Jeremy?"

"Sure. Doesn't everyone?"

"How old are you?"

"Nineteen."

"And Valentine?"

"Seventeen."

I don't think you are grateful enough, Jeremy, Sam Crawford concluded as he got into his car. As he pulled away from the hotel entrance he remembered seeing Jeremy holding onto the cross hanging from his neck and deep in thought. Maybe the kid was grateful, he mused. Some people just don't want show their feelings. Sam stopped the car next to the curb around the corner. He scribbled furiously onto his notepad.

CHAPTER 11

It was Wednesday afternoon when Daniel again appeared at the park. He had passed by the far end of the park and now stood watching a small group of boys and a girl playing a game.

The morning had been spent inquiring about a new carpentry job. It was a small job. He was in install a mantle over a fireplace. The job was another referral from the notice at the synagogue bulletin board.

He found peace in the green of the park and the rush of wind through the trees. He could see through the trees as the group gathered at the game tables at the other side of the park. There seemed to be more people than he recalled gathered there before. He would go over there soon. For the moment he would enjoy watching the game being played here.

Daniel sat on the grassy ground not too far from one of the boys with bat at hand who waited his turn to hit at the ball another player would throw in his direction.

The boy momentarily stared in Daniel's direction.

He took this occasion to inquire, "What is the game you're playing?"

The boy, with a slightly quizzical look, replied, "Baseball." Immediately, he turned to take his turn to swing the bat at the ball. The boy raced toward the base as the ball bounded beyond the pitcher toward second base. The fielder gathered the ball up after dropping it once and threw back to the pitcher. The pitcher jumped up proclaiming, "Out!"

Immediately, the runner standing near the base jumped up and down exclaiming, "Safe. I beat the throw."

"Don't matter. It was to right field side anyway."

"You were standing on second base when you got it," the runner noted.

There upon several of the players gathered in discussion, in disagreement. The runner left the group and approaching a few steps toward Daniel called out, "Hey, mister. You wanta be umpire for us?"

"I wouldn't be suitable to umpire for you. I don't know the rules for baseball. I don't know how to play baseball."

"What da'ya mean you don't know how to play baseball? Everybody knows how to play baseball."

"Maybe he's some foreigner."

"Sorry," Daniel remanded. He did feel like a foreigner. So much around him was strange.

Daniel's pleasant diversion to the baseball game was interrupted by three people emerging from the woods. Though some distance away, he could make out one of the three as Amos who was pointing toward Daniel saying, "That's him over there. See. I told you so. I told you he'd be coming around."

The other two left Amos standing there as they rapidly walked toward him. Daniel watched their approach as Amos continued less rapidly with effort behind them. He recognized Naomi who was conversing animatedly with her companion. He obviously was not one of the usual visitors to the park. His hat partially covered his face. The sides of his seersucker coat flapped beside him. The partially loosened tie waved before the open neck of his shirt. As they came closer, the effect of the August heat and humidity was evident as Naomi's cheeks were pinked and beads of sweat appeared on her tanned forehead and small rivulets gathered from her short blond hair.

Daniel walked slowly toward them. He was not surprised at being sought out by Naomi. He had been appreciative of her vigil during his stay in the hospital.

"So, this is the miracle man," the stranger in the suit stated to no one in particular. He had stopped to catch his breath and wipe with a handkerchief the sweat from his neck and forehead including his receding hairline. Obviously, though slender enough except for a slightly accentuated waistline and appearing physically well developed, he wasn't used to even this small degree of endeavor.

"Hello, Naomi." Daniel had already noted that she was not wearing the short black leather skirt and jacket top. Her green flowery skirt almost looked out of place, it was so different but the off the shoulder sleeveless white blouse was equally revealing as the leather top had been.

"The police released Tom after you wouldn't press charges," she announced and added, "Oh, this is Sam Crawford. He's a newspaper reporter."

"Why did you do that?" Sam Crawford inquired directly not allowing Daniel to acknowledge the introduction.

"As you can see, I am not injured. He had no grievance with me and I have none with him. He is hard of heart, and lonely, and probably doesn't even know why he is so angry. He seeks to control this woman Naomi, probably out of fear of loss. Besides, it was more an accident that anything."

"Well, he wants to see you, to see for himself. Everyone thought you might die, even the doctors."

"But, as you can see, I am well. It was not as serious as everyone believed." He smiled and held his hands out as though displaying his well being.

"People are saying it's a miracle. They're talking about the Plodsky fellow, too. You've got quite a group of inquisitive people over there," he said pointing to the other side of the park.

"It's nothing that I have done."

"Jeremy Plodsky's girlfriend, Valentine, doesn't see it that way. She's telling people how it was. How Jeremy was dead and came back to life."

"Again, it's nothing that I have done."

"Well, you are a strange one, Daniel Adams. You know how to play chess too but I hear you don't know how to drive a car, take a bus every where," Amos said.

"Or, I ride my bicycle."

"I have a feeling you could play a mean game of backgammon. You can't fool everybody, Daniel."

"It is not my intent to fool anyone, Amos."

"There's more to you than meets the eye. I was there when this Valentine was telling about what you did after the shootin'."

Sam Crawford was scribbling notes in his worn brown leather folder. The group now approached those gathered around the game tables. There were many, twice as many as he had seen before.

The young woman broke from the crowd. Her ankle long black patterned skirt rustled as she strode quickly, nearly running, toward the three. Daniel recognized Valentine as she approached. Before he could greet her she was before him. Amid a mixture of smiles and tears she fell to her knees and grasped his arm saying, "Bless you. Thank you. Thank you for saving Jeremy's life."

Daniel looked over the crowd. Over a hundred people had gathered there. They moved irregularly but in concert toward him. In the background, sitting upon his parked Harley, he could see Tom White watching the proceedings.

From the crowd came a scattered 'Amen' in response to Valentine's exaltation.

He had experienced this before. He stepped backward half a step assisting Valentine to her feet with one hand while touching his other hand to his forehead. "Peace to you, Valentine. Peace to all of you. It is nothing I have done. If Jeremy has been healed in a way we do not understand, it was because of love, our love for one another and most importantly the love of God."

"But you were there. It was you who prayed. It was you who made it happen," a voice from the crowd countered. "She said so."

"I was there. I prayed. Valentine was there. She prayed. Jeremy was there. He prayed. But most of all, God was there and he was in our hearts."

Tom White had left his bike and was standing next to Naomi who had moved to the edge of the crowd. Their conversation had joined the murmuring of the crowd.

From the crowd, there emerged a woman leading a boy, a smiling boy who walked haltingly. The right leg of the boy obviously was weak or deformed. The woman fell on her knees before Daniel. "This is Andrew," she said. She grasped at Daniel's shirt and looked up to him. There were tears on her cheeks. "Heal my boy. Heal his leg. Tell God to heal my Andrew."

The crowd grew silent. Many were here because of the 'miracle man'. They were sure their curiosity was about to be rewarded sooner than they had expected.

Daniel knelt down beside the woman and in front of the boy. He quietly said, "I do not heal. I do not tell God to heal. God works his way through our faith, through our hearts." Despite the heat of summer, the boy was dressed in trousers. Daniel rolled the right trouser leg up to reveal the badly deformed knee. "I thought you healed people," the woman stated with a slight hint of disdain.

"Hello, Andrew," Daniel said softly as he briefly examined the deformed knee. Ignoring the reproach of the mother, he inquired of her, "He wasn't born with this?"

"No, it was an accident. A year ago."

"The physician," Daniel began

"They don't care. I have nothing to pay them. There is no insurance."

The crowd began to murmur.

Sam Crawford looked on. A wry smile confirmed his thoughts. A comment from the crowd jerked his head fast to the crowd, 'heal him' he heard, and then to Daniel and the pair, mother and son.

"A physician will," Daniel stated quietly as he stood up and took the boy's hand and looked toward Sam Crawford. "You have a car here, Mister Crawford. Would you drive us to the hospital?"

The crowd now had gathered closer. Words muttered in irritation "poor boy", "why doesn't he do something?" "fake."

"Where should we go, Daniel? This crowd thinks you should do something."

"Don't let them bother you, Daniel," Amos reassured.

Daniel looked at the crowd of people, from one face to another and raised his hand. The crowd became silent in expectation.

"Do not be impatient, my brothers."

"Heal him," a definitely impatient voice from the crowd again demanded of Daniel.

"Quiet," he was answered by Amos.

"I do not heal," Daniel again stated. "I do not command God to heal. God works his way through our hearts. Let us learn to love the Lord. Let us learn to love one another. Let us learn to forgive our failings. Let us learn to forgive one another." Daniel could see Tom White to one side of the crowd staring at him. Daniel Looking at him held his hand forward and said, "Peace be with you," and turned back toward Sam Crawford, "May we go?" As they went as a small group toward the car, the crowd gathered about them leaving a path for them. Murmurs from the crowd filled the park, "Praise the Lord."

Tom White leaned toward the car addressing Daniel. "Will you be back?" He smiled as Daniel nodded. "I want to talk to you," Tom added.

As he headed uptown toward the medical center, Sam asked, "Where are we going?"

"Doctor Solari's office is in the professional building on John R Street across from the hospital."

"I know where that is."

The group of four with Daniel leading entered Doctor Solari's office. Daniel, the mother and son with Sam Crawford entered. Sam Crawford didn't know how all this would turn out but as part of a story he was not going to miss out on the actors.

"It says on the door that this Solari is a neurologist."

"I know. He's the only physician I know. He will see me. He will help Andrew," he replied with a comforting smile as he approached the receptionist. "I'm Daniel Adams," he announced quietly to the receptionist.

The receptionist responded with an inquisitive searching look, "So, you're that Daniel Adams. Everyone's talking about you. But your appointment is not until next Wednesday."

"I know, but if the doctor would be kind enough to see me today?"

"If you would have a seat. It may be a while," she agreed and quickly disappeared beyond the reception area.

Daniel retreated to sit next to Andrew. "We've been so busy getting here, I don't know your name."

"Molly. Molly Perkins," Andrew's mother replied.

"And where is Andrew's father?"

"I don't know and don't care," she asserted. "He left when Andrew was only a year old. Haven't heard from him since. Not a peep or a penny. Almost five years now."

The receptionist appeared at the waiting room. "Doctor will see you now, Mr. Barnes." Then directing to Daniel, "And doctor will have time to see you next, Mr. Adams."

"How you gonna get the kid in?" Sam inquired.

"Doctor Solari will be glad to see that he is cared for," Daniel replied. "He is that kind of a physician. He will see that Andrew is helped."

"How did you hurt your knee, Andrew?"

"It was when I was eight. A year ago. I fell off a garage. Mrs. Olson, mom's neighbor, wrapped it and soaked it."

"And I took him to the doctor a month later when it weren't better. He said it weren't no emergency but wouldn't see him again cause I didn't pay him the first time."

"Well, damnation," Sam Crawford chimed in, "Haven't you heard of ADC and Medicaid? You sure as hell qualify."

"Ain't takin' no welfare. I'll make our way. We ain't the only ones missin a meal here and there, especially these days."

"What is this ADC and Medicaid, Sam?" Daniel inquired.

"Aid to Dependent Children and the other's government medicine. ADC helps support kids without enough money and the other provides medical care. Don't know why she's not signed up. She certainly qualifies."

"Doctor will see you now, Mr. Adams," the receptionist announced. As Daniel, Andrew and Molly Perkins rose to follow the surprised receptionist said, "Doctor only wants to see you."

"It'll be all right," Daniel interrupted softly.

She proceeded to lead the three to an examination room.

Doctor Solari soon appeared. He was a short slender man. His squared mustache seemed to unbalance his body. His slight accent seemed to match the darker tint of his skin. "I understand you're not alone today. I have a feeling you have not come about yourself. It seems I can count on you for the unexpected."

"This young man is Andrew Perkins," Daniel began and nodded toward his mother, "and his mother. Andrew, pull up your clothing so Doctor Solari can see your knee."

"Obviously, this is not a problem for me, Daniel. Why do you bring him to me? Here, son, let's take a proper look. We'll take those trousers off," as he assisted Andrew, "and you sit up here on the exam table."

"You're the only physician I know and I felt assured you would know what to do."

He examined Andrew's knee and leg. He palpated the swollen joint. He moved the leg in every direction. He tested Andrew's reflexes. "Hasn't this boy seen a physician about this injury before?"

"A year ago but we have no money and no insurance."

"They don't receive ADC, there's no husband at home and they're not on Medicaid," Daniel informed, relating information that Sam Crawford had thought important.

"Well, let's get on with this. Put your trousers on, Andrew," Doctor Solari said with a smile. He lifted him off the table, twirled him in the air and deposited him on the floor and handed him his trousers. He dialed the phone and after a moment responded, "Nancy, this is Harry Solari. Let me speak to Peter." After a short pause. "Yes. I have a nine year old boy here with an old knee injury that's never received attention. I'd like you to follow-up. It's a problem because it should be a Medicaid, but never enrolled. Appears other social problems here." Solari listened for a moment. "Knew you'd take care of it. How did I get involved? Why, my miraculous brain injury patient brought him in," he responded with a knowing glance toward Daniel. "Now, you take Andrew downstairs to office 510, Mrs. Perkins. Doctor Owens is going to examine Andrew. He will probably order some imaging, x-ray studies, and he will send you across the street to the hospital. We want you to apply for Medicaid. They will help you with that at the hospital. Andrew will have to have surgery and the diagnostic and hospital costs will be very much. Medicaid will pay for this."

"I don't want no welfare," Mrs. Perkins again asserted.

Doctor Harry Solari smiled as he looked sternly at Mrs. Perkins. "You really have little choice, Mrs. Perkins. We are going to fix Andrew's knee to the best we can." His mustache began to quiver in slight agitation.

"If it will help Andrew," she conceded.

"Fine. You go see him now. He's waiting for you. I want to talk to Daniel."

Andrew had stayed close to Daniel. By now he held his hand.

Daniel led him to the door and assured him, "I'll be down there with Mr. Crawford later. We'll wait until you're through and we'll take you home." He could tell Doctor Solari was irritated when they were then first alone.

"You are full of surprises," Solari began. "How did you know I would take care of the boy? That's not my specialty."

"Ah, my good doctor. That is exactly the kind of doctor you are. You specialize in people. Your life is caring for people."

"Humph," he responded. He didn't have to remind himself of the amount of work that he had done in his years of practice for which he had received little or no payment. His book keeper reminded him often enough. But he would never change his ways. Daniel was very perceptive or more. "Enough about me," he continued. "How about you? Here, hold out your hands. Now close your eyes. Let me see you touch your nose with your right first finger. That's good. Now the other. Very good." He stepped back to observe Daniel. "Looks like you're all right. Have any complaints? Any headaches?"

"I feel well," Daniel assured him.

"I still want to see you next Wednesday. And don't worry. We'll take good care of Andrew.

CHAPTER 12

Sam Crawford had reviewed the notes of this unusual day, which turned out to encompass two stories. The first story was of Daniel Adams and the two unusual medical recoveries he was associated with was his main interest. The second story was the human interest story of the medical problems of Andrew Perkins, the story of Medicaid. This story could wait until it played out.

He had crafted an article relating the seemingly miraculous recovery of Jeremy Plodsky and the association of Daniel Adams and the unexpected, unexplained recovery of Daniel Adams, himself, after sustaining the serious head injury.

He left after midnight after depositing the story on Steve Gillespie's desk.

Now, this morning he stood, article in hand, waiting to see Gillespie, his editor. He glanced at the paper, which had the words 'See me' scrawled across the top and signed with a block letter 'G'. Sam was not used to this happening. After eighteen years perfecting his craft, his articles were usually passed through without much play except to decide which day and where in the paper to run the article. This amounted to as much as a rejection. He looked up on hearing his name called.

"Sam," the editor quietly called out. "Come in here and close the door."

"What do you want with this, Gilly?" He asked waving the article about Daniel Adams.

"You sound pretty emotional about this piece. It's not your usual stuff. Seems a little quick to me."

"It's all the real McCoy, Gilly. Nothing emotional about it."

"Is this all some big coincidence? Is this guy some Jesus freak playing games with us and the police and doctors just screwed up?"

"One thing for sure, Gilly, I've seen the scars on the Jeremy kid. They're big and they're healed. Both the police and the girlfriend know how much blood he lost at the scene. He should be dead but he isn't. And no blood transfusions."

"Don't add up."

"Sure doesn't. There's no coincidence. No one's playing games and no one's screwed up. No one's fooling me. All this checks and rechecks, even Daniel Adams own injury and recovery."

"Seems we need to know a little more about this Daniel Adams character. We print this and it'll turn out to be a television lead. They'll descend on him and us like vultures."

"You're right, Gilly. But I'm not the only one asking these questions. The police, the doctors, and he had a bunch of friends and a large audience seeking him out at Bush Park."

"And I suppose they were demanding more miracles, divine healings, as you say? That could even get to be messy. You never know how a crowd might react."

Crawford was a little concerned over Gilly's viewpoint, but he was boss and had usually been more right than wrong about issues he had questioned in the past. Sam agreed without an argument, "I'll find out more about him and redo."

"You might find yourself on the religion page with this one," Sam heard Gillespie utter as he left the office.

The lone biker sat at the corner near Daniel Adams flat on his shiny maroon Harley. Tom White had spent a restless night with little continuous sleep after he had been released from jail. He could not understand why Daniel Adams had refused to press charges against him. He had verbally and physically hurt this Adams fellow in front of all those people. The park people had defied him and kept him from further injuring the Adams man or further getting at Naomi. He was confused at what kind of man this Adams was when according to Naomi he had been injured so much that they feared for his life and as Naomi had said the police were looking for him because he had been the one who had injured Daniel and could well be facing probable murder charges because they didn't expect him to survive. And now he was home apparently well with no residual affects of his injuries. How could this man survive such serious injury as described by Naomi and recover so quickly so miraculously? What kind of a man was this?

He had waited by his flat because he wanted to talk to him, as he had indicated at the park the previous day.

Daniel came slowly down the side walkway of the house riding his bike.

Tom White started his Harley and sped up the short block toward him. He reached him as he was turning up the street where they both came to a halt. They looked at each other for a few seconds without speaking.

"Good morning, Mr. White," Daniel began.

"You needn't be afraid of me," Tom White answered.

Daniel didn't answer the comment saying, "Yesterday, you said you wanted to talk to me. What would you like to talk to me about?"

"Why did you do it? What do you want? My attorney said everybody wants some thing. They don't do this out of the goodness of their heart. Why did you tell the police to let me go, that you weren't going to hold the charges against me?"

"Oh, I have no grievance against you. There is nothing I want from you. And you had no personal reason for attacking me. Do you not feel double the shame in this case?"

"It does bother me. It ain't natural for some one to act this way."

"Why don't we sit and talk over here," he invited indicating the porch steps.

Tom White sat on the steps inquiring, "Is that what this is all about, to make me feel ashamed?"

"Not at all," Daniel assured. "It's only natural to feel somewhat awkward in this circumstance."

"Then what is it about?"

"It's about some thing you can do for your self, something you can give yourself. It's about forgiveness. It's about following the footsteps of love, hope and caring as with our God. You are a man who has known God, aren't you?"

"There was the day when I was part of such things. But something, somehow, I left that all behind. It isn't important any more."

"But you have become bitter and angry deep inside. Is that how you wish to live your life?"

"What other way is there? That's what life is. Look around. Everybody is bitter and disillusioned. Everybody is in everyone else's way. Those who are successful are taking advantage of all the others. God can't fix it all. Besides, it's just a story. Who can believe it all, anyway?"

"Ah," Daniel began, "our God is real. His way is the foundation of life. His way is the road to peace and contentment in this life and on the road ever after. He has shown us how to live and has given his only son to assure the road beyond."

"How can you know that?"

"It is easier for some to know, to understand, the hand of God. When he is in your heart you are the hand of God. It may difficult for you to understand for you are all alone in the world. Imagine, all these people and you are all alone. Imagine being hand in hand with all the people who know the heart of God and how each life would be."

Tom White sat quietly for a moment. He had never heard someone talk about living in these terms. He had come from a life where bigger and better was always the goal. Always get better grades in school. His father taught him to work harder and longer so that they could have more of every thing, a bigger car, a bigger finer house. No one spoke of the other people in the world except it seemed they were one you had to beat to get whatever you wanted. He had left home because these didn't seem to be the things he really wanted. His father had strongly disproved of his currently lifestyle. Daniel was right. He was alone. "How do I find these people? Where do I go now? My life is a shambles. I have hurt many people, not only you, in many ways. How do I put everything back together?"

"God is very forgiving."

"Can you forgive me for what I have done?"

"I can do no less than God would. I have long ago forgiven you."

"And everyone else?"

"It is what is in your heart."

"My whole life is amuck. I don't know who God is. Where do I find this faith, this foundation of living, as you have called it?" Tom White hung his head down as though lost.

"It is like these steps," Daniel said. "It is the way they are built."

The biker examined the steps. There was nothing unusual except that they were newly built. "They are new. Is that what you mean, a new start?"

"Partly. To begin with, it is the way they are built. Each part is the best piece of cedar that could be found. Like people, each must be the best one can be. And each part rests upon the other so that each part depends on the other or the steps would fall down. Each piece alone would not be very useful but together they have a purpose."

"I can see that but where is this God. Where does he fit in?"

"It is as in life. It can not be seen but what holds it all together is most important."

"You mean the nails."

"Like nails but in this case these steps are held together by sturdy wooden pegs, as God is to man, a part of the whole, unseen but essential as God is to man."

"No one uses wooden pegs any more. That's old stuff."

"I know. I carved them myself, the old way as you say, as I always have. It is as God. It is not something to be seen directly but you know it is there to hold it together. It may be beyond seeing and it may old stuff but is as good today as any time in the past. It is the pathway."

"How can I change? What can I do to find this new path?"

"Perhaps you would like to join me later this afternoon. I am going to meet Amos at a store where we will begin to offer a free meal for those who are in need."

"You mean a soup kitchen."

"That is one name such a place is called."

"To help others like a part of the porch."

"Yes. It is the way of the Lord."

"To help one another. I can try."

Daniel smiled. "I must be going. I have work to do today. I will see you later."

"And I have to call a man about a beer," Tom said with a chuckle.

He raised his hand toward the biker as he rose to retrieve his bike. "Peace be with you, and with your father."

Tom White watched Daniel ride down the street and quietly said, "Peace be with you, Daniel Adams. You certainly are a strange man. You heal and you read minds? You know about my father."

Sam Crawford waited until evening to pursue his story. He rang the doorbell at the front door of the gray frame house. A small gray haired lady looked out the window pushing the lace curtain to one side. The door was opened part way and behind the screened door she inquired, "Yes?"

"I'm looking for Mr. Daniel Adams."

"What do you want with him?" she asked in an inquisitive protective manner.

"I'm a friend of his. I met him at Bush Park after he was hurt there. I would like to talk to him."

"He would be up the back stairs, if he's home."
"Has he lived here long?"
"About five weeks now."
"Where did he live before?"
"He didn't say. You would have to ask him."

"Thank you." He descended the newly rebuilt steps of the front porch and proceeded to the back of the house. A light shone from a window of the second floor. The small backyard between the house and garage was partially illuminated revealing a small plot of mown grass discernible in the dusk. The light reflected off the garage. A narrow sidewalk ran the length of the yard adjacent to a wire fence and extended to the alley beyond the garage. The back stairway led to a small landing of the second floor. There was no doorbell. Sam knocked on the door.

The door was soon opened and Sam Crawford was greeted, "Good evening, Sam Crawford."

"How are you, Mr. Adams?"

"I am fine. This is a pleasant surprise," Daniel indicated. With a motion of his hand he continued, "Please come in. I was just preparing dinner. Would you join me?"

"Well, I didn't plan to eat."

"You are welcome. It is simple fare. You are welcome to share."

Sam was unprepared for this reception. He wasn't used to such immediate acceptance and certainly not the generosity of a meal being offered as he still seemed, still felt, as a stranger in spite of his involvement with Daniel in the care of the Perkins' boy. He watched for a moment as the tall bearded man began to set a second plate at the table. "Thought we could talk about yesterday and some of those other things."

"Yes. Andrew will now be cared for. The physicians will care for him. Please sit," Daniel suggested motioning to the place he had prepared at the table.

Sam sat down as he continued the conversation. "How did you know Dr. Solari would care for Andrew? Other doctors didn't."

"He is a physician. He cared for me. He is concerned with helping people. That is his first interest."

"You mean money. He's not interested in money?"

"He knows that if he does his work well he will receive sufficient reward, not necessarily money."

"But he will be paid by Medicaid."

"And all the other costs, I believe."

"You didn't know about Medicaid and Aid to Dependent Children before I mentioned it?" Crawford inquired beginning to probe the mysteries of Daniel.

"There are many things I do not know about your ways," Daniel affirmed. He had turned to the oven and removed a pan to place on the stovetop. The large fish was placed on a plate and quickly filleted by Daniel. Carrots were next removed from the pan and placed along side the fish.

"I've been around town, Mr. Adams," Sam began.

"Call me Daniel, please," he requested as he placed the serving dish on the table next to the bread rolls, sauce and lemon pieces.

"Been visiting some more people who have some remarkable stories concerning you, Daniel," Sam began as he sat down at the table.

Daniel poured tea, filling each cup, set the teapot on the table and sat down. "Please break bread with me," he requested and reached for a bread biscuit. "The bread is from Arpad's bakery."

Sam understood that he was to follow suit and reached for a biscuit and following Daniel's lead, broke the biscuit and placed it on the side of his plate. He didn't know whether Daniel had uttered a prayer at that moment. If he had, it hadn't been out loud but that seemed the intent of the moment and Sam Crawford considered it to have happened.

"Please help yourself. It is not much but it is sufficient. What kind of stories have you heard?"

He served himself a small portion of fish and vegetable. He sipped the tea thoughtfully. "I thought it all had to be a mistake, someone's imagination. I heard more about the Plodsky boy shot at the restaurant. The police said he was dead. Suddenly, while you are there he's alive again."

"They were mistaken. I can assure you." Daniel replied slowly. He could see that Sam was quite intense about the story he was searching for.

There was a hint of sweat on his forehead as he responded, "That's not exactly what Valentine, the girl friend, said. She said that you each prayed and he came back to life."

"Well, we obviously are two people of faith." Daniel placed another piece of fish upon a piece of broken bread and ate it as he watched Sam searching for the right words.

Sam observed after a fork full of potato and carrot. "It seems a wee bit more than faith."

"Faith is faith, Sam. True faith, sincere faith, is simply a basic truth."

"There isn't too much of that these days. I talked to the Plodsky boy himself. Two days in the hospital. A hole in the lung that would have killed most people, the doctors said at the hospital. There was enough blood left on the floor at the restaurant where he was shot to save two lives. Four days later he's parking cars at the Ponchartrain Hotel. Remarkable."

"He was very fortunate," Daniel stated very matter of fact. His plate of fish and vegetable was now empty. He sipped his tea as he continued to eat a portion of the remaining biscuit. There was no question in his mind the source of these remarkable fortunate occurrences.

Sam vaguely was satisfied that a rational explanation of the two occurrences would not be forthcoming tonight, if ever. The parting words of Gillespie remained in his mind, about, 'ending up on the religion page'. "It's all very remarkable, Daniel" he concluded as he sipped his tea.

"Indeed," responded Daniel. "Let us give thanks for this food and blessings that we received," he stated with bowed head. "Will you have more tea? It is of good flavor."

Perhaps he says grace more than once he thought. "It is good. Thank you," Sam agreed placing his cup forward. "Did you bring it with you when you moved here?"

"No. It is a gift of Mrs. Erdhiem, whom I rent from."

"Oh, the Jewish one downstairs. You must be good friends."

"We get along. Part of my rent is to help with repairs."

"Like the new porch steps I saw?"

"And others. And sometimes she arranges things up here."

"She has a key, then?"

"Oh, no. There is an inside stairway," he explained pointing to a hallway at the front of the kitchen.

"You trust her that much? And her husband?"

"Of course. What's not to trust?"

"Where did you move from?"

Daniel paused because such a question, though expected, was not easy to answer. "I came to Detroit from east of here."

Sam knew his question hadn't been answered because deep inside his being told him there was no answer. Daniel would have freely stated a specific answer. "But why Detroit? Why such a place?"

"I only know I am here. I do not yet know why I have been sent here. For now, I am here to bring a simple message, a message of love and peace. To love one another as you love the God, our father."

"What do you mean, 'not know why you are sent'?"

"It is as in other times, in other places. I will know God's purpose."

Sam Crawford seemed at an impasse for words, an uncommon event in his life for he seldom was at a loss for words.

"You are a religious man, Sam Crawford? You showed great compassion for the boy, Andrew."

"Sure. Sure," he quickly replied. Believing Daniel already knew the answer and found it difficult to lie to Daniel, the trusting one, he continued, "Well, no. I was raised a Jew. A good Jewish family and all that. But later, I sort of fell by the way."

"And why would you do that?" Daniel asked quietly.

"Too busy. No. Well, you know, why would God allow the holocaust, you know, his chosen people, the suffering? Where was He?"

"Perhaps there is no answer, at least, that you would want to hear. You have lost hope? You do not feel the love of God?"

"Why, no. How could you, how could I? Take Israel. Even that, the promised land, is denied."

"Israel? Perhaps Israel is a people, or a place in the heart, and not a place, not a piece of ground."

"God promised Abraham and Jacob and Daniel and led his people, the Jews with Moses, back to the land he promised, Israel and now there is only war."

"That was written at the beginning and became true, once. And the son of God who was crucified and became one with God?"

"Jesus?"

"Of course."

"No one speaks of him in the temple."

"Ah," concluded Daniel. "You are truly lost in the wilderness."

CHAPTER 13

❦

Monsignor Brown had completed arrangements for Archbishop Gregory's reception for the following Thursday and placed that days' itinerary for his review.

Archbishop Paul Gregory sat back from his desk to review the program. He seldom altered the busy work that Hubert Brown prepared for him. Monsignor Hubert Brown had been with him during his previous tenure in Indianapolis. With his experience, he understood how to manage the affairs and activities of a diocese. Placing the program back on the desk, he noted, "This will be fine, Hubert, as usual. I know it's late but will you get the proceedings of the last council meeting from the shelf?"

Hubert Brown retrieved the binder from the lowest shelf of the library stack that covered two walls of the library office where the new Archbishop of the Detroit Archdiocese had settled in as his prime work area.

"We've been here four months and I still have eleven parishes to visit. This recession is playing havoc with our finances, Hubert. For two years now the unemployment problem is getting out of hand. Many parishes are turning to us for financing or help to feed more people. Our schools are beginning to have trouble with enrollment going down. The decreased enrollment decreases the amount of state aid. Of course, other states don't even receive that aid. Bishop Manning, of course, has been able to renegotiate many teacher contracts to keep costs under control. Even so, he thinks we should close some grade schools or consolidate some. I don't want that to happen."

"You might want to look at this article in the paper. It's from the morning *Press*." Monsignor Brown folded the paper so that the quarter page article on page two was face up on the archbishop's desk.

The article titled 'Divine Healer of Detroit' caught his immediate attention. As he read the first paragraph, he commented, "Just another park preacher. We had quite a few in Indianapolis. The difference is these years, even after the year of the millennium having passed, more than a few are still announcing themselves as the 'new savior,' or 'the second coming' or something. Just park preachers causing quite a stir around the country. Some predict the end of the world causing quite a stir. Pour me another cup of coffee, would you, Hubert?"

"This seems somewhat more than that in the article, P.G.," He responded as he refilled the cup from the porcelain and silver coffee service. It's almost nine-thirty and still light out," he noted looking out the draped fenestra windows of the library. "That garden certainly needs tending to. Hasn't Albert found someone to replace the gardener? You know Doctor Snow has told you to cut down on the coffee. The coffee maker is almost empty and it holds twenty cups."

"It helps keep me awake on these long days. The way you go on, I can see why priests are glad they can't marry. At least I can just ignore you or tell you just see it's taken care of," he responded with a chuckle. Leaning back in his chair, he waved the newspaper towards Hubert asking, "Do you know this Crawford person?"

"Don't think so."

"He seems to have some big ideas inside his story about this 'divine' aspect of this Adams fellow."

"Seems so."

"I think you or someone should look into this quiet like. The story sounds rather incredible."

"What do you suggest?"

"Just take care of it and let me know what this fellow pretends to be about."

"Got your attention, did it?" Sam Crawford replied to the sallow faced slender blond inquirer. "Where did you say you're from?" he continued, knowing the answer from Hubert Brown's first question.

Monsignor Brown stood before the desk of Sam Crawford with the newspaper article rolled in his hand. "The Archbishop's office. I'm secretary to Archbishop Paul Gregory. He thought your story bordered on the incredulous."

Crawford reached into the bulging pocket of the seersucker suit coat to extract a pack of 'Sensibles', the no-tar licorice flavored cigarettes. As he lit up a cigarette, he commented, "God damnation, these are terrible. Nothing like the old Marlboros. Why don't you sit down there?"

"They certainly are better for your health. Where does this Adams, Daniel Adams, come from? Is he a Detroiter?" he asked as he sat down across from Sam Crawford.

"Don't really know yet. He just sort of showed up. Your people, the archbishop, feel he's treading on your territory?"

"That's rather absurd," Hubert Brown asserted. No use telling Crawford that he was a priest, a priest secretary to the archbishop. He had been told to look into this quietly. He didn't think that his attire of sport trousers and a tieless dress shirt would betray him. "He was interested in your use of the 'divine' with healing in your article. You surely don't think that this man is endowed with some strange power?"

"Well, there's certainly been some healing going on, from what people have been saying. Some pretty serious stuff, I'd say. And this Adams is somehow a little different from me or you," Sam Crawford affirmed as he stuffed the cigarette out in the half filled ashtray. "Is this an official visit from your archbishop?"

Hubert wrinkled his nose as the dying odor of the cigarette smoke passed him and he responded, "Not really. A bit of curiosity, I would say. We've always had our share of park preachers."

"Adams doesn't exactly do much preaching. Maybe you should make a visit to the park. See what he's about," Crawford suggested.

"What is it that he has to say? What kind of a speech does he give?" He inquired, slightly turning his narrow lips up at the side as though the vary thought of this 'divine' individual having something to say was offensive.

Crawford smiled at this hint of disdain. "I think you're in for a big surprise. No speech. Just a message."

"What kind of a message?" he asked with a lilt of disbelief.

"Just a message of peace and love and service to one to another. You know, almost bible stuff."

Hubert Brown stood idly on the sidewalk near the checker and chess players. It was late morning and he felt equally uncomfortable in the humid morning as the late July temperature began to rise as he felt less than adequately clothed in the denim sleeveless shirt and trousers he wore. He already felt out of place. Everyone appeared older than he except the women and the children beginning to congregate in the shaded wooded area near the swings, slide and wooden climbing structure. Although in his mid forties, he looked even younger being slight of build and blond hair.

Charles noted him first. "You're new here, sonny," he declared and waited for a response. Seemingly unheard, he continued, "You better stay in the shade. Those white arms will get burnt in the sun out here."

Hubert's uneasiness was reinforced by Charles' garrulous greeting. The white skin of his neck and face flushed pink slightly as he responded, "Right. Just visiting."

Amos intervened as he noticed Hubert's discomfort, "Don't let him bother you any. He only pretends to be unfriendly. Makes him feel good. That's Charles and I'm Amos."

"I'm Hubert. Hubert Brown," he replied.

"Didn't mean nothing, Hubert. Just blond people like you seem to sunburn easy. Play chess?"

"Not really."

"That's what all you youngsters say. Just like Daniel. He'd liked to whoop me at chess though. But he didn't."

Hubert Brown's senses were immediately alerted at the mention of Daniel Adams' name. He was surprised at the size of the gathering in the park, which continued to grow in size and now numbered close to a thousand. Some had folding chairs and had assembled in small groups and were busy in small conversation. Others were seemingly unoccupied or reading the newspaper. The crowd now had become of mixed age, some younger than he was. The hum of the chatter was surmounted by the grinding engine noise of the motorcycle that came to stop curbside. The young rider, dressed in black leather, now stood next to the motorcycle conversing with his woman companion. The whole crowd of people exuded an aura of expectancy. Many seemed to repeatedly glance either to the north end of the street or toward the boys playing baseball beyond the wooded area. Hubert noted Sam Crawford getting out of his red Contour parked up the street. He was lucky to find a place to park, next to a fire hydrant, as each side of the street was occupied by parked cars of the growing visiting throng. The circular parking area at the opposite end of the park was filled with cars and people were flowing from that direction. He watched as Sam lit up one of those ugly smelling cigarettes as he leaned against the car and surveyed the growing crowd.

The expectancy seemed fulfilled as the attention of the crowd became directed to the north side of the park as a lone bicyclist appeared slowly pedaling toward them. The movement of the crowd gradually became oriented toward the visitor and the murmuring increased with comments of 'there he is', 'I told you he'd be here today'.

Hubert surveyed the man on the bicycle who was much the same age as himself. He noted the hair to the shoulder, the small black beard and the long sleeved white shirt. As he came close enough he could see the shirt was collarless and he wore gray trousers. A young woman in an ankle length brocade print skirt and white blouse trotted, almost running, toward the biker. Her approach caused the biker to stop. He leaned the bike against a signpost and was in a conversation with the woman.

The crowd now was mostly standing and had moved as a staggered group toward the visitor leaving lawn chairs and the checker and chess tables behind them. The visitor disappeared within the crowd. Hubert stood at the border of the crowd. He could feel an uncomfortable internal excitement. He could feel his heart beat against his chest and his eyes moisten. A mother nearby, smiling eagerly, raised a small child above the crowd saying, "See, there his is." Hubert's momentary emotional response was chilled by a feeling of being an intruder as he found Sam Crawford at his side commenting, "Quite a sight, eh, Mr. Brown?" Crawford continuing, "The archbishop must be pretty interested in Daniel Adams to send his Monsignor secretary Hubert Brown to spy", further deflated Hubert.

Monsignor Hubert Brown felt invaded and offended by Crawford replying, "A spy? You're the spy. Why would you want to know about me?"

"This is a story here, monsignor. When things don't make sense, you check it out. I checked you out with the news people at the religious desk. Now it makes more sense. Like I said, there's a story here."

"The archbishop wouldn't like to be part of a park preacher's story."

"Oh, this isn't a story about the archbishop, yet."

Their conversation was interrupted by the voice of Daniel Adams. The voice was quiet but penetrating, easily heard as the crowd grew silent to hear what he would say. He seemingly stood alone, separated from the crowd, and appeared a head higher than everyone.

"Is he standing on something?" Hubert asked Crawford.

"Oh, no. He stands on a knoll, a little hill. It just works out that way."

"Shrewd," replied Hubert as he too awaited the words of Daniel Adams.

"Peace be with you," Daniel repeated again raising his hands out above and toward the people.

"And with you," responded several from the assembled crowd.

"Many of you have asked of little Anthony Perkins."

"He's the one with the injured and deformed leg," Sam Crawford whispered to Hubert.

"So?" he replied, raising his hands gesturing. "So what?"

Daniel continued, "The physicians at the medical center have examined him and are going to operate on his knee next Friday. They offer great expectation that they can help him. Pray the Lord gives wisdom and skill to the physicians."

The crowd murmured.

Hubert Brown grunted.

Sam Crawford smiled as he scribbled in his note pad.

"May our love for one another and for the Lord bring strength to each of us that we may serve those in need. While the work of the physicians is in the faith in the Lord others like Anthony Perkins and his mother among us find these times very difficult. There is much hunger. Many are without work. I have come to you to serve."

The crowd grew restless.

Hubert Brown turned to go commenting, "Nothing divine here."

Sam Crawford goaded him a little. "Give up so soon? You would deny him so soon?"

Hubert was not amused at Sam Crawford's challenge and turning to leave, commented, "Just a do gooder."

He stopped momentarily as Daniel Adams continued, "We should look among us to help those in need. Amos has been able to provide space adjacent to his place of worship, a vacant store front on Grand Boulevard, to bring us together and provide a meal for those in need."

Amos stood tall with a beaming smile.

"Who is this Amos?" Hubert Brown inquired.

"He's one of the regulars here in the park. Daniel says he's a Moslem."

Hubert Brown grunted.

"We are in need of bread and cheese, and vegetables for soup. We are in need of strong and willing hands to serve the Lord. Tom White and Naomi will be at our new kitchen this Thursday morning and each Thursday."

The crowd spoke out 'the biker?' 'why would he?'

Tom White stood beside Daniel. "I was wrong," he said. "I have much to make up. Do not be afraid of me. Daniel has forgiven me. The Lord forgives me. I have had much bitterness until now. The Lord has freed me from this bitterness. We need only a few hands to help, to prepare and to serve the food and to clean up afterwards. Those of you who have bread, cheese, crackers, vegetables and can help, please come Thursday morning."

"How will those who need know about the free meal?" a voice asked from the crowd.

"They will know. A few at first," Daniel replied.

"We are not rich. Where will the food come from?"

"Have faith. There will be enough."

"A soup kitchen. That's what I call divine. Who's this Tom White?"

"He's the one who smashed Daniel Adams' head on the curb last week ago. You read my article."

"Peace be with you. Go and love one another. Let your work be in the name of the Lord," Daniel invoked to the assembled crowd.

Hubert couldn't explain the chill that surrounded his body beneath the sweaty denim shirt. His mind was blurry and confused as he turned to leave the park.

Sam Crawford sat at a park bench, his blue seersucker coat beside him. Sweat slowly drained into his loosened shirt collar as he scribbled in his note pad. He smiled and blew a wisp of cigarette smoke in the direction of the departing monsignor. "You should meet the man sometime, Hubert," he called out. "You're in the same business."

Bishop Manning had completed presenting his projected school consolidation program to Archbishop Gregory and was leaving as Monsignor Brown entered the library. "Stay a minute, Roger. Hubert has been looking into the newspaper story of the park preacher. I suppose you read about it in the *Press*. Seems to be a topic of discussion."

"Indeed. Sounds like some preposterous story of some mentally imbalanced vagrant. You know the lack of state funds has most of them out on the street. All the more for us to feed," Bishop Manning declared.

"Well, Hubert, what did you find?"

"This Adams is a tantalizing personality. Attracts a crowd as if by magic."

"A 'divine' attraction, Hubert?"

"I wouldn't say that but he sure makes you uneasy inside."

"And the miracles? The divine cures?" he asked with a smirk.

"Just Crawford's word, so far. I intend to talk to the police who saw him and the doctor who treated him, the sources that Crawford noted. He sent some deformed kid to see a doctor and he's got the crowd into starting another soup kitchen."

"Now, that's something I can appreciate," Bishop Roger Manning affirmed. "We can't feed everybody ourselves. Where does he expect to get the food from? Don't tell me he expects to multiply the bread and the fish?" he chuckled.

"No," Hubert Brown replied with a serious semblance of a frown. "He expects to rally the people to help other people, to have faith, he said."

"Let me know what you find out. These certainly are difficult times. A little faith certainly is needed. A lot of faith, indeed."

"Don't forget the meeting in Cincinnati on the sixteenth. We have some serious decisions to make. Either we stand together now or go our individual ways. It is not likely our new pope will make a visit during the winter after the pilgrimage to the holy land in September. Hopefully, he will wait until spring. That would give us more time. We have no idea how he may respond but it is time for Rome to understand the world is changing. The issues of marriage for some priests and of the dignity of death are important."

"I understand we have eleven more signers. That gives us ninety-one aboard."

"Hardly close to a plurality. We need some of the older bishops. This must be carried on in a very orderly fashion. Good night, Roger."

Archbishop Gregory glanced at Hubert Brown busily arranging papers. He knew Hubert was not sympathetic to the proposed changes. "This all bothers you a lot, doesn't it, Hubert?"

"I'm not familiar or comfortable with such things."

"We are only interested starting a dialogue. The suffering of so many is so great. They deserve a dignified option."

"It is not our business to decide these things. We are to support their being, their hearts and especially their souls, not their body. We leave that to God and the physicians."

"You argue well but it is time for many changes. The church is standing still leaving the people or vice verse they are so far ahead they are leaving the church if not in body in spirit. Our ranks of priests are so diminished; those that remain are unable to serve the people. The question of celibacy and marriage need to be discussed.

"The church welcomes the married Anglican priests from England and Africa into the church. I don't know how much future they have in the church. I don't see any of them becoming any more than bishops. And then there are over twenty thousand ex-priests who are now married. They are well organized. Many wait and have expressed the hope that the church may find a way to accept them back."

"I am not part of this. I can leave this to you bishops."

"Be careful, my friend. It will not be long before you are a bishop. It is a different responsibility."

"In the mean time, I will look into the story of this Daniel Adams."

CHAPTER 14

Daniel had spent a long day. He retrieved the notes from his bike carrier basket. The notes and sketches had been just made at the home of the Steiners. The bookcases would take several days and he was concerned because he must learn about the plastic or metal.

He had spent the morning with Amos and Tom White at the storefront building discussing the arrangements for tomorrow's first day meal gathering. There would be table area for over twenty people to eat. The kitchen area was small with just a double electric burner to cook the big pot full of soup. Somewhere, Tom White had gathered together an abundance of vegetables for the soup. All this would be kept in the refrigerator of the National food market near the storefront. Daniel hoped the food had been begged, freely given, rather than borrowed or stolen, for there were other Thursdays to follow.

The afternoon was partially used to visit Andrew Perkins. Surgery was scheduled for Friday and Andrew was very excited. "Then, I will be able to play real baseball," he had said. "And, you will come and watch me?" he had asked.

"Now, you just leave Mr. Adams alone," Molly Perkins had tartly chastised him.

"Certainly. And your mother, too," Daniel had assured. "Dr. Solari said you had signed all the papers for your Medicaid."

"Not because I wanted to. Just for Andrew," she informed Daniel, still a bit defiant about taking 'welfare'. "People don't look up to others that take welfare," she had repeated.

"Well, tomorrow you can help those who also need help," he had quietly continued.

"Don't know rightly how I'm to do that," she bemoaned.

"Those who help each other help themselves and do the work of the Lord," Daniel said. He continued, "Tomorrow, noontime, there will be a gathering for a noon meal for those in need. You can both partake and serve."

Molly Perkins' look lost a bit of harshness as her pinched forehead and tight lips loosened slightly. "And where's this supposed to happen?" she asked.

"At the storefront a block north of the National Market on Grand Boulevard," Daniel explained. "All who want to help are welcome. All who are in need of a meal are welcome." He had smiled inwardly as he noticed a faint smile on Molly Perkins' lips for the second time since they had met. "Tell your friends who might share."

He placed his bike inside the garage. It was an overcast muggy evening, still, with little breeze, and humid from the morning rain and even though only shortly after five o'clock it was approaching darkness because of the cloudy overcast. As he approached the back stairs to his flat, he noticed a light in his window. Mrs. Erdhiem again, he thought. She often tidied up his flat; "as long as he didn't mind," she had said the first time she had offered.

Indeed, it appeared that she had as he closed the door to the flat. He opened a window hoping the night air might be a little cooling. He immediately entered the bathroom. Disrobing his sweaty damp clothes, he entered the tub shower. He relished the lukewarm cooling shower as he soaped and washed his salty sweaty body. He then, partially dried, stood before the mirror to comb his hair and dry and partially trim his beard.

As he stood there before the sink and mirror, a shadow altered the light from the doorway of the bathroom. Daniel drew the towel about his waist simultaneously thinking "Mrs. Erdhiem wouldn't still be here" and looked toward the doorway.

The naked light-olive form of Valentine Baden framed in the door way took a short step forward. The lithe olive body burned an unrest within Daniel. The curvaceous outline was pleasing. He could feel the thunder within his body as the pert breasts pouted toward him. She shook her dark flowing hair saying with a soft smile, "I am here, Daniel."

Daniel Adams turned his back to her and asked, "Please go, Valentine." He could feel her warmth and her vibration continue to slowly approach.

She said his name, "Daniel." She spoke almost in a whisper.

"Please, you must go. It is not right to treat your holy body this way. The Lord will not—"

She now stood close behind him with her taughtness just touching his lower back. Her hand gently held the side of Daniel's arm. She stood there a moment slowly drawing him closer. "The Lord will be pleased that I thank you for saving Jeremy's life."

"Not this way," Daniel affirmed. His body was warm in an embarrassed discomfort of guilt as the moment was pleasing. His hand touched her hand for a moment. He could feel her vibrating warmth close to him and now grow cold.

"Daniel, what is happening? It is so cold. I feel numb all over," she murmured.

He felt her cold hand slip from his arm. Her body slowly fell to the floor where she lay as asleep.

She awoke fully clothed. She lay barely awake in a cloudy cold darkness. The chill in her body caused her to draw her legs and arms close to her body seeking warmth. Suddenly, she sat up on the bed calling, "Daniel, what has happened?"

He appeared at the doorway.

"What am I doing here? I feel so cold."

"For moment you will not be able to remember that which you do not wish to recall. The coldness does that. But in a moment you will remember most. When you are fully aware come to the kitchen. I have prepared some tea, tea and toast, and perhaps some cheese if you would like."

Valentine lay back a moment. The coolness abated. Her thoughts came nearly whole. She arose swiftly from the bed and to the doorway. "Who dressed me? Did you?"

"Unfortunately there was no one but me."

"I am so embarrassed," she began.

"There is no embarrassment in being grateful. Sometimes things get out of hand, overstated, you might say. Come. Sit. The tea is hot and strong," he continued as he poured a second cup of tea and replenished his cup.

"I am ashamed," she began again. "I don't have much to give for such a great gift that you gave." She sipped the tea. She applied a small shaving of cheese on a cracker.

They sat in a moment of silence.

Daniel smiled and sipped the tea.

Valentine chided, "You are laughing at me. You think I am a little girl."

"I was smiling," Daniel said, "because you have expressed the greatest gift that one can give, the gift of love. You have very much to give. You are rich in love. For the moment you only mistook the way to express your love in your quest to show your feeling of gratitude."

"Jeremy has meant so much to me and I wanted to thank you."

"It is not me that you must be grateful to, it is God to whom you must give thanks."

"But it would not have happened. He would not have survived if you had not been there."

"We do not know that, do we?" He sat his cup down. He paused and Valentine did likewise. He folded his hands before him on the kitchen table and bowed his head. Valentine did likewise.

"Lord, our savior—"

CHAPTER 15

ROME

It was the fifth day of fast, almost a week, of only liquid and reluctantly the daily prescribed supplement of vitamins urged by Dr. Marcus.

The staff was notified that Pope John Alexander would have a light meal in his quarters that evening as soon as the barber had been discharged from his hastily scheduled visit.

The message was sent that he would audience Monsignor Majee and Dr. Marcus at seven in the evening.

Anna exited the quarters at seven o'clock carrying a dinner tray piled high with service pieces and dinner leftovers. She was smiling and exuberant declaring, "He's a new man, almost his old self today, well, really since yesterday."

Majee and Marcus rose from their seats of expectancy.

"Why didn't you tell us when we asked you how he was?"

"Oh, he's been very busy, too busy to be interrupted," she declared knowingly. "Said he could see clearly but needed his privacy. I told him you were asking about him, about his health. But he said, 'In due time'. I guess that time is now," she concluded.

Majee and Marcus watched Anna recede. They indeed had inquired of his health several times in addition to sending frequent messages of wishing to meet with him. Even more disquieting to them, they had been personally deferred abruptly when they had knocked at his door. To be treated in such an off-handed manner had alarmed them as they saw this as a change in Pope John Alexander's personality. He was forever a man of courtesy, a man of gentle dignity. They knocked at the door and opened it in response to the familiar voice of their life-long friend bidding in Hungarian, "Come. We will talk."

He continued in their natural Hungarian, "We will share a brandy. We will talk."

The visitors stood for a moment relieved of their fears for the well being of their friend. He stood at the side-table pouring three couplets of brandy. He stood erect in a clean white shirt with the gray streaked black well groomed hair. He turned with a smile, a tired smile, embraced by a clean-shaven face of strength. His heavy black eyelashes seemed to cause his eyes to penetratingly embrace his friends.

"We are glad to see you are in a better disposition," Majee noted accepting the proffered brandy.

"You have lost weight," Marcus observed.

"But, of course," John Alexander replied, "always the doctor," he observed with a smile.

"Always concerned about my friend."

"Come, we will sit," they were directed. "We will talk of our young friend, Marie," he continued looking down into the amber depth of the brandy he slowly rotated at the end of his strong long fingers. "The prefect here has notified me that the investigation of her death following your visit Janos has been completed. He said he had signed the matter out as a suicide. I informed him that her death was not a suicide but an unfortunate accident. He agreed to amend the report."

"Did you explain the nature of the accident to the prefect?" Janos Majee inquired. The monsignor looked up as expecting as explanation which to his displeasure and disappointment was not forthcoming.

"No. I didn't. I thanked him for his devotion and dedication." He paused to sip his brandy and retrieved the wrinkled envelope with the letter inside. The leaf was open so it was evident that the letter had been extracted and read.

"What is this?" Marcus inquired.

"It is a note that was in Marie's pocket that I retrieved from the prefect," Janos noted.

"And I appreciate that you sent it on to me. Of course you know its contents." John Alexander opened the letter, leaving the fifty thousand lira note within the envelope, and glanced across the half page message written in Hungarian. Without reading it to himself again he felt the warmth of emotion expressed as Marie had proclaimed her devotion to him as a person and as her priest and had continued to apologize for her actions as she had been in need of money. She had died before she could give him the envelope. But the message mystified him as he had no insight how anything related to money and why the fifty thousand lira was included with the note. He began to read the letter aloud. "'My priest and precious friend,' she says," he began. He stopped and let the paper fall to his side.

His two close friends had sat upright, at near attention, without moving. As he stopped speaking, they look at each other and Marcus asked, "And?"

"And she apologizes for everything that led to the 'dreadful story' as she called it."

"She meant the one in the *Gazetteer*."

"I suppose so but she had written the note before the stories appeared, but she had related the 'story' to her mother and Anna, and who knows who else." There was a silence, a silence long enough for each to enjoy the diversion of the brandy.

"What about everything that led up to the story? And what are we going to do about that story?" Majee inquired.

John Alexander had selected a cigar from his small tabletop humidor. He proceeded to unwrap it, pinch the end off and savor the end of the unlit cigar and before lighting, looked up at the two friends and with a slight smile at the corners of his mouth replied, "We can do nothing about the story. Marie's death and the story are unrelated even though the *Gazetteer* has chosen to link them." He stopped speaking to light the cigar with the silver lighter. He puffed gently on the cigar and pointed to the bottle of brandy suggesting that a refill was indicated.

Pope John Alexander sipped his brandy and toasted towards the cross and nodding affirmatively toward his companions. "It is a lesson. For three days I denied my Lord in my perceived depth of despair, in failure. I may be a sinner but I am blessed. It is I who abandoned the Lord. It is I who forgot the Word is whole in my soul. He would not abandon me."

"But is no statement to be issued?" queried Majee.

"What is there to say? I remember nothing from the event that has been alluded to. The last time I saw Marie on the day they specifically speak of, among others, she was standing right next to the chair that Marcus is sitting in." He did not relate the memory of what he had seemed to remember but not too clearly remember. He had a faint distant memory of Marie beginning to disrobe. He found such a memory difficult to believe. "Never the less," he continued after contemplating the growing ash on the tip of the cigar and tapping off into the ashtray, "There is the story and of course the conversation with

Marie's mother. My problem, my friends, is that, in the eyes of some, I have sinned, sinned grievously. For this I have anguished and looked for guidance in abstinence. As God is in my very being, I have found no truth that is of my knowledge to create this heavy heart."

The pause, the silence, of friendship did not require an inquiry of statement of understanding. Their years together had created a band of unspoken allegiance. The simple things of man to man sealed the band, a brandy, a game of backgammon, brash talk in private.

"You should know that there is a diary of Maries. The *Gazetteer* spoke of it. You should know I have hired a private investigator to search for it. He is reliable, confidential and will be well paid if successful, more than the *Gazetteer* would want to pay. I have my secretary determining the names of the employees of the *Gazetteer*. We will discern the parish of any of the employees. We will find at least one devout parishioner to assist us and who also would be well compensated on recovery of the diary."

John Alexander seated himself after pacing during the explanation of Monsignor Majee's plan. He flicked the ashes from the cigar and slowly sipped the brandy. "As you will, Janos," he responded as though the problem was behind him. This was John Alexander who now left disappointment and personal attacks upon himself behind him looking to the morrow and anticipating the expected joy of another day in God's service. "I understand that the September trip is as yet incomplete. Probably because I have changed it to include the Patriarch and the Israelis?"

"Cardinal Vittoria and I, with others, spoke of it only several days ago," Majee replied slowly. He could see the glitter in John Alexander's eyes and could feel an anticipation in his speech. "You disturb them, I think."

"Well, I am what I am. These few days have cleared my vision. I am only one person, a servant of God, a servant of the people, all the people."

"You are pope."

"Of course. But foremost, I am a human being, a simple Christian who is pope and believes in the joy and hope of being a Christian as millions of Catholic and non-Catholic believe in the salvation of Christ Jesus." He sipped the brandy, paused, smiled towards Marcus and raised his brandy. "A simple Christian with a blistering backhand," he said to Marcus.

"Monday night," Marcus confirmed. "You better eat something to bolster that backhand between now and then."

The diversion was momentary.

"The symbolism is fine. We will delay the mid-east trip exactly thirty days. The weather will still be good there."

"You are going to upset many people."

"I am pope." He smiled as he said the simple words. "There are no religious or political moments to prevent the change in plans."

"It is time to minister to the Christians of the world and others who wish to hear."

"You have something in mind?"

John Alexander turned to his desk and returned with a sheaf of hand-written papers. He held them toward his two friends.

"The Christian ecumenical dialogue," he stated. "The last day and a half I have pondered and set down a sequence of activities. One God, one salvation, one people. First to the Americas. In August we will go. We will go to Detroit first. I haven't decided where to host the next assembly."

Marcus and Janos were momentarily taken back. Marcus looked at John Alexander with a physician's critical eye. Had he embarked on a mystical brainstorm? Was he enjoying a flight of fancy? Had the stress of the recent events created some mental or emotional imbalance? His appraisal was interrupted by Janos who asked, "Why Detroit? Why not New York, Chicago or Los Angeles, some major media city? If it doesn't happen in New York or California, the media doesn't know it happens."

"Detroit," repeated John Alexander. "For some reason I see God's hand leading me to Detroit. People say Detroit is the workingman's city, a city of common people. That is where we will go. Don't worry about New York. As you said, I am pope. They will know. You can be sure television will cover not only the event but also the preparations. The world will know what we do there."

"You said assembly, a Christian dialogue?"

The excitement in John Alexander's decision was pervasive. Marcus could see that this was his true self. It had taken these months to be able to clearly express his basic person, his basic relationship to God and to set it in motion.

"Yes, it will be an assembly of Christians, all Christians. We will extend invitations to all those who believe in Jesus Christ, the savior, to attend. The leaders and the people will be invited. We will begin a dialogue of love and understanding. I will meet with any Christian leadership privately who will respond to my invitation." John Alexander paused and sipped the remainder of his brandy. He flipped the ash off the cigar and noticing it had extinguished discarded it with a crush into the ashtray. He smiled resolutely. "In fact, I will meet with the non-Christian leaders privately, if they wish. After all, the unity of those who believe in the one God, the God of Islam and the God of Judea, must dictate the rules of civilized society."

"In one assembly?" inquired Janos Majee.

"There will be several," he replied and appeared to stop mid-sentence as though he was in a moment of contemplation. His lips quivered in a pursing motion and his eyelids blinked repeatedly. He sat there unmoving staring at his two friends.

Marcus observing this change in attitude of John Alexander, "What is wrong, my friend?" he inquired as he rose from his chair. There was no reply. He approached his patient.

There was no recognition from John Alexander who sat back in chair, closed his eyes and appeared to be asleep. Marcus approached his patient more closely and raised one of his eyelids. There was no response. Marcus however observed the rapid constriction of the pupil in response, took his pulse and satisfied with the condition of his 'patient' and spoke to Janos Majee, "He will sleep for a while, perhaps half an hour."

Janos had also risen to observe the startling event. As Marcus indicated he and Janos should leave the pope alone and allow their friend to sleep for 'he appears exhausted'. Janos noted out loud, "That is just as Marie's mother described Marie's description the day of the debacle!"

"That is interesting. Then I believe I know what the story is, the answer to what happened with Marie, her story, Maries' mother's story," Marcus declared.

Bewildered, Janos threw his hands into the air and exclaimed, "Well, I wish someone would explain it all to me."

Marcus was unrevealing to Janos. The secret of petit mal that afflicted the pope was a medical confidence. Well controlled for years, for some reason the current medication was at this time ineffective or had my patient failed to take the medication during this time of stress and excitement. He would look into that later question when his patient reawakened. "Perhaps he will discuss it with you, himself. The excitement and lack of nourishment have obviously taken their toll."

"He will be fine," he assured Janos as they were leaving the papal suite. "Sometimes stress and high anxiety accentuate and precipitate his problem. I will have to look into his medication. We will return later."

"But what's wrong with him?"

"Perhaps you should know. Perhaps he will want you to know. That will be his decision. We will wait here with him. He will awaken in a short time," he went on as he looked at his watch, "perhaps thirty or forty minutes, about nine o'clock.

"Trust me. He will be just fine and your story is most important. It can help explain much that has happened."

Monsignor Janos Majee wished he could not hear the hushed conversation of John Alexander and Marcus. The partially opened doors allowed the words to leak out. "No, it is better if no one else knows. You are my doctor and responsible to this confidence. The world need not know."

"Janos knows more about your current misunderstanding and if it weren't for him, we would not know the answer."

"I wish you would explain it to me."

"Janos and I can explain together."

"I guess so."

"You can trust him with your life let alone this confidence," he affirmed as he opened the door to motion Janos to the bedroom suite.

"I can understand your reluctance to extend your confidence to me," Janos began as though he were treading in forbidden territory.

"It is not you, my friend. I am partly ashamed and afraid of my affliction. When I was a boy, some said I was crazy, while others said I was demented, stupid."

"Of course, that's all nonsense," Marcus continued. "What you witnessed an hour ago was an episode of petit mal, a non-convulsive form of epilepsy. For some reason, his medication has become less effective. He assures me he has been faithful in taking his daily medication. Some call them absence seizures, which mean the brain is dulled for a few moments and instead of an uncontrolled violent seizure, simpler body movements occur, as in our friend's case, movements of the eyes, lips and sometimes the nose. During this minute or several minutes, there is no control. The brain is focally in overdrive, so to speak, so it's called petit obviously for 'small' seizure. Then many times he goes to sleep for a variable length of time and awakening with no remembrance of most of the time." Marcus held his hands up as a signal of conclusion of the short lecture.

"Everything fits the description I heard from Anna of the events that Marie's mother described," Janos slowly projected, "You have no memory of anything that happened that moment with Marie?"

Pope John Alexander hesitated, "Well if we are to explain this. I must say that I have a vague recollection of her beginning to remove her blouse. That is all. I awoke on the bed after that. I don't know what happened while I was unaware in the bedroom."

"Nothing happened," Marcus interjected sharply. "Nothing could have happened."

"But she said or her mother said she told her."

"Nothing," Marcus again spoke up "Nothing could have happened."

Janos had told no one of the so-called evidence or the story of the unholy wager but the diary if found would probably reveal the bragging of Marie in the deception of her friend involved in the wager.

CHAPTER 16

❀

"We will arrive in Detroit for our first visit on August fourteen," the pope continued as he outlined his gospel to the people to be delivered to the people of North America. He had explained, "As Paul had outlined, critiqued and delivered the message two thousand years before, the children of God, each and every one, shall know the love, hope and dignity of the living word of Jesus Christ. I will speak to them as the father of the children of God, those born and unborn, those of tender age and those who have traveled the long road of life. They will know me as the Church and as such as their Good Shepherd."

The twenty-one cardinals that he had gathered sat in stunned silence as he delivered his plans. As he continued they began to mutter in low tones one to the other. Pope John Alexander knew that his next presentation would rouse their curiosity with great discomfort. The larger group sitting behind the enclave of cardinals, clergy, bishops, archbishops and a few administrative laypersons understood the discomfort of the chosen.

"We meet here at St. John Lateran because as we will meet in the future as the third council convenes and as we begin our journey to North America we bring the rock that was Peter to the traveler that was Paul, we bring the essence of each that rests here in this cathedral.

"We will begin our dialogue of the council this winter but first I will initiate our dialogue with the rest of the Christian world.

"We will listen!

"I will listen!!"

He paused. He had made his announcement to cardinals and clergy who had been called to this convocation of faith. They had no prior knowledge of the reason for the summons. Cardinal Vittorio had been given the order directly by John Alexander and members of his office had made the calls as directed for the "convocation of faith." They had also made the calls to the clergy and others for the luncheon meeting to present the outlined plan that he had labored for two days to conceive a labor of love, God's love.

The pause allowed the words, the terms of John Alexander's faith and mission, to settle in. The first seconds were accompanied by slow negative appearances that then dissipated to immobile silenced bowed heads as they finally heard.

"This is the vision I have. This is the mission I feel is the moment of the church in the world. It is a calling I feel necessary to respond to." With these words he placed the visit to North America a step above his own personal decision. He left the feeling with the words of vision and calling that this was a mission of faith, a mission that his faith required.

"I am in need of legitimate guidance and abundant logistical support and am open to any suggestion to assist in accomplishing this mission and am open to general questions at this time." There was a stirring among the clerical. There was low chattering from the back seats. A new relationship from the congregation had been requested publicly.

"We have all read, as we hope the faithful through out the world have read, your Determinate letter espousing in the first part the shepherdhood of all Christians and expressing the joy and hope of salvation based on the authority of scripture and the second part to explore and define the elements of the apostate among Christian leaders. We understand the wish for dialogue but the path is not clear. Dialogue must lead to communion. Communion must see the face, the heart of God. How does this journey lead us there?" was the first question from the learned cardinal.

John Alexander paused as he could see such dialogue could continue for hours. He had determined the mission. He had opened the character of his leadership. He would be a shepherd with ears. But it became obvious that to continue to answer every legitimate query publicly would cause confusion. He continued to answer the question by explaining the methods of his mission. "Not only will I meet with the leaders, we will attempt to have laity involved in the dialogue. More importantly, we will endeavor to achieve the widest television coverage possible so that the message, the homily, based on the essence of the dialogue will reach the people of the world, the people of God, and they will know that Pope John Alexander is their shepherd, shepherd to all people of the world in the name of he who gave his life for their salvation."

There was a brightness that emanated from the vibrancy of John Alexander's voice that entranced those listening. The quiet of St. John Lateran was recognition that John Alexander's mission and vision was now theirs also. No new questions. He had left no doubt that his will be done.

"Let us pray," he continued.

John Alexander had no idea where his extensive dialogue was supposed to lead. He knew that a better understanding and a trend to collegiality of the belief in one common God, to expel the hostilities of heritage, resentment, economics, politics and the host of other origins of hostility, was a useful goal.

Deep in his unspoken vision was that all Christians could over generations find a common communion.

He moved almost as in response to a revelation.

CHAPTER 17

DETROIT

"There were three thousand people there to listen to a park preacher, Hubert?" Archbishop Gregory exclaimed with darting wide eyes of disbelief. "Three thousand, you say?"

"At least. To see him for themselves. All ages, young people even," confirmed Monsignor Brown, nodding his head to accentuate.

"Must have caused quite a commotion."

"All quiet and quite orderly," Hubert Brown affirmed.

"Bound to be some disorder if it keeps up," the archbishop forecast. "Not likely though, to keep up that is, without some type of disturbance with all those people. There were no police there?" he added thoughtfully.

"No police. It's unbelievable, almost," Hubert related.

"What's unbelievable?"

"The hold he has over these people. The aura he presents. They look to him and believe in him. His first words are, 'Peace be with you.' and many in the congregated reply, 'Peace be with you.' Just like he was beginning mass."

"Thinks he's a priest or something, does he?" interrupted Archbishop Gregory.

"He doesn't claim anything except to bring a message of God's love."

"Sounds like he's a nuisance to me, a public nuisance. By the way, this is the latest news about our new pope," he quipped handing a copy of the newspaper to Hubert Brown.

"*The American Informer*?" he observed.

Bishop Gregory turned to the coffee maker to refresh his depleted morning coffee mug while Hubert reviewed the article and the archbishop added with a quirk chuckle, "The 'Pope's Girl', it says. Isn't that something? You know what that means."

"I wouldn't believe what the *Informer* says."

"It's not really their story. It's a story, pictures and all, from *The Gazetteer* in Rome. They know what's going on over there. Besides, the church would take them to court over it if there weren't some truth in it. Imagine, the girl commits suicide in despair over a relationship with the pope. Says she was his housekeeper and laundress. Who knows what else?" A sneer twisted the archbishop's face.

"I wouldn't believe everything they write. I understand that they don't like the church. They want to sell newspapers."

"Good looking, too. Be prepared for questions over this one."

"I wouldn't convict the holy father on the basis of this story. All these rags have had trouble keeping their circulation up the past several years. He deserves more credit, more faith."

"Well, it goes to his credibility and to the celibacy question. There will be changes some day."

"I'll look into this Daniel Adams more," Monsignor Brown indicated as he left the room

Archbishop Gregory, as Brown left the room, picked up the telephone. With a stern look on his face he awaited phone to be answered. "Sergeant Sweeney, please." He waited with shifting feet and sipped his coffee awaiting Sweeney's attendance at the phone. "Sergeant Sweeney? This is Archbishop Gregory."

"I'm fine. How are you?"

"That's fine. Look, there's a problem in town that needs a little taking care of."

He moved his feet impatiently as he listened to the response. He sat the coffee cup down as he replied. "I realize you 'owe me' as you say and this is a public nuisance problem that should be taken care of."

"What kind? You know the commotion at Bush Park created by the park preacher?"

"Well, good. You should look into it. I am sure he doesn't have a permit. That's unlawful assembly. Someone could get hurt and besides, it's not worth the cost to the city to control it with police. Maybe he doesn't get a permit if he asks for one."

"Free speech, you say? Well, I'm talking you as a public servant and as you say 'you owe me.'"

"That's right."

Gregory looked at the clock and shuffled his feet as he listened to officer Sweeney's response.

"That's right. Wait, there's more. He's opening a food kitchen this morning, giving free meals. I'm sure he doesn't have a public health permit. You should look into it."

"Right again. On East Grand Boulevard today."

"His name? His name's Daniel Adams. You better take a good look at him. He's probably a vagrant, you know, no job."

"I'm glad you understand. You're a good man, Sweeney. God bless you." Archbishop Gregory replaced the phone, looked to the floor and smiled, thinking, 'You have to deal with religious super fanatics anyway you can.'

The sign in the window said "Bush Park Welcome to Thursday Meal" in hand painted printed letters. The chairs had been arranged at the sides of the two long narrow makeshift tables.

Molly Perkins was struggling to cover the tables with the large roll of white paper.

"Here, I can help you with that," the slender blond man said as he stepped forward to grasp one side of the roll. "Two people can do it much easier together."

"Can use some help, 'spect. Should be cooking, but there's 'nuf back there now," she responded to the new helper. "Those new jeans you're wearin'? My name's Molly."

"I'm Hubert. Hubert Brown."

"Seen you at the park, I think. Didn't I?"

"Yes, maam. I was there."

"Thought so. Just fold that over the end while I cut it off. Don't mean to be bossing you around, any," she apologized with a slight blush coloring her neck. "Cept I usually don't have anyone helping me. Used to doin' myself."

"No problem."

"This here's butcher's paper, just wide enough to cover this top. These ain't regular tables," she concluded pointing to the tables made of various used doors resting on wooden sawhorses.

"Quite ingenious," the monsignor indicated.

"Oh, lots of people do that. The church I used to go to used these in their meeting room. Just put a cover on 'em and nobody knows the difference."

"What church is that?"

"The Baptist church over on Van Dyke. Just keep that side even over there, Hubert. It's getting a little crooked."

"I don't know that church."

"You go to church?"

"Why, yes," the monsignor replied a little taken back. The question of attending or not attending church, mass, never occurred to him. "I attend the Cathedral on Woodward Avenue," he continued.

"The Cathedral," Molly Perkins repeated. Then, with a slightly curled lip and cheek, stated, "Oh, you must be one of them."

Hubert Brown, surprised, stepped back from the table a moment letting go of the paper roll. The paper tore slightly on Molly Perkins side.

"Now see what you done," she spurted.

"I'm sorry," he hastened."

"I didn't mean nothin. Some of you Catholics just act too high and mighty fer me, like you're the only one's right."

Hubert didn't know whether to begin the teaching or desist and decided on a center ground. "Well, we all worship the same god, don't we?"

"I suppose. Let's get this finished," she urged. "I have to leave soon to visit my boy in the hospital."

"Is he ill?"

"Why no. He's the one goin to have surgery on his knee tomorrow."

"Oh. I didn't know."

"Most everyone knows."

"I recall. He was the one at the park."

"He's the one Daniel got the doctors to see."

"Well, I will certainly pray for him," assured Hubert Brown. "Andrew is his name?"

"Seems like there's a lot of that going on since Daniel showed up. Yes, my boy's name is Andrew."

"Prayer is a powerful thing," Hubert assured.

"Guess so. You pray much?"

The question beguiled Hubert Brown. Prayer was a part of his daily life. Prayer and a prayerful attitude surrounded eating, sleeping and doing the work of his clerical office. He felt dislocated from himself to be denied a basic part of his life because he was not dressed in his clerical garb. He did not have a chance to respond as simultaneously the store was a beehive of activity.

People had approached the front door inquiring about the Thursday meal.

A panel truck stopped in front of the store and it's driver got out to open the rear doors of the truck.

Naomi appeared from the back of the store and announced, "Soup is soup, Molly. Oh, I see you've found a helper."

"His name's Hubert."

"People are at the front door already," Naomi noted.

"You better take care of that," Molly demurred.

At the door were a young woman and a girl. Neat and clean, the woman stood with the girl clinging to her blue jean covered leg. "There'll be free eats?" she inquired from her pale narrow face. The words were sharp and distinct matching the severe dark hair pulled back and gathered in back with a small ribbon. "My daughter and I are looking for the free meal."

Before Naomi could respond to the woman and daughter, the deliveryman edged his way into the door asking, "Where do you want these things?"

"What is all that?" she inquired. "I'm sure we didn't order this."

"Carton lettuce, carton tomatoes, other vegetables, ten loaves bread, other stuff," he replied, not waiting for directions, and stacked his delivery inside the door.

"Tom," Naomi called out. "Tom, look at this!"

Tom White appeared at the back of the store. He wore a white partially freshly stained apron to the waist. The domesticated Tom White looked a little unbalanced, top heavy, with the broad shoulders and shoulder length hair. A light sweat glistened highlighting the prominent shoulder and neck muscles.

"Who's going to sign for these things?" the deliveryman inquired.

There was a moment of silence as no one had been designated to be in charge. The obvious question of who ordered the items and who would pay for them was on Tom White's mind when he asked, "Is there a bill with it?"

"Naw. It's all paid for," the driver indicated.

The red Contour pulled up to take the place of the departing panel truck. Sam Crawford peered out the passenger window. Assured this was the right place he picked up his seersucker coat and approached the store.

The young black boy with his nose against the glass looking into the window turned to ask, "This the place?"

"What place?" Sam Crawford rejoined.

"Place for a free meal?"

Sam could see the bustling inside the doorway and the long tables set up. He paused, loosened his collar and tie with one movement of his hand and was about to answer when the woman with her daughter came out of the door.

Seeing the two men she stopped to inform, "No food till noon, another hour. Of course you can help them get things together if you're a mind to." Taking her daughter's hand continuing on her way, "Be back then," she concluded.

The two men stood for a moment observing each other.

Sam Crawford had quickly surveyed the boy, seventeen maybe nineteen years old, slender as a twig and about the same height as himself. He was packaged in a Detroit Piston cap and oversized black and white athletic shoes, which appeared more like weights than shoes designed for athletic endeavor. Black denim trousers and a thin white tee shirt draped in between. He thought his light chocolate skin coincided with his narrow nose attesting to dilution of his black heritage somewhere in his history.

The young man quickly appraised his new acquaintance noting, "Don't expect you interested in a free meal," as he nodded toward the red car from which Sam Crawford had emerged.

"No, but I'm not afraid of a little free work. How 'bout you?"

"Not me."

"Let's go in, then," he indicated grasping the boy gently by the elbow and approaching the door. "My name's Sam."

"Edgar," he replied. "My name's Edgar J.L. Who are you?"

"I'm Sam Crawford, a reporter for the morning *Press*."

"Well now," Sam Crawford announced. "What kind of work do you have for two good workers?" He halted his greeting in midstream as he saw the incognito monsignor Hubert Brown engaged in arranging place settings. "Well, what do we have here?" Again he was halted in midstream by the shushing motion of Hubert Brown's finger to his lips. "Hubert Brown. Surprised to see you here. Can we help? This is Edgar, Edgar J.L."

"Meet Hubert Brown, Edgar."

"Hi."

"Guess I'm not surprised to see you here. You must think there's quite a story here."

"Let's just say I'm fascinated by all the things that don't completely add up."

Now who's the spy, Crawford thought. A spy or just an attraction to something not easily explained? The last person in the world that he had expected to see here was the Monsignor Hubert Brown. The Office of the Archbishop must have an interest in the activities of Daniel Adams to dispatch their monsignor secretary to the work of Daniel, incognito even.

Molly Perkins stopped placing the place settings of paper bowls and plastic utensils and looking up the three in conversation began, "We're never going to get finished if you're going to keep gabbing there. Oh, it's you, Mr. Crawford. Said you two want to help? We have to add a salad bowl and fork to each setting. Thanks to the unexpected delivery, we can add a lettuce and tomato salad to the meal. Whose your friend?"

"This is Edgar J.L. Edgar, this is Molly."

"S'pose you can help too, Edgar."

"Be glad to."

"What's this Edgar J.L.? Just put a napkin under each fork. What's your last name?"

"Louis. My mother always called me Edgar J.L. Edgar Joe Louis."

"Joe Louis!" Molly said with a big smile on her face. "Your mama wanted you to be a prize fighter. You gonna be a prize fighter?"

"No maam, Miss Molly. I be a preacher."

"You will have to finish up whatever Tom and Naomi have in mind for you. It's most twenty-five till and I have to get to the hospital," she informed the group as she took off her white apron. "Oh my," she said. "There some more out there now."

There was a pause in the bustle in the front room, the makeshift dining room. Molly had left. Edgar J.L. was stationed at the front door to greet and inform the gathering group of hungry patrons. In the background he could be heard, "Welcome, welcome," just as though he was the noonday host. "It'll be just a few minutes before everything is ready," as he disappeared to the sidewalk.

Sam Crawford withdrew a folded tabloid sized newspaper from the pocket of his coat, which had been draped over the back of a chair. "I suppose you've seen this already, Hubert," he began holding the face sheet forward displaying the bold face headline 'Pope's Girl' with accompanying pictures of Pope John Alexander and the girl Marie.

Hubert Brown waved his hand in partial dismissal and partial discomfort that matched the slight blush of embarrassment replying, "I have."

"Seems they caught your leader being earthly."

"I have grave reservations regarding the veracity of the *Informer* story. It's all based on the *Gazetteer*. His Holiness is not that kind of person. I have faith in his fidelity."

"They hint they have real evidence and expect more. They even question that the girl's death was accidental. As they say, eighteen feet to fall is not a suicide threat, only a threat or a tease."

"Or if one lands directly on their head as she appears to have done."

"I'm sure that when the investigation is completed the truth will be known."

"What investigation?" The sudden appearance of Daniel had not been noticed.

"Why, this," Sam Crawford replied holding out the *Informer* to complete his answer. "That's the problem. The investigation is said to be completed."

Daniel had taken the paper to read the article and rapidly scanned the two page story. He dropped the paper to the side. "This can not be. This cannot be true. This pope would do no such thing," he stated with finality. "He did no such thing."

"Well, he wouldn't be the first pope to stray from the fold."

"Not this one. I know him. I was close to him when he was a boy!"

A pause, a quiet, came between the three men.

"How can that be?" retorted Hubert Brown. "He is almost seventy years old."

"It does not matter. It was in a town call Gyor. He was twelve years old then. He is a favorite son."

"Preposterous," concluded Hubert. "The Archbishop had questions of your mental status. Now I wonder."

"I wouldn't be too hasty, Hubert. You barely know the man. Daniel, this is Hubert Brown. Hubert is a priest. He is monsignor secretary to the archbishop here."

Daniel looked to his latest protagonist with a smile. "Then you are a disciple of the living God?"

"Yes. I am a Catholic Priest."

"Then you know that your pope, the Peter of today, the living word of the son of Daniel and the son of Abraham would not defile the name of God in such a way as this paper, the *American Informer,* relates."

Hubert stepped back. The feeling of awe, the uneasiness as he had first experienced at the park once again overtook him. His calculation of reality faded. "I believe that to be true." Turning to the reporter he inquired, "You said the *Gaz-*

etteer suggested that further evidence might be forthcoming. What might that be?"

"I dunno, but I'll sniff around the religion desk at the paper. See if they have heard anything."

The three engrossed in their private discourse had not noticed Edgar J.L. had let the waiting diners into the dining area at Tom White's direction. An elderly man stood at the chair where Sam Crawford's coat was still draped.

"This seat taken?" the man asked.

Sam retrieved his coat.

The throng of at least twenty-five had descended into the hall and were seating themselves.

Tom White appeared at the back of the room. Daniel appeared at the front of the room "My friends," he began raising his hands upward. The general murmur of the room became quiet. He continued, "It is fitting that we pray."

Two uniformed policemen appeared at the door, took a few steps inside, looked around the group busily eating and officially asked, "Who's in charge here?"

There was an immediate hush. One of the older men partaking of the free meal recognizing one of the officers spoke up. "Why, Officer Sweeney. What are you doing here? Didn't know you were back on the beat, you being a sergeant and everything."

"That's okay, Nestor. We just have to check things out here. Who's in charge here?"

Daniel Adams had made his way from the back workroom responding, "I would believe I am."

"Well, we just need to see your Public Health license to operate a restaurant."

"I am afraid we don't have one of those."

"How much are you charging these poor folks?"

"This is a free lunch, a free meal, program sponsored by the generosity of the people of the community."

"No license. Free food. Don't add up. What's your name?"

"My name's Daniel Adams."

"Can I see some I.D, your driver's license?"

"I don't have a driver's license. I don't drive a car."

"Your social security card, a credit card, anything?"

"I don't have any of those."

"Daniel Adams. Daniel Adams," Officer Sweeney repeated several times. Sounds familiar. Aren't you the preacher fellow from over Bush Park? Seems there's some disturbance everywhere you go. Who do you work for?"

"I'm not a preacher. I do part time carpentry work."

"Well, seems we have a problem here. I think you ought to come down town and answer some questions."

Tom White, now dressed and out of the apron stepped between Daniel Adams and the officer. His leather jacket immediately set off Sergeant Sweeney's fuse. "Some biker you've got here with you."

Tom White inquired, "You're not arresting this man? What for?"

"Don't get in my way. We know what to do with your kind," Sweeney observed as he took his night stick from his belt.

"It is nothing, Tom," Daniel interjected.

"We're just going down town to the station."

"He's done nothing wrong," Tom White continued. "Is he under arrest?"

"The preacher's got some explaining to do. This meal's over. This place is closed."

As Sergeant Sweeney ushered the compliant Daniel Adams from the store, Edgar J.L. asked of anyone who would listen, "What are we going to do about Mr. Adams?"

"Don't know much to do," Tom White replied raising his hands hopelessly.

"What was that reporter with the red Contour?"

"Sam Crawford."

"I think we should call him."

CHAPTER 18

Sam Crawford slowly drove his prized red Contour back to the office. His mind continued to recall Daniel's statement, "I was close to him when he was a boy" and Hubert's retort as he was leaving, "How can that be, Crawford? Nonsense."

Nonsense, indeed, he mused. Who was this Daniel Adams? A nut? Perhaps. Perhaps not. Was it just a delusion that he had been in Guuy or however you spell it, wherever that is, when the pope was a boy? A rather specific time and place for a delusion. Adams certainly wasn't eighty years old. Other thoughts passed his mind. Where was Adams from? Adams had spoken as a stranger at their evening of dinner with the strange comment of 'as in other times, in other places' he had written this in his notes and that 'he would know God's purpose'.

Another time and another place, this place, Gujor, whatever. Charles Evans might know he thought.

Sam Crawford passed his desk, picked up a nest of phone messages and sorted through them as he passed on through the room and down the hall to the small room shared by the religious desk, that was primarily Evans, and a sundry of transient newspaper departments, such as food and entertainment, at the moment merely P.C. terminals.

Charles Evans was considered a scholar, a student of religion. A devout Baptist, he never the less was a student of religions. He could describe the three hour Hindu wedding ceremony and what each flower and plant meant at a Hindu funeral service. He knew the Hindu and Moslem leaders in town. He was a friend of Archbishop Gregory and had had dinner with Bishop George of the Methodist church just the previous Thursday evening.

Sam seldom asked him a question because Charles Evans was a born teacher and never answered a question with a one-sentence; more often it was a fifteen minute discourse with historical facts interspersed.

As Crawford entered the room, Evans was almost jumping up and down holding a printout from the computer in his hand. He was talking to no one in particular, "What a day. What a day and he's coming to Detroit," standing before his desk and talking to the window.

He jumped with surprise and turned around to Sam Crawford's question, "Who's coming?"

The small man with a bright smile that matched the red bow tie replied enthusiastically, "Why the pope. Pope John Alexander. Next month." He calls it an ecumenical revisit of the Pentecost of the millennium."

"How can he do that in face of this mess, Charles?" Crawford asked waving the *American Informer* before him.

"That is a bit of a quandary," he stated thoughtfully with his clipped almost British speech. His accentuated speech matched his small well trimmed black mustache and grease like groomed tapered hair.

Crawford sat himself on the edge of an adjacent desk as Evans returned to the printout.

"Whatever," he continued. "The pro-nuncio has indicated that Detroit will be the first city he will visit and that the leaders of all religions will be invited to at least two public and numerous private meetings."

"Can't you see it? The television. Hundreds of millions of people will attend by television. This will be bigger than a president's inauguration and just before the trip to the holy lands. I didn't think he would make a trip here so soon."

Charles Evans paused a brief moment to catch his breath in all the excitement he felt.

Crawford seized the moment to change the subject. "This article about the pope. It suggests more evidence might turn up. Do you know anything about that?"

"I wondered also. I called Stafford of the *Baltimore Daily*. He's close to some of the people in the pro-nuncio's office. They're usually pretty closed lipped about sensitive things. Stafford had already read the story in the *Gazetteer*.

"He reads Italian?"

"I don't know, I'm sure. Someone there must have. However, he had a head start on the rest of us because of that. We have our copies of the *Gazetteer* but nobody reads them. Stafford has heard some conversation about snips of letters or perhaps a diary."

"A diary?" he commented picking a copy of the *Gazetteer*. "Well, that's not for certain. He thinks he heard that mentioned."

"Do you know this Fazio, Roberto Fazio?" he inquired holding up the copy of the *Gazetteer*, "who wrote this story?"

"No. Why?"

"You could call him up. Talk to the horse's mouth, so to speak."

"I'm afraid my allowance wouldn't quite stretch that far. I'm afraid I would get a horse laugh from Gilly instead of the horse's mouth if I asked," he said with a smile at his play on words.

"Mind if I keep this, Charles?" he asked proffering the paper.

"You can borrow it if you would like," he replied with an officious attitude as he felt Crawford hadn't appreciated his 'horsey' pun of a comment.

Crawford, however, had switched his thoughts regarding the original intent of visiting Evans. "Do you know a place called Guyer?"

"Guyer?" Evans repeated. "Guyer, where?"

"Guyer, some place the pope was a boy."

"Oh, you mean Gyor, Gyor," he spelled. "Gyor, Hungary."

"Yeah," said Crawford," maybe fifty-sixty years ago when he was just a kid."

"Of course. Gyor, Hungary, 1945."

Crawford settled back in a chair. His question was about to be answered. He wasn't sure he wanted the whole story or not as Charles Evans continued.

"Very important time in Hungarian religious history. Bishop Apor, Vilmos Apor, was killed protecting his residence, his church, from Soviet military officers who were trying to enter in search of women. There were many women including nuns hidden in the recesses of the cathedral. He was beatified as a Christian martyr, several years ago."

"So that's where he was," Crawford murmured getting up from his chair to conclude the lecture of which he was sure there would or could be more.

"Where who was?"

"Oh, nothing, Charles. By the way, Charles, you'll be getting tickets for all the events when the pope is here. Get tickets for me. I'd like to observe."

"You getting some kind of religion, Sam?"

"Just a great curiosity," he concluded and turned to return to his desk to answer some of his phone messages.

The phone rang at Sam Crawford's desk as he sorted out his several messages. "Crawford here," he answered. He listened to his caller.

"This is Tom White, Mr. Crawford. You have to help him," he heard blurted into his ear.

"Help who, Tom? Slow down, now. Help who?"

"Mr. Adams. They've arrested him?"

"Something about a public health permit for this place. And did you know, he doesn't have a drivers license or other identification?"

"I can believe that," Crawford confirmed. Crawford's thoughts sped through the visible Daniel Adams. A man from no where who seems to be a man of many times and not exactly one of only this present time, some one associated as far as he was concerned with real miracles, healing miracles, a religious person without a real religion, calls himself a messenger. "You say they arrested him?"

"Well, they took him in for questioning when he had no identification or real job, mentioned vagrant," Tom White excitedly continued. "He's no vagrant. He's a holy man."

"You think so?" Crawford queried.

"Well, you seen what he done. Edgar J.L. says he is."

"Who took him in, Tom?"

"Two police were here. One of the men at the free meal called one of them Sergeant Sweeney. This Sweeney did all the talking."

"I'll look into it, Tom. It's probably some kind of mistake. That would be the second precinct. I know Sweeney." Crawford pondered the story. Another story that didn't add up. Sweeney was not a patrol cop. Spent his time in the second precinct station house. It had been a long time since he had been a 'beat cop' and how did the police know to look into the 'free meal' deal so soon or was it look into Daniel Adams? The free meal wasn't even in the second precinct, out of Sweeney's precinct. When things didn't add up, it smelled of a story.

Crawford entered the main workroom of the second precinct. He was familiar with the station house. He had done his stint on the police beat. He had known Sweeney when he had been a 'beat cop', walking the beat, same precinct, knew his way around. The storefront where the 'free meal' was offered wasn't even in his precinct but for some reason Sweeney had crossed precinct lines to hassle Adams.

Crawford stood at the back of the room of desks and stamped out his cigarette stub. Officer Ashe noted the reporter and asked, "What's up that brings you down here these days, Sam?"

"Glad to see a friend," Crawford answered. He sat on the corner of Officer Ashe's desk. "Just nosey," he replied. "Got a call that Sweeney's on the muscle."

"Don't know anything about that. He came in a few moments ago. He's in the corner office there," Ashe continued, pointing to the offices in the front of the room.

"Buy you a cup of coffee sometime, Ashe," Crawford murmured leaving Ashe and slowly walked toward Sweeney's office. He stopped and watched Sweeney as he talked to Daniel Adams sitting in the chair near Sweeney's desk. Sweeney was doing all the talking. It looked like a lecture or chewing out that Sweeney was directing toward Daniel. Crawford stood leaning against a wall, with his seersucker coat draped over one shoulder and an unlit cigarette resting between his lips. He was trying to decide whether Daniel required rescuing or not. As far as he was concerned, from what Tom White had related, this was a hassle Sweeney was involved in. Daniel Adams had done nothing warranting his arrest. Why was Sweeney hassling Adams? While Crawford was deciphering this quandary, Sergeant Sweeney exited his office without noticing Crawford, secured a nearby phone, and dialed the number. Crawford moved along the wall closer to hear Sweeney saying, "No good reason to hold him. He agrees to apply for a public health license. I warned him about public disturbances at the park."

"What did he say? He said that he never organizes anything at the park. The people just show up, he says."

Crawford watched as the officer listened intently. Some one was giving him instructions.

"Oh course, I'll warn him. But you know the park isn't in my precinct."

Before Sweeney hung up he had listened again to a long discourse. As he hung up, "Thank you," followed by, "your eminence."

This was Crawford's clue and his opening. "Well, damn. Your eminence, it is, eh, Sweeney?"

"What are you doing here, Sam?" the red faced round faced Irishman inquired. "Eavesdropping, too. I be ashamed of you," he continued with what was left of his Irish accent.

"Now, that wasn't the mayor, or the chief of police you were talking to was it? And it wasn't the pope. So that only leaves the governor or the new archbishop and I don't think you have the guv's phone number," Crawford jibed with a big smile at the embarrassed sergeant.

"I don't see it's any of your business," Sweeney retorted rising to his full six foot-four and reclaiming some of his calm.

"It's my friend you have in there that you're putting the hassle on. Does he need a lawyer?"

"Not yet, he doesn't."

"Why the beef? What's the archbishop's interest?"

"Nothing special," Sweeney observed. "Nothing the *Press* would be interested in. You know the pope's coming to town. Just a good idea to get these preacher types under wraps."

"You mean all of them or just this particular one? You sure went out of your way. The archbishop must have a very personal interest to ask for such a favor," Crawford observed as the two men approached Sweeney's office door.

Daniel could see the conversation that had taken place between the officer and the reporter. He had risen to his feet facing the two who approached the door.

Sweeney looked up saying, "You can go, Adams."

"I'm glad to see you, Mr. Crawford," Daniel said.

"Call me Sam, I told you."

"And remember what I said about unlawful assemblies. We don't want any disturbances, Adams. You need to get a permit for assemblies the size of yours."

"I arrange no assemblies," Daniel quietly replied.

"Then maybe you shouldn't show up there."

"You know better than that, Sweeney. From what I know, maybe you should let the proper precinct take care of whatever needs taking care of," Crawford reproached Sweeney.

"He knows what I mean."

"And you know what I mean. This would make a lousy embarrassing story. Come on Daniel, let's get out of here."

CHAPTER 19

SOMEWHERE IN TURKEY

The bar was poorly lit. Only a few customers occupied the booths at the wall opposite the bar. A young woman made her way from the bar to an occasional booth where a stranger might be newly seated to announce her wares. The booth near the window, with better lighting, lighting good enough to enhance the stained blue oilcloth table covering, was occupied by two young men in deep conversation.

"She's a nice one. Look at that!"

"She'd eat you alive, little man. Besides, you couldn't afford her. Anyway that's not why we're here," The taller one declared between large draws of beer from his glass "This new pope is a brave one, a brave stupid one. He didn't take his so-called 'pope-mobile' to Hungary on his visit there. Another beer, waiter, here," he summoned. "Another?" he asked of his companion.

His companion indicated he was only half through with his hand at the middle of the obvious half full glass. The smaller man sat there contemplating his tall swarthy leader, leader in the mission, in the planning. He ran his hand without effect through the thick black disheveled hair, too long in length, too long since a haircut and too long since being adequately combed. It stuck out in different directions like a wild black rooster crow. For certainly he was the rooster. At five feet-eight inches his attitude was his protection before he might need to demonstrate his facility in martial arts that had surprised and felled taller larger adversaries picking on the 'pip-squeak'. He sat forward with both thumbs in the armholes of his black wool vest, "Do you always drink this much?" Without waiting for a response he continued, "And now the pope is going to America."

"And that is why you are here." He stopped to wipe his nose with a paper napkin. The smaller man as a reflex wiped his nose with a brush of his shirtsleeve. The stained sleeve was an abundant balloon design with buttoned cuffs in need of washing. "You speak English, good English, better than mine."

"Oh, I speak very fine English," the smaller replied in English so distinctly different from the deep throaty language of home.

Several turned from the bar at hearing the English tune tones not commonly heard here. This was a stopping place for the local furniture factory workers, workers likely to have finished six grades of school. They were good in math, simple math, and a smattering of English but none of the high class English they had just heard.

"No. No. No English here," he was told in his native tongue. "You will stand out. People will wonder why you are here with your smooth English."

"Like I said. That is why you are going. Student visas are being processed for both of us as we speak. We will go by plane several days before the pope. We will get this pope."

He continued, "This man is a curse on our people. He would have the world come to despise our people. He lulls our faithful with calls of unity, all the time despising the truth that he knows in his heart. He is wrong. Our leaders know his true purpose, to destroy both our dignity and our homelands. This one is more dangerous than the last "He stopped and raised his glass of beer in a toast. "Praise be to Ali Agca even though he failed in stopping the last pope. This time, we will succeed." This thought seemed to suddenly bring his message of purpose to the uncompleted ending.

"We will be able to move about freely in America. Where he goes we can go." He finished his beer and was about to request service of another when the thought of freedom struck twice.

"I would like to go to America and get this pope. I would like to see this free America also," the little man opined. "Another beer," he asked of the waiter. A smile spread over his barbed face in need of a shave as he thought of experiencing the freedom of America.

"Your identification, friends", was the second blow to the thought of freedom. A military officer of serious demeanor stood before them.

The taller man rose with a smile. "Of course," he responded presenting his abundant stained teeth as the smile persisted afraid to display the inner tugging of fear in his stomach. He stood tall, a gangling, stooped shoulder young man attempting to brace his shoulders and attitude in military fashion, responding to the inquiring officer. He straightened his suspenders and tucked in his wrinkled shirt. He extracted his identification from his wallet and handed it to the short rotund almost obese officer.

After examining the papers, the officer offered his sincere apologies. "It is a mistake. I apologize for any embarrassment. And this man?" Pointing to the smaller associate who had his papers ready to present, he waved his hand at them as not necessary when the taller one explained. "He is with me."

"But of course," the officer acceded. "It is his English, you know."

"Very good?" the taller man asked smiling.

"Very good." the officer concurred.

"It will be of great service to us."

"Good luck." He tipped his hard brimmed military hat with his baton and smartly exited.

The taller man appeared both elated and afraid to have been deferred to by the military officer. Afraid because the local patrons at the bar may believe he is a sympathizer or even an informer for the police. He said loudly so many could hear, "Fortunately, he was a friend of my father." More quietly he said to his associate, "He is one of the military who is sympathetic to our cause and does know my father."

The taller man continued, "Our passports and visas will be forgeries right from the ministry. Another tie to our movement. The workers there support our cause. We will see Anton this afternoon, as students, to have our photographs taken.

"You will examine all your possessions, everything you take on the plane. You will take one suitcase."

"I have no suitcase."

"I will see that you have one and a travel bag, also. They will not be new. As I said, one suitcase and everything must be examined that your name is not present, even your money folder. You will have new papers with a new name." He paused, finished his beer. "Another beer, here."

"After the photos I will show you some of the various methods according to our opportunities that may present to get rid of this pope. Some things are being sent ahead now. Others, a few, we can take with us. Security at the air terminal is severe."

They drank their beer.

"You know," the taller man began, "this is our fate. We have been chosen to carry out this affair. We may never survive. We will try of course but if not," he raised both his hands above his short black brush cut hair and declared, "it will be a glorious death. We will be honored warriors even more for what we have done, both among the people and among the martyred ancients."

CHAPTER 20

DETROIT

"This pope will cause us and the church harm. He is weak, spiritually weak, this one with the 'Pope's Girl'. He makes us all look unholy," the priest noted derisively.

The private room of Mike Varga's restaurant was barely lit well enough to compete with the decor. The festooned maroon tapestry, dark gray walls, subdued the recessed lighting and the interspersed gilded heavy framed oil paintings, each with its own illuminating light.

The six tables were unattended except for the corner table occupied by two men in deep conversation and engrossed in the meal. One in the black garb of a priest was leading the conversation. The second slender man was dandily attired in a soft gray suit with matching gray suede shoes. A paired paisley tie and handkerchief tucked into the suit coat pocket decorated the suit. He sat upright as his delicate fingers worked at the pasta taking care to keep the white French cuffs from scraping the marinara sauce.

As a first generation Italian in America and naturally of catholic dedication, Mike Varga had long been a soft touch to the priests of the area and was pleased that the archdiocesan priests found his bill of fare to their liking. They ignored his murmured history of scrapes with the Detroit police and politicians. How could any of these murmurings be of significance when both beat police and officers were commonly his guests? Priests, jocks from the Detroit Lions and police were favorites of Mike Varga. Besides the lasagna was the best, and the privacy, deference and service exceeded their expectations.

Archbishop Paul Gregory continued, "One of the first things was his invitation to a convocation on church affairs it said. Everyone on the invitation list consists of the fifteen who met last week and the other signers of the position paper on assisted suicide. The others and I are at great risk. He intends to address us directly as a group and the leadership will no doubt receive the most attention and no doubt our future will be in jeopardy."

"Well, you certainly are destined to be on his cardinals list for appointment at the end of the year. You should be concerned about that. As a should be retired monsignor, I have no future to be concerned about so I have no similar risk."

"We're gonna surprise him, Gerald. We might just see him go home early this trip or receive extremely bad press that his moral authority will be diminished. He may not have the courage to reprimand us when he meets with our group." He sat back contemplating the older priest's comment. The truth was evident. He might be on the cardinal list this coming winter. He always believed it would happen the following year. He relished his leadership role of the liberal voice. It was always a small group of vocal priests with the percentage markedly decreasing at the bishop level. He had never been privately or publicly restrained about his public comments or writings. Now that be had lead a position, an organizational position, it appeared that this pope was going to confront him and the group and without any intermediary contact. Well, he could injure this pope who had demonstrated his personal moral weakness but he would still be pope and the cardinal list, the cardinal list. That was most important. He would injure this pope without the pope knowing whom, this pope who had stepped up to challenge him. Such a weak defective pope, the compromised pope, should be compromised. Then he would reconcile his differences with the pope privately.

"How do you plan to do that, Paul?"

Paul Gregory broke another piece of bread from the loaf and passed the breadbasket to his conspirator. "Not me, exactly. Alfred has found someone with the resources who will be meeting us tonight and he'll be able to arrange a distressing encounter for this ladies man," he explained as he caressed the red sauce from the side of the dish. He looked up and laughed. "We'll have pictures of him in living color."

"That won't get rid of him," the dapper monsignor noted.

"No, but it will soften him up. Take some of the aggression out of him. Where is that man? He was supposed to be here by now."

"He may have changed his mind."

"Not for what he'll be paid."

Monsignor Gallagher contemplatively sorted the peppery marinated shrimp and scallop pasta that was his main course wondering why he was here. He had served in concert with the archbishop in espousing liberal causes but was now a conspirator in a plot to discredit the pope in the eyes of the world. In theological controversy he was comfortable. In direct contradiction to the pope he was very uncomfortable. He had never knowingly, publicly disobeyed the direct edict of the pope or the papal office. He, for this moment, thought about his actions within the confessional. He had often found a point of extreme leniency with the women who carried the heavy load of contraception on their conscience. He had frequently found himself discussing the position of the church with the petitioner. After listening to the various family stories of there being several children, limited financial resources, illness and threats to the family structure he had found himself discussing personal decision in view of the stated church position and finding a way out for the parishioner. He knew that he was not alone as a priest that practiced this liberal confessional theology. However, overtly he never espoused this position. He, however, felt this discussion of these problem positions was in the province of the clergy. The present conflict was still considered a legitimate conversational event to enlighten and strengthen the decisions of the church. He had thought this dinner meeting had been to discuss how to present their position. Now he was involved in this plot.

He was caught between the loyalties of the philosophical leader Archbishop Gregory and the pope to whom he owed total obedience. He still wondered why Archbishop Gregory had not been privately remonstrated during the previous years like Curran being released from teaching at Catholic University or Father Dalton in Los Angeles choosing to leave the priesthood after twenty-four years in defiance to having his surveys of priests' attitude on marriage of priests and the ordination of women disparaged and destroyed. It was easy to understand a lay professor, as Curran, being dismantled for his candor in discussing questions of theology. Even Dalton, a priest, had been forced to toe the line in discussing controversy. Of course, he thought, Jesuits as Father Dalton were a different lot. But why hadn't Gregory been cornered?

"Are you sure?" he began and was interrupted by the archbishop's expected quest.

Standing in the doorway was an impish thirtyish blond highlighted by a twisted smile. If the monsignor thought that he was well attired, this sprig of a man was one in full bloom. He was a dandy in a doeskin shirt with a paisley ascot and pinkish trousers sitting on pointed pink loafers with a tassel. An ample suede jacket rested on his shoulders. He stood there with his hand perched on one hip revealing a brash bronze belt buckle fronting a noticeably narrow waist.

"Well damn, which one of you am I doing business with?" the dandy inquired stepping into the room to allow the waiter who had been standing blocked by the visitor to exit the room. "It must be the pretty one. Never had a priest call on me yet," he decided advancing toward the monsignor in mufti with hand extended. "I'm Max."

"What is this?" Monsignor Gallagher inquired of the archbishop waving his hand toward Max with no intention of returning the greeting.

The priest sat back in his chair and wiped the sauce from his lips and held up his hand. "There will be no introductions, Max. This is strictly business. Would you like some wine, Max?" he offered picking up the decanter of red wine. "It's very good, Bardolini, a dry Italian wine, northern Italy."

"Sure," he agreed sliding his glass forward, "and something to eat, too."

"We've already eaten, Max. We expected you forty-five minutes ago."

"Well damn. I have business, you know."

"We know. We know. Perhaps some antipasto would be nice."

"Yeah, that would be nice," Max agreed, "and something real to drink."

Paul Gregory motioned to the waiter who had returned. "Bring our guest a nice antipasto."

"With shrimp," Max chimed in.

"With shrimp and some fresh warm Italian bread and what to drink, Max?"

"Scotch, scotch on the rocks. Good scotch. Dewers. Dewers on the rocks."

Monsignor Gallagher leaned toward the archbishop. He was slowly burning inside and wished to bring this conspiracy to a halt. "You mean you're going to do business with this, this fagot?"

Gregory reacted with a mixture of a smile and a twinge of distaste at the thought.

Max reacted before the priest could respond. "Well, damn. Look who is talking. Aren't you the dandy. It takes one to think of one. Look, I'm a businessman and my company is good. I've got the best girls in town. Not the most, but the best."

"Just you listen," Gallagher began in response to the rebuff.

Gregory sat forward and wiped his balding head with a napkin. The peppery spices of the pasta always made his pate sweat and the moment of confrontation made him sweat all the more.

"Let's hear what the man has to say," Gregory suggested.

The waiter returned with the order.

"Alfred said you were looking for some dirty tricks. Who's the patsy?" he inquired as he sniffed and sipped the scotch as though it was a fine brandy.

"That's not important."

"You have an enemy or is this just for fun?"

"Let's just say this is political. We want pictures that fall into the hands of the newspaper, you know. What do you have in mind?"

"We establish an embarrassment. One of my girls and I got a good photographer. Where is the patsy staying?"

"He'll be at the Westin hotel. The presidential suite."

Gallagher cringed as Max made a blob of shrimp encased in proscuitto and impaled it against a wedge of melon with his fork.

"Well damn. A big shot, huh? Big money, huh. You know my work doesn't come for peanuts."

"How much?"

"Two. No, three grand for this one. The presidential suite can be trouble. Too many rooms. Too many people!"

"What do we get for our money? Give us the scenario."

"Got two. The Westin's good, know my way around. Pass keys. Nice to know if the mark likes an evening snack. Can use the evening snack routine. Waiters and waitresses deliver evening snacks as a courtesy of the house. Have to feel sure he's alone. Once inside, the waitress, that's Dolly, sheds her uniform and in her skinny does her thing, does a pose, a little dance, makes an offer or two. All the time the waiter is taking pictures. Nobody knows there's a camera. If the mark agrees, it's easy. If he don't, Dolly does whatever she can."

"Won't work. Forget it," announces Gallagher.

"I agree. Not the best," agrees Gregory.

Gallagher feels a moment of relief. Maybe Gregory will pass on the idea. Max continues attacking the shrimp, proscuitto antipasto.

"But the one I like best," Max continues "is a lot quieter. Does the mark like a little drink? Maybe he visits the bar?"

"Not likely the bar but he likes a drink or two."

"Then we deliver the evening snack some way. Have a selection bar. Leave the snack tray, pour the first drink, leave the bottle and leave."

"Then what?"

"The first drink is fixed to put him to sleep. Takes maybe fifteen minutes after it's finished. Last's maybe an hour or so. Call the room, you know, to see if the order was received then Dolly and the photog use the passkey to go in. We get some good stuff that way."

"I don't think we should go with this. I don't think this is necessary," Gallagher asserts.

Max has finished the last of the antipasto and sits sipping the cubes of ice of the scotch.

"You've done this before?" Gregory inquires.

"Well, damn. We're pros, your eminence or whatever. The spiked drink works like a charm. Sometimes, we have Dolly wait till the mark wakes up and demands to be paid for her services. It's really a laugh, sometimes."

"Not this time. Just the pictures if we decide to use you. Alfred will discuss it with you."

"Of course, many times the presidential suite sets up a courtesy bar like some other rooms, conventions, you know. That's another way. I can slip a waiter into one of them at the Westin," Max continues.

Gregory smiles. He likes the last move. "Like I said, Alfred will get back to you. It won't be for at least a week. And you will only have two nights to get the job done. The rest of the time he will be elsewhere." The pope and his immediate staff would occupy the archdiocesan rectory and also had a suite of rooms, the presidential suite, at the Westin Hotel for convenience to the others attending and for his many meetings. He knows the pope intends to stay two specific nights because of convenience. He rises and offers his hand. "Thank you, Max."

Max shakes hands with the priest. He smiles at Gallagher and leaving imparts to the observing monsignor, "Take care of yourself, dandy."

"I don't think this was a very good idea, Paul, meeting directly with him, especially you."

"You mean because he knows I'm a priest?"

"Mostly."

"Max won't do anything rash. He's caught between his world and the rest. Alfred is a driver for me some times. He's a parishioner who'll do anything for me. He got in some small problem with the police a while ago. I got it fixed up. Alfred can turn Max. Max won't turn me because of Alfred. I can turn either one."

Monsignor Gallagher felt subdued by the evening events. The Archbishop was determined to implement his plan. The brash provocateur, Max, had insulted him. "I beg you to call this off. This is insane. You are planning to attack the pope. All your life you have been a faithful priest."

"He disgraces the name, the church."
"You don't know that for certain. These rags print a lot of trash."
"He is weak."
"And you are wrong, wrong."

CHAPTER 21

The early evening was stifling. Mid-August was fulfilling its history of hot muggy days and nights. Arpad's Ford was hot and humid with slight relief afforded by the breeze of the open windows. He didn't find the opportunity to explain to Daniel that the car was so old that the air-conditioning needed a new compressor and he was so poor he didn't have the money to pay for that repair. He was just happy to have a car with an engine that ran well and tires with tread left on them. Daniel had not complained of the oppressive weather.

As Arpad turned the corner many cars occupied the adjacent vacant lots overfilled from the spaces on the street. "This is an important evening. It's St. Stephen's Day and Father Dizon will hold the prayer service."

"You mentioned that. I look forward to the service. He has been your priest for a long time?"

"For over twelve years since we lived here. He's the priest at Holy Cross Church here.

"I noticed there are very few homes here."

"Mostly vacant lots now, all torn down," Arpad agreed. "When I was a boy, the shoe shop was right there." He pointed to an unpainted, partially boarded up store. "And Sarkisian's grocery store was next door, the store that's burned. No one lives here anymore. Delray Hospital used to be a couple of blocks down from the center," he stated. "Torn down," he continued pointing to the spot where the hospital once stood. Daniel was sure that moisture, almost tears, welled at the bottom of Arpad's eyes. They talk of some kind of government development zone being planned here."

"People come from miles around to church and to the center, people who grew up here, Hungarian, even Armenians. Some bring their parents. Some bring their kids. They come for special events, usually Friday and Saturday. Tonight's special. We'll eat." Arpad maneuvered his car into a parking spot waving to friends on the sidewalk. "And Father will be there. We'll have a beer, play cards, maybe dance," he continued with a big smile on his tired face. As they got out of the car he asked, "Do you dance, Daniel?"

Daniel smiled. He knew their dances, the line dance, with the leader with his or her handkerchief. The men were often the leader with discrete demonstrative movements and steps that the rest seemed to know. "I know some dancing but not yours. It is beautiful and wonderful. I will watch and enjoy."

They had reached the corner of the building. The tri-color Hungarian flag hung moist and unmoving above the door. The American flag was draped to it's right. The bronze sign, obviously recently rejuvenated, beside the door announced, 'The Hungarian Cultural Center'.

As Arpad and Daniel approached the door they were greeted by a sweaty, pink-faced, Sam Crawford. "Surprised, eh?"

They stood aside as others entered the building.

Others, as Sam Crawford, stood in small groups at the corner enjoying a cigarette and talking.

"Surprised I'd be here?"

Arpad and Daniel in unison assured, "We're glad you're here."

"Been talking to some of your friends here. They almost expect Daniel to give a speech from what you have been telling them," he jibed Arpad.

Sam wiped his perspiring balding head and neck with his handkerchief. His loosened tie hung down limp as his softened wet open shirt collar. His seersucker jacket hung over his shoulder.

The contrast of Daniel's open neck collarless shirt and calm appearance was evident. His forehead was slightly moist. The shoulder length hair and short beard seemed unruffled in the heat. He responded, "I have no speech to give."

"People will want to hear you."

"Mostly see you," Crawford countered.

People who knew Arpad, and there were many, slowly began to gather about the three men for they guessed that his guest, the one without a tie, was the Daniel they had heard so much about the previous weekend.

"I'm Frank," one of the men spoke out extending his hand. "You must be Arpad's friend, Daniel."

"Yes, I am Daniel," he affirmed grasping the hand in return. "Peace be with you." He continued, "You are a friend of Arpad, also?"

"These are all my friends," Arpad said waving his hand to include all of the gathering group. Then to the group as a whole, raising his voice slightly he announced, "And this is my good friend, Daniel, Daniel Adams. He would like to meet each and every one of you but we are hungry" and with a big smile, as he was pleased with the attention announced, "the chicken paprikash is ready. I can smell it. Let's eat. I'm sure Father Dizon is waiting."

The room opened from an entryway that had a long row of hangers on one side. Above the entrance to the main room was an alcove large enough to house a standing figure of a saintly male figure, St. Stephen, the first king of Hungary, crowned King of Hungary by Pope Sylvester II.

The meeting room was filled with many round tables with a buffet table at the rear where the kitchen was situated. The room was humid, warm with ceilings higher than usual. The accompanying tall windows on each side were open. The chatter of the gathering crowd, a part of whom were passing before the buffet line, was augmented by the rushing sound of the fans at the top of several windows extracting the hottest air accumulating at the ceiling of the room.

The men who had worn coats had taken them off on entering. Scarcely a tie remained, most having been set by the coat. Sweat mingled with the smiles and the animated discussion. Father Dizon's invocation had been longer than most desired but was appreciated by the Hungarian gathering. Father Dizon had invoked the blessing of St. Stephen for the many favors and support over the difficult past, including the tragedies that had befallen the Hungarian nation over the one thousand years since St. Stephen had been ordained and invoked his blessing for those honoring him this evening.

Now that the meal was over, there was still almost half an hour before the small band would show up. Tables of card players had assembled to one side of the hall near the open windows. Others had sought the relative coolness of the outside air. It was just after seven and Fort Street was busy with traffic as the sun hung heavy and gold down the street to the west. A small crowd had gathered about Arpad and Daniel. Sam Crawford had looked forward to this moment and was well rewarded. Daniel deferred to Arpad the first questions with the excuse that he was 'just a guest'. As Arpad was relating the events that had occurred across the street from his bakery, Daniel quietly interrupted directing his comments in Hungarian to two of the gathered group having their own animated discussion. In Hungarian he spoke to them, "No. I do not perform miracles." As they had been carrying on their discussion in Hungarian they were embarrassed momentarily. One other replied in Hungarian, "It is true. You are a holy man, as Arpad has said."

All nearby could hear and most became silent. Sam Crawford had switched on his tape recorder and held his scribble pad near at hand.

Arpad was of course surprised and amazed. "You speak Hungarian," he murmured.

"If I am a holy man, it is because I am a follower of Jesus, the Christ. If you believe as Arpad has said that miracles have happened, it is the work of God through the living word of His Son."

Sam listened to his recorder to be sure he could hear the buzzing of the tape revolving, recording, and smiled and wiped his sweaty brow.

"But no one else we know has done the things you have. Who are you?" one of the men asked.

"I am but a messenger."

"That's what Arpad has said."

"A messenger of the living word of Christ Jesus," he continued.

The crowd had increased. Daniel stood in the middle of the crowd. They stepped back and had cleared the area immediately around. Father Dizon stood at the edge of the crowd. He made the sign of the cross.

Daniel looking at his direction said, "Peace be with you." He could see the lips of the priest respond, "and peace be with you."

Daniel then raised his hands to the crowd surrounding them and turning slowly repeated, "Peace be with all of you."

He was not a speechmaker. In all his travels he had found these occasions almost distressful. He thought of Moses who had deferred to his brother Aaron to speak for him. He quietly beseeched God for strength to respond to the gathered children of God for he had no such brother to speak for him.

They stood expectantly.

Arpad quietly spoke, "Tell them, Daniel."

Sam Crawford wiped his sweating neck with his handkerchief and checked his recorder again in anticipation, smiling, enjoying the moment.

"I did not come here this evening to disrupt your celebration in honor of your St. Stephen, so significant to your history and important in your daily lives. Our friend Arpad has brought me as a guest. He has told some stories of our times together. I'm sure he has told you that I am, as you, a follower, a messenger, of the living Christ. I practice and am a messenger of the word of Christ and His kingdom." He paused, smiled, and continued. "We are all one people of the Christ, the God of all people on earth and the message is the love and hope of the living word of His salvation. Peace to your brothers and to strangers as they be your brothers who have not known the Christ." Daniel raised his arms to the crowd.

The band had assembled and was testing their instruments.

Attention was suddenly directed to the front door. All heads turned as a new rumble of mumbles in English and Hungarian slowly grew.

The entrance door of the hall seemed filled with priests. Three priests were more than enough to seem to fill the doorway. The several other visitors who were not in priest garb completed the party who momentarily stood contemplatively at the doorway.

Father Dizon had moved toward the doorway. It seemed appropriate that the priest of the gathering would greet the visiting priests.

The buzzing of the crowd eased slightly as Father Dizon proceeded more rapidly toward the doorway and the priests. Lips could be seen to move among the visitors but no one could hear what was said. It was clear that the congregation was not accustomed to visiting priests with wide red-colored sashes at their waists. They watched, wondering what the visit, the strange visit, was about.

"Who is that?" Sam Crawford inquired of Daniel.

"They are priests," Daniel replied seriously.

"I know that." Crawford's impatience uncommonly was showing.

Father Dizon had reached the group now well within the entrance of the hall. There was an occasional sharp utterance from the crowd when he suddenly knelt before the tall priest dressed in white. He grasped the visiting priest's forearm and kissed his hand. The visiting priest in white quietly placed his hand upon Father Dizon's head while speaking as Father Dizon rose to stand before the group.

The congregation had pressed forward.

Daniel said quietly to Crawford, "That one, the tall one in white who smiles is truly a holy man. The sullen one to his right with the red sash only pretends to be holy."

"What do you mean, 'pretends' to be holy? That's Archbishop Gregory. I know some things you don't know. But 'pretends' to be holy?"

"He is unfaithful to the word."

"Well, I know he's very liberal."

"He does not believe as he should."

"You can tell that?"

"I just know."

The crowd's anticipation was rewarded when the tall priest raised his hands. "Peace be with you," he said.

The crowd responded irregularly enthusiastically, "Peace be with you." Some kneeled and many made the sign of the cross, as the murmured word was heard, "It's the pope."

"The pope," exclaimed Sam Crawford!

"He is truly a holy man. He is a chosen of God," Daniel said quietly.

"What in the world is he doing here?"

Daniel began, "He is a man of the people. These are his countrymen."

Pope John Alexander interrupted all who were speaking with his simple words in Hungarian. "I heard you countrymen were having dinner tonight to celebrate our glorious St. Stephen." He paused to cross himself. He continued, "Is it too late for a humble Hungarian to get a meal here?"

The crowd pressed forward to see, perhaps to touch the unexpected visitor. Marcus and the other dress-suited man had placed themselves before the crowd. Father Dizon had responded, "Most certainly. Our house is your house. We will find you a table."

Pope John Alexander had removed his suit coat and handed it to Archbishop Gregory to care for. "I will ask the driver to come in to eat," Archbishop Gregory informed John Alexander as he received his suit coat from him.

Commandant Raymond immediately stepped forward to request, "Your Eminence. It would be wise for him to stay with the car at all times. His absence would create an undue risk."

"What is that?" Archbishop Gregory asked evidently miffed at the commandant but not because of the message that he didn't understand. "Why can't he speak English around here. Why French?"

"My commandant speaks French, Italian, Swiss and German. He is learning some English. I thought you would be fluent in French and Italian," John Alexander stated almost as critical observation.

"He suggests that your driver stay with the car for security reasons."

"You let the policeman tell you, tell me, what to do?"

Immediately the intemperate interpretation of Pope John Alexander and his security chief relationship suggested a lack of respect for John Alexander's judgment. Gregory retreated to his usual sullen presence as John Alexander continued, "Raymond is responsible for our safety to the best of his judgment. He will see that Henry is well fed." He turned to Raymond who stood in ignorance of what was said but understood fully the manner or as he thought, the ill manner of Gregory's interruption and attitude.

"Please assure that Henry has a good meal and perhaps a beer, Raymond."

"He will eat well and have one beer," he responded likewise in French accentuating the 'one' beer. "I will also have the car placed in a secure location."

John Alexander dismissed Raymond and the whole affair with a wave of his hand. "I know you will take care of everything." Raymond understood the assurance of the smile as he was assigned this task at his convenience.

John Alexander continued, smiling, to the assembly feeling as the center of attention that as a matter of truth he was, "Here, we will eat among the 'people,'" he began and followed Father Dizon to a table. "We will eat. We will meet our friends." He motioned archbishop to an adjacent table. "You, Marcus and the archbishop there," he pointed. "The commandant and I will eat here with this priest, this Hungarian priest." Commandant Raymond of the Swiss Guard was pleased and relieved to be able to be close enough to feel he could protect his charge from any threatening acts. He not only was responsible for the pope's well being but felt responsible for the visiting group.

Pope John Alexander was not used to such close security. He had refused the use of the security vehicle on his trip to Hungary. He had developed a fondness for this Swiss guardsman, the French Raymond, commandant of the elite Swiss Guardsmen at age thirty-eight. As long as his presence was paramount at special events and on trips outside the Vatican when his affection for racquetball became known he became one of the Monday night gladiators with Marcus and Pope John Alexander.

This particular evening, Pope John had excused himself from an afternoon evening reception, which would be a continuous occurrence on the twenty third floor of the Westin Hotel during his stay here.

His room at the hotel instead of the archbishop's residence, indeed, had been his initial point of refuge. Being five o'clock, he had had other thoughts on his mind. Marcus had inquired as to his health. "You are tired. It is good that you rest. This will be a fatiguing journey."

Marcus was surprised at the response. "I am not tired. I have some place I want to go."

"Oh," was the surprised response.

"Find this archbishop here, this Gregory, and his driver and Raymond. He would be furious if I went without him. This Gregory, you know, leads a group of bishops interested in changes. He has no idea how to go about it except by starting a revolution unless he only thinks about himself. We will meet informally tonight. He will be surprised."

The trip to the Hungarian Cultural Center had begun.

As John Alexander had requested while he ate, first the young people with their parents were escorted to meet him. He motioned for the music to play. He had exchanged one reception for another reception this night. His smile was continuous and contagious. In Hungarian or English, he greeted each as they introduced themselves. He ate slowly, sparingly. "Where are you from?" "Oh, Szeged, a beautiful city on the river."

At another moment, "Your father still lives in Gyongyos? I'm sure I know him." "Yes, he will be pleased to know I have met you," he answered with eyes bright. "Have him send me a letter about things at home."

He watched the dancing and occasionally clapped his hands to the rhythm. He blessed each youngster with a hand on his or her forehead. A hug was forthcoming to those who were not awe-stricken. He smiled. The white collar was loosened. After the eldest of the congregation had individually met John Alexander they gathered in small groups to discuss this remarkable memorable event. Others joined the dancing lines. Many sought to meet and engage their archbishop. Between the varieties of greetings, hand shakes, crosses, kissing the ring and an occasional embrace, John Alexander's gaze repeatedly returned to the bearded man in a group conversation a few yards away and who alternately watched with evident enjoyment the dancing and with smiling satisfaction the activities of the pope.

At one moment, he leaned to Raymond and gesturing toward Daniel asked in French, "Who is that person with the small beard?"

"I do not know, my eminence, but I will find out. He does not come to meet you?"

"No, but his one friend there, the baker, whose family is from Baja, has."

"Would you like to meet him?" Raymond inquired prepared to arrange such a meeting.

"I know this one from elsewhere," John Alexander avowed. "Later perhaps."

The main course and salad had finally, slowly, been consumed. French coffee, strong black coffee, was an endless cup. The reception line became thin and staggered. As dessert was served, Raymond tugged at the waiter's sleeve and unheard to anyone, "I'm sure there's brandy in the kitchen. This would please your guest." The waiter smiled agreeably and quickened his pace to the kitchen.

John Alexander sat at the table and enjoyed a sipping brandy that had mysteriously appeared. Archbishop Gregory joined him at the urging of Marcus.

Gregory was not comfortable at this sudden personalized socializing with the pope, one who controlled his destiny, one against whom he had conspired to bring about liberalization of church actions even beyond the so-called 'confessional church', and who he had held in contempt as the unchaste one with the 'Pope's Girl' and even was plotting, at this very moment, to embarrass his pope to the point of ineffectiveness, he thought.

A pope eight thousand miles away and a pope at your hip pocket were two different people. The first was a vulnerable seemingly inanimate figure of a name with a face fronting as a statue while confronting the flesh, living words and actions here was daunting. He felt a smallness that was indescribable. The stature of the man who could make him cardinal was overwhelming.

"The people are wonderful, my friend, Gregory?"

"They love you," Gregory replied internally cringing at being received as a friend.

"Such dancing. Have you ever seen such dancing. And the prysiadka. Just marvelous."

"The what?" inquired Gregory.

"The prysiadka, the squat dancing." The pope smiled at his prince in waiting. Every archbishop saw a cardinal's hat in his dreams. "You have not yet visited this parish, I see."

"No. Not yet, your holiness," the subdued archbishop conceded.

"Well, of course they are a poor parish," he inferred their importance of neglect was economic. "Their wealth is their love, commitment, and hope in the Christ." He glanced again at Daniel and Arpad. He turned his attention to the dancing, so familiar to his own family gatherings at home in Hungary. His feet subconsciously moved to the rhythm that he felt from the dancers. John Alexander, the man, the Hungarian, rose from his chair and moved toward the dance floor. He moved gracefully with slightly increased speed. The crowd began to slowly applaud in rhythm and raise their voices as he reached into his pocket extracting a folded white handkerchief. He stepped to the front of the dance line as he shook his handkerchief to unfold it. Holding the hand and handkerchief shoulder high, he assumed the lead of the dancers. He began slowly moving his feet adroitly, deliberately to the rhythm of both the crowd now concentrating their attention and presence and the music in union. The line of dancers reflexly followed the lead of the new lead dancer who performed deftly stately holding the handkerchief high with his left arm to lead the second dancer who grasped the opposite end of the kerchief.

Daniel watched with great interest near the dance floor and was not surprised when after four or five minutes John Alexander with a turn and flourish handed the lead to the second dancer. He stopped, smiled toward the crowd and wiped his sweating forehead with the handkerchief and rubbed his left shoulder. The crowd roared in approval.

He moved from the dance floor and walked smiling toward Daniel. Crawford and Adpar stepped aside a bit. Daniel addressed John Alexander quietly, "The old shoulder wound still bothers you, my friend?"

John Alexander subconsciously grasped his left shoulder with his right hand to contain the throb of his aching shoulder. He, as quietly, replied with a smile, "Only when I dance."

Daniel knew the pope knew to whom he was speaking.

"You have me at a disadvantage," Pope John noted. "I have not met you tonight." There was a knowing silence.

John Alexander again wiped the accumulated sweat from his forehead as he surveyed the small gathering before him. His thoughts rambled as he watched the balding man in the seersucker suit wipe the sweat from his head, face, neck and then his head again. His mind dug deep to recall this man who stood before him, whose presence seemed to transcend time. His shoulder ached and his thoughts were gathered to a dark time so focused that the words that Archbishop Gregory was speaking were blurred, disregarded. He saw the night, not here but in his thoughts. Soldiers. Gunfire. Good Friday. Oh, Holy day, as he had always reminisced, not a day for bloodshed and transgression. His shoulder ached and he was on the ground in the light rain. He was only twelve years old and his shoulder ached beyond belief and this man was kneeling above him with his hand in the wound and his shirt in the other hand pressing into the wound. The noise and clamor about them continued on the steps of the cathedral.

He shook his head to clear the darkness and looked up to Daniel, for that was his feeling. He would always look up to him. He said, "You are Daniel and you were there." He began to fall upon his knees to pay homage to this visitor but Daniel speaking to Arpad said, "Help me. Our friend is in pain. Let's get him to a chair."

"Leave your hands off him," Archbishop Gregory interrupted. "He needs no help from a heretic street preacher."

The words of the interfering archbishop went unheeded. He was in no great pain. He only knew the sweetness of the moment as Daniel and Arpad did assist him to a chair.

"Get that man away from the pope," the archbishop continued.

He was waved away by John Alexander who again asked Daniel, "You were there?"

Crawford was now scribbling furiously and had turned the tape recorder on again. He had heard those words before. Now, he was sure he would have more of the story. He was disappointed when Daniel responded in Italian.

"I was there. There are those here who would not understand."

Pope John Alexander was a committed devoted disciple of Christ Jesus, the living word of God. He now was the lead apostle. He had prayed with faith for the communion of saints. He had visited the miraculous sites of the church. He had been part of ecclesiastic reviews of proposed candidates for sainthood, for canonization. He had read the verified miracles supporting these supplications. He believed. He had prayed to the saints. His limousines embraced the symbols of St. Christopher.

But now he knew. To speak of something unseen, to revere a mystery, to participate in acts of faith had unquestioningly filled his life. However, the mystic always remained.

There was no mystic in what was now happening. Nodding his head, "Those were terrible times," John Alexander responded also in Italian. "I was just a student and thought I would die."

"You have always been a chosen one."

"In those terrible days we lost two of God's great men. Bishop Apor died that night and his friend and classmate Cardinal Mindszenty soon became only a symbol in prison or exile."

"But you remain and you will be exalted."

John Alexander smiled, "There is only one to be exalted and I will hope to speak for him."

Crawford assured his tape recorder was still running.

Archbishop Gregory again, whose proficiency in Italian had been neglected could not follow the conversation and being left out, directed, "Your holiness, that is a dangerous man and should be avoided."

Crawford could not resist the opening. He had lost his religion. Why? He did not know for sure. But religion. He knew what religion was supposed to be. "I'm sure you know what a dangerous man he is personally."

The Archbishop's face did pink slightly beyond the sweat of the humid evening and his sullenness became fused with unspoken anger.

Daniel continued in Italian. "It seems your bishop is of a dark side. Love and hope are for the few."

"It seems I have had bad advice," he responded in Italian to Daniel. Then turning to his archbishop, he continued in English, "This is just a poor man for whom we serve, eh? Look at his clothes, he and his friends, like the baker," pointing to Arpad, "are the common, the meek of our Lord." There was the mixture of a smile toward Daniel and a plea of compassion toward Gregory.

He then turned to the gathered congregation who by now had gathered about the central figures and announced, "It is time for us to go. We thank you for your hospitality. It is always nice to be at home."

The assembly cheered, prayed, blessed and rejoiced as each felt the moment required.

He turned again to Daniel, to inquire in Italian, "You will not leave us?"

"I will be here for you."

"Is there a way you can come to me tonight? I have great need to see you. My soul is in great despair."

"Where you are I will be tonight," Daniel responded in Italian. "Peace be with you," he continued in English.

"And to you," John Alexander concluded. "We can go now," he declared. He turned to his faithful commandant who was the only one to understand the words that had been spoken in Italian.

Only the two understood the depth and meaning of the conversation. Only they could or would believe this to be true.

"My friend, Raymond. What you have heard will not be repeated. Believe and your faith will be increased. We have just spoken to a truly holy man."

Commandant Raymond did not respond. The truth of what he had heard was greater than he wished to examine. He would leave it to faith.

No one had paid attention to the dark green Ford and the two occupants. They were parked at the curb a block north of the Cultural Center with the black limo in view.

No one would have understood their discussion. They sat with the motor running and were cooled by the air conditioning.

"Do you have air conditioning in your car at home?" the short occupant of the passenger seat inquired. He looked up to the driver.

"Air conditioning in my car? You joke. Who has a car?"

"But I thought you were an official?"

"I only do what I'm told to do with what I am given, what I need. I receive a small stipend each month from my cell leader." He smoothed his black thick brush cut and rubbed his short stubble beard. "Of course I am an official. I am number two, a trusted patriot," he asserted to reinforce his authority. "That is why they sent me to Camp Ibn Awad. I can kill a man in a thousand ways. They taught me well."

"I wish they would send me for training."

"You would not survive the training, the heat, the desert of Africa. They are mean people. Besides, it is very expensive. You are only here because of your loyalty and your good English. Enough. We are here with a job to do. If we can get near the limo, we can do the job the easy way."

The driver retrieved a small package from the glove compartment. "This can be easy. Just tuck this magnet pack near the back seat. The plastic will do the job." A grin filled his dirty face.

"We know these cars are reinforced with bullet resistant glass, too."

"This is Czech stuff, E-27. It can blast a bunker open from inside or out. Let's see if we can get close enough. The driver is still there. Perhaps he will leave. And don't tell me my plan won't work," he snapped, "I am the leader."

They disembarked, the tall dark leader and the shorter man, Mutt and Jeff, the taller man with shinny smooth hair and the smaller man with ragged black hair irregularly peaked and shaggy. The smaller man grinned through his bearded face, a short beard but as shaggy as his hair, saying "Wonderful place, America. No one asks you 'who are you?' or 'what are you doing?'" He stuck his thumbs in the armholes of his rough woolen vest that was half buttoned from the top down saying as he strutted. "Just like an American," he said evoking a grin from the 'leader'.

The taller man ceased to grin as they approached the limo parked beside the center. He ceased to grin for at least two reasons as he stated, "You might look too American. You like to be American?" He did not wait for a reply, an answer which was not forthcoming for the little man was deep in thought. A sober thought for he did have a legal student visa and to be an American was not an idle thought. The second reason, a tall officious individual was approaching the driver of the limo. A second man, a cook in an apron, who was carrying a tray of food, accompanied him.

They continued toward the limo, "Perhaps we can engage in a conversation and find the right opportunity."

At the limo they heard the tall man say, "Eat. Good." The cook handed the tray of food to Henry, the driver.

Raymond turned to return to the hall and noticed the two strangers who had begun a conversation with Henry.

"Nice car," the smaller one had begun.

Raymond interjected, pointing toward the street, "You. Go."

Armin, the cook, smiled, "He doesn't want anyone near the limo. You fellows eat yet? Most everyone has eaten."

"No," the smaller man replied. "Is that fellow some police?"

"Big doings inside, visitors, the pope himself. Can you believe that? And that fellow is the Swiss Guard to protect the pope."

The two men knew well that the pope was the visitor. They looked at each other. Knowing they would appear to be part of the congregation, the smaller man agreed, "It is time to eat and we wouldn't want to miss seeing the pope."

He wiped his sweaty bearded stubble face on his abundant flounced shirtsleeve, turned and led his taller accomplice into the hall.

They could see the priests seated at separate tables. People had gathered about each table. "There he is," the smaller man said nodding his toward the Pope Alexander. "The big policeman is standing right near him."

"Do you think I could get close enough? I have my denbi. It would be over in minutes."

"We better eat. Only a few people are at the food line. Better you use the denbi with a propellant. That Swiss Guard has seen us close at the car. We might not get out of here."

"I do not care about my life in this mission."

"There will be a better time. We have a week."

Each, by this time, had a full plate of chicken paprikash and stood to one side watching the dancing, the crowd, and especially the pope and the reception line that passed by him. The pope was less than twenty feet away. On one glance toward the pope, Raymond's ever roving eye made contact with the taller man and nodded in recognition to him.

"I think we should eat and go," he whispered. "We have his attention, this policeman. There will be a better time."

CHAPTER 22

It was nine o'clock when Pope John Alexander reappeared at the reception room of the presidential suite. He was refreshed. The shower had washed away the heavy sweat of the evening as the night air would cool the fetid day. The clean clothes now covered a body whose spirit glowed with both contentment and anticipation. His smile and movement through the room of invited guests was with a noticed new vigor. His absence had been noted. His common response was always, "I feel refreshed and renewed."

The contentment of the evening with his Hungarian community of friends had indeed been refreshing. The fatigue of the overwhelming crush of people and conversation was lost for the moment.

The anticipation fostered by the 'holy man' Daniel was beyond examination, a fulfillment of faith, a truth of all believed faith.

He had asked Archbishop Gregory to likewise join him at the reception after refreshing. This could easily be accommodated because significant number of local clergy of the archbishop and others were roomed in the hotel. Archbishop Gregory, in particular, as other archbishops and cardinals honoring the pope's visit had accommodations on the same floor.

Gregory knew this was a semi-command performance and eventually appeared. It was near ten o'clock. John Alexander still carried the same brandy sniffer that be had begun with at nine o'clock. It remained half consumed.

"Wonderful evening," Gregory opened as he approached his internal adversary.

John Alexander had made the rounds of the guests making up for the lost time and felt comfortable in dedicating this moment to his irascible archbishop. "It certainly has been," he agreed. Leading Gregory to a table for two, he asked, "What would you like to drink? The day is long. It will be good to sit, my friend." He sat at the table with the brandy before him. He twirled the brandy glass between his long fingers and contemplated the swirling dark fluid until the vortex focused his mind on a path of conversation.

"Black coffee will be fine," Gregory ordered. He sat down across from his commanding host. He glanced around, as it seemed uncommon that these two should consort in such a private manner.

The apparent friendliness of his pope and to be singled out for both the evening visit to the Hungarian Cultural Center and now this tête-à-tête was a bit perplexing. The first event was diplomatically appropriate. To request the local archbishop, the host archbishop, to accompany to a local ethnic, a parish activity was protocol but now Paul Gregory, cardinal in his heart apparent, but in truth, a knave, a deviant adversary of the pope had been addressed as 'friend' by the target of his personal ventures.

The whole truth of the living flesh present before him here contrasted again with the paper words extant when eight thousand miles away.

Guilt and search for conciliation rattled through his heart and mind bringing shortness of breathe to his soul.

As a school child called before the master, he sat there awaiting hopefully a friendly conversation if not a verbal thrashing. A few present recognized his aggressive stance. He blushed at his personal feeling of a squid caught between two rocks. He picked up the cup of coffee, added two ice cubes to cool it, and slowly sipped it awaiting the teacher's words. He felt small as many eyes glanced their direction.

John Alexander sipped the surface of his brandy and as he placed the glass of brandy back on the table, leaned forward and quietly asked, "Why are you so unhappy, my friend?"

Gregory had heard from many that this Pope, John Alexander, was a quick study, a consummate judge, of individuals and of character.

"It is not that I am unhappy, your holiness."

"Call me, John Alexander, Paul."

The very soul of Paul Gregory squirmed at this further encroachment on his person but continued, "It is not that I am unhappy, John, John Alexander. There is so much to do."

"I understand, Paul. We both are here to lead the church, the priests, the laity, to serve the people of Jesus Christ. We are here to bring the word, his living word, of love and salvation." There was a long pause as John Alexander again sipped the surface of the brandy he was carefully conserving and savoring. "I have seen you tonight. The people, the little people, the poor, the workers trouble you or, may I say, you do not trouble over them."

"I love them all," Paul Gregory protested.

"Tardy words do little good. Some place the love of God has evaded you. It appears you are empty of God's virtues at this moment."

"It seems you have made up your mind," the Archbishop declared. He refrained from uttering the defaming comments of the 'Pope's Girl'.

"I speak not of the past but of now and tomorrow. Somewhere you have lost your way. We need your vision but your vision clouds your person. It is not more important than who you are. I have read your positions on change. You make too much noise. You divide as an adversary. People become polarized."

"I have not wanted to offend you personally. We, I, look for change."

"You do not know me and what offends me. What offends me may not be important. What is in your heart and the convictions of your soul, the gift of Jesus Christ that you carry to the people of the world, is important. Love of God and one another is contagious."

Paul Gregory heard the words of rebuke, questions of heart and soul, delivered in the name of love. Bitter sweet love. 'I may not be offended', the teacher had said. What he really said is that I have offended God, that I have failed my calling, my position, my leadership. This one man who stands between me and the red hat has suggested that I have failed God. The conviction of the unconvicted.

He unbuttoned his collar after carefully hanging his suit coat on a hanger. He rinsed his face in tepid water and peered at his face in the mirror for a moment and questioned himself without an answer, "was I right to bare the conscience of the ambitious archbishop?" He sat in the cane-back captains type chair. The floor lamp at his shoulder provided sufficient light to read. He flipped through the pages of the well used Bible to familiar passages but could not settle on the one of importance at the moment. His mind passed from a favorite psalm that applied to his wayward archbishop Paul Gregory. "His mercy endures forever" and to himself, "My strength and my courage is in the Lord" and waffled to his encounter with Daniel. Would Daniel meet tonight with him? Would there be a knock on the door? Whither is this Daniel who has met me before, who I have known? He is of the holies, a prophet, an angel. He calls himself a messenger passing through time in substance. His thoughts blended with slumber with the conflict, "Blest are they who have not seen and have believed". Oh, Lord, I have always believed but to see in flesh. His chin nodded forward as his eyes flickered partially closed and irregular snoring created an irregular nodding awakening. Despite the fatigue of the long day, deep sleep was not to come with the internal excitement of the encounter with Daniel.

In the haze of slumber, John Alexander, heard the words, "I am here, my friend."

He shook his head. The words were surely a dream as of his last thoughts before slumber.

"It is I, Daniel. I am here as you have asked."

The thought of a dream had disappeared as Pope John Alexander sat straight up in the chair, wide eyed and awake. He stood up to greet the expected visitor.

"You call me by my name. It is true. We did meet before in those troubled days. Would you sit," he asked indicating the second chair at the table.

"And I was there. We were there. It was I who tended your shoulder wound. It was you, a student only twelve years old."

"Only twelve."

"Yes, only twelve when you stood before your Bishop, Bishop Apor, when the Russian officers began shooting when he denied them entrance to the cathedral. One of their bullets tore your left shoulder, a second the skin of your left hip. The wounded shoulder appeared destroyed. You were lucky to live."

"You saved my arm, probably my life."

"I was only there. If your life was saved, it was God's work."

"But that was over fifty years ago."

"Fifty-six years ago."

"You are not that old."

"I am as old as I am," Daniel replied.

"It is a strange coincidence, the same name."

"I have always been Daniel."

"As have I," John Alexander responded with a smile.

"Where are you from, if I may ask?"

"It is rather, where am I?" Daniel replied. "I am where ever God wills me to be. Where ever he sends me."

"And may I ask, why are you here?"

"I am here once again where you are."

"You were willed to be here. You were sent here by God?"

Daniel smiled. "I have no other reason to this point."

John Alexander searched the face of this other Daniel, the face with the short beard, slightly more than a goatee, a very slight gray mottling. He wasn't more than fortyish. A holy man. He smiled to himself. Did he expect an aura, a crown, some distinguishing exhibit? Was he a person, a man of flesh who wasn't of flesh? He saw a man such as himself.

"Are you here because of the millennium that has just passed?"

"I believe I am here because you are here. You are a favorite son, a child of faith as I am. You speak of needing me. That is why I am here at this moment."

John Alexander sat across from the man he believed to be his ultimate vicar, his penitentiary in man, human form.

He left his chair, turned first to the cross that graced his dresser, "You must know, that very cross was a gift from the wonderful Bishop, Bishop Apor. He took me in when my family was lost, killed in the war, the revolution. No one else would take me because I was possessed they said."

"Your malady. Your flights."

"You know?"

"I know. I knew."

"He took me in when others were afraid of me."

"You were an orphan of the war. You were, you are, a child of God."

"You were there. Why wasn't the Bishop saved? Why was I saved?"

"It is not for me or you to say. It isn't a question."

"I wish you to be here because I wish to confess to you," he continued and knelt before Daniel. "In my despair, I abandoned my God, an act of intolerable faithlessness. I placed myself in a moment of selfpity. For a moment I thought I might have been guilty. I have brought shame to the church, to the name of Jesus Christ. The death of the child, Marie, even though I didn't cause it, my association with her led to the tragic accident."

Daniel quietly listened. After John Alexander has ceased his simple statement, he, in incanted tones, said "Go in peace, Daniel."

There was silence, individual meditation. John Alexander remained kneeling before the knees at the feet of Daniel. Urge to prostrate himself before this being, urges to grasp his hand and kiss the ringless hand, and urge to rise and embrace this messenger, this man of God passed through his mind. It felt as though he was before God, the Holy Spirit.

John Alexander instead broke the silence. "I am at peace as never before. I search for the true words of love and salvation to speak to God's people." He rose.

"Like me, my friend. The truth is not in our words but in the love of Christ and the love of God's children in the name of the living word. God is the father of all children on earth and his son the savior of all who believe and act in his name. We are the teachers and you are a chosen one."

"As you, also."

"But you are chosen to lead the flock at this time. The word of the God, through the salvation of His Son, through the love of Jesus Christ in the word of the Holy Spirit, as one in God as truly as I live, says the Lord. I do not desire the sinner dies but that he turns around."

CHAPTER 23

"Missed you at the gathering in Delray last night," Crawford queried with a big grin across his face.

"I wasn't invited," Monsignor Brown informed the reporter who stood before his polished red Contour. "Must you smoke those awful smelling cigarettes, Sam Crawford?" He continued assuming a position upwind from the cigarette smoke. "The story is that Pope John Alexander really mingled with the people. Wish I had been there."

"He even had a few words with our friend Daniel. No one could understand what they were saying. Most of the conversation was in Italian but I got it on my tape recorder."

"In Italian? This Daniel can speak Italian?"

"Yup. Even Hungarian. Got it all on tape. Had a friend translate it back at the office. Looked like they were some kind of friends, he and the pope, like old friends. Said something knowing the pope when he was twelve years old in Hungary."

"How could that be?"

"Don't know that but today's crowd is bigger than ever here and still growing."

"Think he'll show up?"

The park north of the trees and picnic tables was filling with people standing between the parked cars. The humdrum noise that filled the park was interrupted by a crying child here, a laughing conversation there, a complaint about how far away it had been necessary to park.

Two motorcycle policemen appeared at the furthest north end of the park and closed the cross street that now filled with waiting people.

"There's over five thousand people filling this park, I bet, Hubert. He'll show up. There's some kind of destiny at work here."

The police arranged one way traffic on each of the adjoining streets as honking horns expressed the frustration of drivers of those cars obstructed by the commotion and who had no interest in the happening at the park and had places to be and things to accomplish.

"It's almost noon," Hubert Brown observed. "Maybe he isn't coming."

"You know the police showed up yesterday after you left and closed his first weekly free meal down."

"You're kidding!"

"Something about not having a public health permit to serve food. Took him down to the station house."

"He was arrested?"

"Oh, they couldn't do that. It was just a hustle, some kind of harassment. Your archbishop doesn't like him much."

"Why would you say that? The archbishop believes he is probably demented, delusional. You know how the state has emptied out the psychiatric hospitals. He believes he is one who was set out on the street. You know how he never answers any questions of where he comes from, doesn't have a driver's license. We were talking about him just this morning."

"Your archbishop has you convinced?"

"Not necessarily but it is all so strange."

"It certainly is," the reporter agreed. "Truth sometimes is stranger than fiction. Things we don't understand are hard to accept. Besides, your archbishop is afraid of Daniel, I believe."

"I doubt that."

"He called Daniel a trouble maker, a dangerous nuisance last night, even a heretic. Big coincidence. Daniel, your archbishop and the pope at the same place last night."

"How come Daniel was there?"

"Arpad wanted Daniel to meet his Hungarian friends and his friends wanted to meet Arpad's 'holy man' friend. It all came together, the Hungarian pope making a surprise visit with the local archbishop to his Hungarian friends and Daniel just happened to be there. Like I said, destiny."

"You seem to imply some kind of pre-determination or fate. Not just random, a coincidence?"

"It certainly is strange."

"You seem to think he is some kind of 'holy man', Sam, and not just some end of the world, millennium, park preacher. You know we passed the millennium, already, and like yesterday, his delusions, knowing the pope when he was twelve years old. Nonsense."

"Maybe not, Hubert. That conversation they had in Italian last night referred to the pope being injured, shot in the left shoulder. Daniel knew that the pope, as a boy, had been shot by the Russians. He said he had been there. It was the same time that the Hungarian Bishop Apor was assassinated. Daniel's comment about knowing the pope at age twelve was not preposterous, not nonsense, as you surmised, Hubert."

The murmuring of the crowd changed from one of nondescript anticipation to one of electric recognition as the word passed quickly from one to the other, "He is here."

Daniel had indeed arrived. He pedaled his bicycle to the edge of the waiting throng. As he leaned the bike against the light post, he was immediately engulfed by the adjacent people and seemingly lost within the mass of sweating people. An ordinary man would have been alarmed at the moment of seeming confusion. People were speaking to him continuously simultaneously, "Where have you been, Daniel?" or "Are you really a prophet?" or "Please, here is my daughter. She is deaf and cannot speak." While others reached out to touch him, to touch his shirt, a clatter of noise and confusion engulfed Daniel. It seemed he would be lost in the torrent, trampled and injured or carried along as a canoe in a raging current. Carried along within the crowd, a woman held her small child above the crowd, saying, "See, there he is." As though written by script, the moment of confusion and noise dissipated as Daniel raised his hands above his head softly saying, "Peace be with you." The crowd quieted and parted leaving Daniel as a solitary figure. Despite the softness of his voice the words penetrated the crowd as he turned slowly to repeat the words. From the crowd an irregular chant came as, "And peace be with you" echoed and enchanted the congregation to a low murmur as stillness overcame the park awaiting his words. "My friends, it is gratifying to greet so many." he began only to be interrupted by several from the crowd saying, "We can hear you but we can't see you."

Again as the script unfolded, the movement brought of the crowd brought the space occupied by Daniel adjacent to a picnic table. It was not his intent but with the unrequested aid of several of the crowd he found himself ascending to the top of the picnic table. "Here, let me help you," he heard as a hand extended to assist. "Why it's you, Edgar J.L.," Daniel noted.

"Yes, sir. Now you just be careful up there," Edgar J.L. exhorted.

The crowd responded as though a well known dignitary had just taken the stage. The hot humid crowd erupted in an extended applause.

Monsignor Hubert Brown and Sam Crawford were now less than thirty feet from the perch of Daniel.

"What do you think now, Hubert?" Sam cajoled the priest in whispered voice penetrating the din of the applause. Sam wasn't any different than the rest of the people. His head was red from the heat of the day. His hair was disheveled and, his tie unloosened with his shirt collar wet and wrinkled as the sweat rolled down his face. His wet shirt clung to his body. He held his seersucker coat draped over one arm. His hand sought the tape recorder because his expectation of a speech or words, at least, from Daniel was great.

"These people are as irrational as he is," Hubert Brown whispered back.

"Then why are you also applauding?"

If Hubert Brown's face weren't already pink from the heat, the blush of his blond skin would have revealed the feeling of his embarrassment. "It seems contagious," he replied.

"He attracts a crowd just like your pope does," Sam Crawford continued needling the monsignor.

"I certainly wouldn't compare the two in the same sentence."

Sam Crawford turned his tape recorder on as the applause began to lessen just in time to hear the soft exaltation of, "Hallelujah. Amen" by Edgar J.L.

Daniel stood within the crowd with a patience and calmness that betrayed his internal emotion to the demonstration of adulation directed toward him. He slowly turned to face the crowd in several directions raising one hand toward them in recognition and as an attempt to bring the reaction to a termination. What is it they expect of me, his thoughts ran? "Father find the words for me, as you did for Moses and Jeremiah," he silently pleaded.

"Amen, Daniel. Amen," echoed from several of the congregated throng.

"See, Hubert. Some think his gesture is a blessing being bestowed on them."

"His presence here brings great expectations, thanks, in part, probably to some of your newspaper articles. Why must you insist that he has some sort of mystical or religious power? You spread false hope among the people in need."

"You haven't denied what he has done as far as I can see." Sam Crawford wiped his sweaty brow and continued, "If he were Catholic, what he has already done would be sufficient to qualify for sainthood."

Hubert Brown remained silent to Sam Crawford's attestation.

As Sam was about to reinforce his argument, Daniel began to speak. Sam Crawford checked to reassure that the recorder was running.

Daniel spoke in a quiet voice. The quiet tones were succinct and penetrated the humid air.

"You ask many questions of me," he began slowly. "I am a simple man of God and I bring God's message to all who will listen. I receive your generous reception in the name of our Lord. May you find peace and joy in my words in His name."

The poignant voice of Edgar J.L. could be heard by all, "Blessed is he who comes in His name."

Daniel continued as scattered "Amens" darted from the gathering.

"The voice of God is one of hope and joy for all men. We are bound together by His love for each of us and our love for each other."

"Amen," Edgar J.L. responded.

"Amens" again resonated from the audience from scattered areas.

"You will find the strength and sweetness of the Lord in what you do to and for each other. You will find His gracious and giving hand in all that you do. When you give to the poor, and we have all have something to give, when you assist the lame and less fortunate, and some are stronger than others, you are the hand of our Lord."

"Hallelujah. Amen," incanted Edgar J.L.

"Amen. Amen. Amen," echoed from the crowd.

"You, who see the goodness in the hand of Lord, know that God's love endures forever, for each and every one on earth."

"Amen."

"Amens," echoed again from the crowd to Edgar J.L.

"Sound like he chooses quotations from the bible."

"It rolls off his lips. Edgar J.L.'s got a gift, too. What's that?" Crawford interjected. "It's the damned police."

A police car slowly made it's way through the crowd. The blue and white rotating flashing lights signaled to the throng to make way for the slowly oncoming police car that was directed toward Daniel.

Daniel continued, "Let us all know the strength of the love that binds us one to the other. Let us know the love and gift of salvation that the Lord has promised."

The police car had come to a stop adjacent to the picnic table pulpit of Daniel Adams.

As the two officers began to exit the car, Edgar J.L. stood next to Daniel and raised his hands to the crowd, "Hallelujah, Amen."

The crowd resonated, "Amen, amen."

"It's that damned Sweeney again," noted Sam Crawford exuding a bit of anger. "It's your no good archbishop who's up to this, Hubert."

"How can you say that? He wouldn't do that."

"Oh, you don't know how this Adams frightens him. Sweeney is doing what the archbishop has asked. This isn't even Sweeney's precinct. Just like yesterday."

They watched helplessly as Sweeney approached Daniel.

"Now, I told you yesterday not to stir up a commotion like this at the park. You don't seem to understand the law."

"These people have done nothing wrong." began Daniel

Sweeney wasn't to be deterred in his mission. "Now, you just come down from there and come along, mister. You and the boy here can't be disturbing the peace like this."

Muttering from the crowd in protest slowly began to rise. Several men had grasped the side of the police car in a bouncing motion.

"Now, you all just back away," Sweeney ordered the crowd.

"This can become nasty," noted Crawford.

"He seems to bring trouble with him," Hubert responded.

Daniel turned to the crowd. "There is no need to interfere."

Sweeney had reached up to lead Daniel down from the picnic table as the other officer had approached Edgar J.L.

"This man has done nothing wrong," Daniel said in defense of Edgar.

"He's obviously a trouble maker," responded the accosting officer.

The crowd retreated still with muttering protests as Daniel and Edgar J.L. were led to the police car.

"That's a fine howdy-do. They're really going to be arrested this time for disturbing the peace. Rocking that police car was a real mistake. You gonna help me bail'em out, Hubert?"

The holding cell was barren and cool. The air conditioning contrasted with the humid outside weather at the park. The sweat laden clothes of Daniel and Edgar J.L. created an accentuated coolness. Edgar J.L. grasped his arms about himself to warm his body as he continued to sweat in disguised fear and anticipation.

"I never been in jail before," he nervously noted as he paced before the seated Daniel. "Have you?"

"Many times," Daniel replied as his mind traveled through history. "Many were a lot worse than this and in more troubled times."

"You really been around."

"Have no fear, Edgar J.L.," he quietly continued. "You must know, our faith is in the Lord."

"Amen," he responded. This Daniel must be a real troublemaker, he thought. Three other detainees occupied the holding cell. "What do you think these others are in here for?" he asked Daniel as he gestured toward the other 'guests'.

"Who you pointing at, boy?" protested the elderly man. He stood up as he spoke holding his beltless trousers up with one hand. He advanced toward Edgar. "You just mind your own business," he remanded.

"I didn't mean nothin."

The other man stood up from the bench nearby leaving the remaining occupant asleep, snoring a stuporous sleep, curled up on the bench.

"He didn't mean anything," Daniel said softly to the belligerent cellmate. "I think he has had a little too much to drink like the sleeping one," he added quietly to Edgar and stood next to Edgar.

"You just can't mind your own business," the protagonist continued raising his free arm to strike Edgar.

Daniel stepped forward and placed his hand on the assailant's shoulder. The flailing arm stopped in mid air. His whole body motion came to a halt and he slowly slumped to the floor.

Edgar stood in amazement.

The observing prisoner looked on in amazement.

The fallen man seemed momentarily asleep. Within seconds he slowly awakened exclaiming, "I'm freezing." He grasped his body with his arms in an attempt to warm himself.

"Just like Spock," observed the watching prisoner. "You have some mysterious power, mister? You sure handled that drunk."

Daniel said nothing returning to his bench seat.

"Why, he's a holy man," explained Edgar.

"You're kidding."

"You read the papers?"

"He's that one? What's he doing here in jail? He's not a drunk like these other ones."

"It's a big mistake."

"Those things in the paper true about him? They true about you, mister?" he addressed Daniel.

Daniel slowly responded, "Whatever Mr. Crawford has written is the work of our Lord and not of me."

"You really are a holy man?"

"He sure is," assured Edgar J.L.

"You believe in all that salvation stuff, all that born again stuff, for everyone, for anyone?"

"It is true. It is a truth. You are a Christian?"

"Sure. Well, I was."

"You question your faith?" Daniel asked.

"It's kind of hard to believe all this stuff, salvation and everything."

Daniel waited expectantly for the troubled man to continue.

"You say it's a truth, salvation is for everyone?"

"Everyone."

"Even the worst sinner?"

Daniel waited.

"Someone who steals?"

Daniel waited.

Edgar and his now dulled protagonist watched, listened in silence.

"Someone who has so sinned that God would not want anything to do with him?"

"God's love endures forever. He has given his only son and became one with the son to forgive man's sins."

"You is that bad?" inquired Edgar J.L. "What you done that's that bad?"

"I ain't saying. Ain't telling anyone."

"You killed someone," Edgar J.L. concluded.

Daniel raised his hand. "My friends. Let us pray." He kneeled on the gray tiled floor.

The troubled man kneeled on the gray tiled floor.

Edgar closed his eyes as Daniel began, "Lord, we beseech thee." His mind was clouded as he listened. His mind conjured the vision of a temple. They kneeled before an altar. The light of the window streaked in across the multifaceted stained glass windows reflecting off marble columns. A tear crept from each eye and he bowed his head to the figure he could see in his vision on the cross at the altar. The preacher in the pulpit in reassuring terms continued, "Let us live in the joy of Christ, in the salvation of faith. Let us reaffirm our faith in the atoning death of Jesus Christ. The Lord puts to death and gives life. He raises up again. Repent your sins in faith. Remain faithful until death and I will give you the crown of life."

The clanging of metal jolted Edgar. He looked up to the reality of the holding cell door being noisily opened and the curse of the guard.

"Lookee here. Everybody's praying. Well, your prayers are answered, you two. You're outa here." He stopped for a moment. "Oh, it's you, the preacher man. You here again? You gonna be a regular visitor like Bert, sleeping it off again over there? You won't like it. The food is no good in here and the company's lousy."

"But what about me?" The troubled man asked. He raised himself from his knees. One hand held his beltless trousers up and the other was extended toward Daniel.

Daniel smiled. "Seek the Christ, the one who saves. Follow His path. He will know what is in your heart. He is the path to salvation."

The officer led Daniel and Edgar J.L. around the corner into the office area.
"I can't be bailing you out like this all the time, Daniel."
"I appreciate your concern, Sam Crawford. These things just happen."
"Well, actually, we didn't have to bail you out. It was Hubert, here. Monsignor Hubert discussed the problem with Sergeant Sweeney, as secretary to the archbishop, that is, and Sweeney, on the phone over there, thought you should have another chance. I explained it wouldn't do much good, this second chance, because you had your work to do and you'd just go about doing it."
"I thank both of you, especially for Edgar J.L. here."
Sweeney approached the group.
Crawford slipped in a comment. "Talked to his eminence, I bet, Sweeney. This would make a sweet story."
"You don't know nothin', Crawford. Anyway, we go way back, you and me. You wouldn't be printing anything like that now. He looked at Crawford with a knowing smile and a wink, his Irish brogue now coming on a bit to accent his declaration. But you, Mr. Adams, if you're to be going to that park and expecting a crowd, you better be calling me first. It does cause a problem, so many people in one place, the traffic and all, and in this heat, you never know how some people might act. You hear, now," he concluded. "Here's my card, now you call, hear, the number is on there."
"And monsignor, the archbishop isn't too pleased with you," Sweeney avowed. "Says your ideals and practicality are mixed up."

"Humph," interjected Crawford as he sipped on some free station house coffee. "You might have to choose between your archbishop and the pope before the week is over."

"I don't see where Daniel Adams comes into this," Hubert queried.

"Oh, but you will. You two are tinkering with destiny." Crawford winked toward the waiting Daniel and Edgar J.L. and turned with a satisfying smile towards Sweeney. "Yes sir. Destiny is at work here."

He turned to Sweeney. "Everybody's free to go now. Right?"

Sweeney nodded in agreement, gesturing toward the door. "Just please, don't complicate my life. O.K. Mr. Adams?"

"I'm sorry if we have caused you difficulty, Officer Sweeney."

"Enough. I'll drop you off at your place, Daniel. You must have work to do, Hubert, as I do. It's almost five o'clock now."

"And Edgar J.L.?"

"Yes, sir. Let's get going.

"It's fortunate, the time. I'll have time to eat before my appointment this evening," Daniel noted.

"How's that? What happens tonight?"

"Oh, I will be playing racquetball, hand ball with a racket within four walls, not only one wall or three walls."

Crawford shook his head. "Well, damn. You play racquetball? Have you ever played racquetball?" inquired the surprised reporter.

"No, I haven't but I have played hand-ball and he says this is easier with the racket and the four walls," Daniel explained.

"Who says it will be easier?" The alerted reporter inquired. "There's nothing easy about either one, handball or racquetball."

"Why, the priest from Rome, the Hungarian, John Alexander."

"The pope. You are to play racquetball with him?" exclaimed Crawford, interested and bewildered.

"Here you sit in front," and directed Edgar J.L. to the back seat. He stood by his open car door and lit a cigarette as he absorbed the tidbit of news he had just heard. Unbelievable but obviously true. What a story, he thought, as he puffed on his foul-smelling cigarette. This was a human interest story of a lifetime he thought as he got into the car.

"Where's this racquetball game going to be, Daniel?" he asked trying not to reveal his level of excitement.

"I don't know that. A driver will pick me up at seven-thirty, tonight."
"You have shoes and stuff?"
"They will be provided."

CHAPTER 24

Sam Crawford sat at his desk content to enjoy the air conditioning of the office in contrast to the humid first days of August. He reviewed his notes of his experiences of the past several weeks of Daniel Adams. His scribbled notebook contained impressions and events, the conflict of the Archbishop and the secretary Monsignor Hubert Brown, the unreasonable aggressive actions of the archbishop in maliciously engaging the police, Sergeant Sweeney, to harass Daniel. He turned to the story of the upcoming city council race, which was beginning to crystallize. He had a deadline to get that story finished. But, this evening he was going to try to play tag with the pope's entourage and chase the amazing racquetball story.

The phone rang. "Certainly I'm interested, Charles. I have about a half an hour before I chase another story. I'll be right there." He rose and put on his seersucker coat jacket.

The invitation of Charles Evens was a pleasant surprise. Charles had been scurrying around in constant motion every moment since the notice of the pope's mission to Detroit had arrived. Sam had scarcely been concerned with that story as other events in the city had occupied his time let alone his preoccupation with the Daniel Adams story.

He entered the conference room used by the feature writers. The bright morning sun reflected off the polished oak conference table.

"I want you to meet Monsignor Majee."

The tall slender Majee, dressed in his black suit with clerical collar rose to shake Sam Crawford's hand. "A pleasure."

"Likewise," assured the reporter. Getting my exposure to monsignors he thought. Wonder what this is all about?

"And this is Peter Stone," Monsignor Majee informed. "Peter is an American in public relations and employed by the church, the Vatican, especially for this mission of Pope John Alexander. He has spent many years in Rome in his work so has been very valuable in understanding our needs and has been very effective in arranging the media coverage of this mission." Crawford and Stone exchanged quiet 'hellos' while all were again seated.

"First of all, Sam, Peter has provided tickets for both you and me in a group of media at one side of the podium or altar at the stadium."

"That's great," Sam acknowledged with a smile and a thumbs up sign directed toward the PR man.

"Monsignor has informed us," he continued, "that Pope John Alexander wants this Daniel Adams to attend. The pope has asked him and he has indicated his great desire to attend. Transportation and proper seating for this man, Daniel Adams, is the issue. We would like you to be his escort of sorts. He seems to have attracted the fancy of his holiness for some reason and your acquaintance with him is fortuitous."

"Well, damn. Excuse me. I'll be glad to. He's to sit with us, the so called media?"

"Yes, this is a small seating, a group of eight," Stone affirmed. "Myself and an associate, Charles here and a photographer, two cleric paper reporters, you and this Daniel fellow."

Sam could sense a general questioning of the status of Daniel Adams in all this. He deigned to broach the subject. His deep feeling that the coincidence of the two events, the occurrence of the timeless Daniel Adams and Pope John Alexander in this place and time, was more than coincidental. Destiny, fate, some predetermining force was at work here and he was privileged to be a witness.

"I must say, Sam, your articles in the paper about the 'divine' character of this Daniel Adams have come to the attention of quite a few people. An out of town reporter from the *Sentinal* has inquired of the meaning of your articles. Several Rabbis have used him to make an indirect query. I have referred them to you. Have you had any such inquiries?"

"No. But I'm not surprised. He's caused quite a bit of uneasiness among the cleric. He's so real to cause them some kind of concern."

"Concern. What type of concern, Mr. Crawford?"

"Well, he seems to agitate the local Archbishop Gregory and his presence coinciding with occasion of the visit of the pope arouses a certain curiosity."

"Well, that's all coincidental. The second reason, this morning following your suggestion and using the Vatican resources, Peter, at Monsignor Majee's urging, has been in repeated contact with a Ricardo, a reporter at the *Gazetteer* in Rome. Urging him on with certain incentive, monetary to be specific, he has both discovered that a diary did and does exist of the late Marie, the housekeeper of our Pope John Alexander. The story is that through a lot of search this Ricardo is certain that Marie's mother has the diary, so he says."

"And what's in the diary?" Sam almost impatiently inquired.

"We don't know," Charles affirmed nervously fingering the edge of his black waxed mustache. "It is locked. Her mother doesn't have the key and has not forced it open."

"Well, damnation," he began and stopped in mid sentence with a slight blush warming his neck. He raised his hand in apology and continued quirking a small apologetic smile. "Sorry. These are all generic locks. Any diary or notebook or suit case key will open it," Sam decried.

"She won't give it to Ricardo and he's afraid to go to his paper now that he has found it secretly."

"Well heck. Can't you buy it from her?"

"It's not all that easy."

"Look. You get a letter from the pope in Hungarian. You get a bag of lira. Peter Stone flies over there today. With Ricardo, the letter, and the lira and you'll be back tomorrow night with the diary."

"And I can assure you that whatever is in the diary, Dr. Marcus has assured me, will not harm Pope John Alexander," Majee asserted.

"Then the day before the ecumenical service we have the scoop of the year clearing the pope, if he allows us. Even make the portions of the diary a public document."

"As you suggest, to recover the diary would be a blessing and again as you surmise, I don't believe John Alexander would allow the personal diary to become a public issue. I agree with Mr. Sam Crawford. Would you do this journey for us, Mr. Stone?"

Peter Stone looked at his watch. "Six hours," he said. "It's four-twenty in the afternoon in Rome. Getting to Boston, to Rome, pick up Ricardo, meet with Marie's mother, an hours drive. It could be done by noon tomorrow. I will take Annette with me. Her Hungarian and Italian will help. A woman's touch. Annette could charm an ice cube."

"Agreed," confirmed Monsignor Majee. "How much will you need?"

"From nothing to perhaps two million lira, about five thousand dollars, maybe more."

"Two and one-half million lira will be waiting for you in Rome. The diary is that important."

"That's peanuts," Same Crawford interjected. "The *Informer* will pay fifty thousand, fifty thousand dollars, sight unseen for that diary."

"Ninety million lira," Majee pronounced startled at Sam's revelation.

"Yeah, the price of sleaze is high."

"Let's hope the *Informer* is not involved and Ricardo does not become a greedy accomplice. Whatever it takes, Peter."

Peter was already on the phone to confirm reservations.

CHAPTER 25

Commandant Raymond had become accustomed to Pope John Alexander's peculiarities of embarking on unscheduled excursions unknown until the last moment such as this one to the Sacred Heart Seminary as on this trip as the seemingly impromptu visit to the Hungarian Cultural Center in Delray. Now the trip to enjoy an hour of racquetball, seemingly a surreptitious event betrayed, however, by John Alexander's comment to Marcus and Raymond in Rome that he would be packing his playing bag hoping for just such an opportunity. Therefore, this trip was not as unexpected as the Delray trip had been. Such escapades were the bane of Raymond's protective responsibility. Raymond's abilities, tested to the limit by such excursions, were brought to forefront. Pope John Alexander could in no way complain when told that a two man security team had been sent ahead to survey their destination. Actually, John Alexander restrained his smile of admiration or any such comment opting to await the appearance of the advance security men in silent satisfaction. He had often expressed to Raymond that he should do as he thought best in his protective role but he had no intention of being a 'man in a cocoon', standing his ground as Raymond would describe the characteristics of the "fringe radicals and crazies in the world who want your hide, your holiness".

Raymond and Pope John Alexander were still waiting in the chauffeured black town car when a similar car carrying Dr. Marcus and Daniel arrived at the Sacred Heart Seminary.

Only one car was parked in the circular driveway in the front of the clustered attached red-brown brick academic buildings. A blackgarbed cleric was engaged in conversation with the occupants of the waiting car.

"Commandant, this is Andre. Is everything in order?" the driver inquired in French.

"He awaits the signal from Raymond for us to enter the building."

"I understand," Daniel commented.

"You understand French?" Doctor Marcus queried.

"I also understand that Raymond, Commandant Raymond, is quite nervous about John Alexander's wanderings," he added nodding his head to Marcus that he indeed did understand French and had understood the driver's previous conversation as they drove over.

"That's why Raymond has replaced the drivers, the chauffeurs, with two of his own security, of the Swiss Guard," Marcus explained. "There. There's the rector with Raymond's advance security coming out of the school now."

Raymond and Pope John Alexander were disembarking at the moment. Following a discourse with the security guard, Raymond said, "We can join the party now," he stated turning to the two passengers with a smile, adding, "The other driver will stay with the vehicles."

"Come on, Daniel. We'll have some fun. Just follow me."

They exited the air-conditioned car into the hot humid August evening. The sun was still lowering in the western sky. It would be over an hour before the moon would clothe its long shadow.

A seminarian ushered them as Marcus noted, "Thank goodness this ancient place is air-conditioned."

No one noticed the dark green Ford again in pursuit of John Alexander. The occupants were thwarted by the front entrance approach of Pope John Alexander's car. There was no recourse other than the general parking lot. Even with the small number of cars this lot provided an uneasy surveillance. Fortunately, parked at the rear edge of the lot, the occupants could observe the target vehicle.

"What are they doing?" queried the short shaggy haired passenger.

"They are waiting, obviously," the taller man explained condescendingly to his passenger cohort, "probably for a second car."

"He has a different driver."

"They have many drivers," the taller replied. "See, there's a second car," he informed confirming his obvious deductive ability.

"They still stay in their cars."

"They are waiting for someone to greet them. Someone so important would wait to be formally greeted," announced the tall one, the leader. "There, they are getting out now. Some one is coming from the building."

"He's not dressed like he was the other night."

"This is something less formal," announced the leader.

"What kind of bags are they carrying?"

"They look like overnight bags, maybe athletic bags. That's what this is. The pope likes to play racquetball. That's what my biography sheets said. They are going to play racquetball. See if a driver stays with the cars."

"They have gone into the building," the shorter agent announced.

"And the driver?"

"One driver stays with the cars. You can see that very well."

"Of course, I can see that and I can see that he walks and acts like a military person. That is why the driver is replaced."

"He would be a Swiss Guard soldier you know, the ones in the black and orange stripped baggy pants."

"Of course, I know. You don't tell me anything. You are here only because you speak English."

"Awful good English, therefore," replied the short one in English.

"Don't talk to me in English. Anyway, this Swiss Guard is only for show, for ceremony. They are not real soldiers. We will get ready and in a few minutes we will go in ourselves. After all this is free country. We will go in with our own athletic bag, our surprise bag, and go to this racquetball room. All will pay the price. I can kill in a hundred ways."

He opened the trunk of the green car, emptied out a green canvas bag. Wrinkled shirts, socks and underwear fell into the trunk. Into the bottom of the bag he placed four hand guns and six cartridge clips that had been secreted under a brown plaid blanket.

"Is enough for an army," said the short one.

The tall one covered the weapons with two of the wrinkled shirts and zippered the carrying bag shut. "Must be prepared. Come, we will play racquetball," he concluded with a laugh. "You carry the bag."

"Now you use your English. Why you are here. You will inquire directions to racquetball room." He opened the school door facing the parking lot. With a grin of satisfaction he declared, "See. Door's open. Is free country. Follow me." He led the short man inside the building. He looked to the two doors that led from the reception room and were separated by mail slots. The left one was open. The right one was open. He turned to the left wall opposite the windows.

"Ah, a message board. Is there anything there to tell us which way the racquetball rooms are?"

"I do not read that kind of English much. You know that, only signs, money and food."

"Don't tell me what I know. We will go down this passage. There will be someone you can ask," he ordered turning toward the left doorway.

A young man appeared at the doorway. His stare at the two men was accompanied by a half step to the rear that reflected the uneasiness of being approached by someone speaking a foreign language and dressed as no one else frequenting the school.

"Can I help you?" he inquired.

"You student here?"

"No, I teach here," he replied calmly and evenly trying to overcome the sweat that suddenly softened his shirt collar and ran from his armpits. The feeling that these strangers threatened his being was reinforced by the force of his heart beating against his chest.

"You, please," the rooster asked, "direct us to the racket room?" He held up the green canvas bag.

"Oh, racquetball," he squeezed from his throat that seemed constricted by his tie. He pointed behind him down the hallway saying, "the left hallway", without taking his eyes off the two men, the intruders, and continued, "to the end of the hall, then turn right."

The taller man swept by the professor as the smaller man said, "You are thanked," showing a broad close-mouth grin and followed.

Commandant Raymond stood in his athletic shorts and sneakers with racket in hand. He stood shaking his head while in conversation with his Swiss security guard driver. "This is not good, Dieter. We should call this off. I don't want him down in that court. Look at that," he said pointing to the court. "There is only one entrance. The ladder from the top. It is just as you described. No door at the bottom."

Marcus and Daniel exited the locker room across from the court as Marcus inquired, "Those shoes are not too tight, are they?"

"They feel fine."

"Dr. Marcus," interrupted Raymond. "Excuse. It would appear that this is a dangerous, unsafe, arrangement. This ladder entrance provides extremely limited access with no rapid exit possible, like being in the proverbial barrel," he concluded and awaited Marcus' response hoping for concurrence.

"You have men stationed here?"

"Yes, Andre is in the hallway through that door and Deiter, here, will be in the adjacent basketball court through the other door. Your driver is with the two cars."

Leaving Raymond to his decision making, Marcus led Daniel to the racket court ladder. "Come, we'll practice a bit. You will see. It is just as you have played handball. The four walls make it even easier. John Alexander won't be here for a few minutes while he changes in the rector's rooms and makes his way here."

Marcus climbed over the ledge and began down the ladder. "Call me, Raymond, when he gets here. You're right, but do you think there's any danger?"

Raymond looked down as the resounding impacts resonated as irregular racquetball shots caromed off the rackets and the walls. He shook his head again. Marcus was telling Daniel, "Now return this one off the back wall. It then must reach the front wall."

John Alexander accompanied by the monsignor rector and the security guard appeared at the basketball court doorway and on entering he could see Raymond was waiting for him. It was obvious that he was in a delaying mood. "What? What now? You are not loosening up."

The two faced each other in apparent contention. Two six-foot men had apparently reached a point of unspoken disagreement. This would be a verbal disagreement. The only advantage otherwise would be of age as each were muscular men, shoulders able to joust with the best and legs able to create an advantage in any tug-of-war. The curly black hair of the commandant's chest on inspection would win the age contest compared to the graying mottled hair protruding above the more modest garb of John Alexander's tee shirt.

"It is the court. The only way in or out is this ladder. Like fish in a barrel." He repeated the descriptive phrase.

John Alexander contemplated the situation.

"Dr. Marcus feels likewise," Raymond added trying to forestall the decision. "We can find a safer place," he concluded.

"We should be safe within this sanctuary. No one knows we are here."

Raymond raised his hands in combined frustration and condescension knowing that he should have known John Alexander would perceive no danger or perhaps would prefer perhaps not to concede that danger existed.

The monsignor rector watched in silence. The security guard was disagreeing, was arguing with the pope. His feelings were mixed that someone would openly confront the pope. Was this disrespect or were his fears justified?

"You have men stationed close just in case?"

Raymond nodded in the affirmative adding, "In both directions." He watched as John Alexander straddled the wall top then turn to begin the descent down the ladder.

"You will stay and watch?" he asked of the rector.

"Only a moment. I have several things to attend to."

Raymond began to follow down the ladder pausing to tell Dieter, "You will watch the doors. Stay in communication with Andre. You have no time to watch this game." He waited until the guardsman indicated that he understood the directives and descended the ladder.

The professor watched the two strangers proceed down the hallway for a moment. Then he rapidly approached the phone and urgently dialed the rector's phone number. His feeling of urgency was quickly fulfilled by the answered phone but quickly deflated and replaced by concern when the secretary answered his query. "He's not in the office right now."

Professor Max Ernst objected, "But."

"But what, Max?" the secretary countered. "Just slow down a bit. You are excited."

"But, he must know, there are two strange foreign speaking men here who have entered from the parking lot."

"There are several foreign men visiting here this evening," the secretary agreed. "Did they say what they wanted?"

"They asked where the racquetball room was and then left in that direction."

"But of course," the secretary continued, "that is where they are meeting."

"Who is visiting?" queried Professor Ernst momentarily relieved that these men may have been expected visitors.

"Why, some priests, foreign priests."

Max Ernst fears were now reignited. His voice raised half an octave. His soggy collar chafed his neck again just as at the first encounter as he exclaimed. "These men were not priests!" Feeling a sixth sense of apprehension and that precious time had been lost in this useless conversation he ended the conversation, "Find the rector and tell him what I have told you." He replaced the phone, turned and rapidly trotted down the hallway in wary pursuit of the strange appearing and speaking visitors, one of whom had spoken poor English of sorts.

He reached the end of the hallway and turned to the right entering the hallway to the locker rooms and the racket court. He immediately flew forward, launched several feet in the air, having stumbled over a soft but unyielding mass on the floor. He rolled quickly to a stop. A cold griping knowing grasped within his stomach. Subconsciously, he knew he had stumbled over a body. He rolled to one side disregarding the ache in his shoulder to view the unmoving body. The man, the fallen man in a dark suit lay unmoving with his head askew twisted slightly upright against the hallway wall and one hand inside his coat jacket. The sun shone through the window illuminating the shadows of his face. His eyes stared toward the sunlight. Ernst lay in equally unmoving dismay, near fear, with wild thought s traversing his mind. A voice darted out at him from the shadows, the darkness of the body. "Andre. Andre. Parle. Andre, are you there, Andre. Parle," in French the voice spoke. Ernst looked for a moment. The lips of the fallen man were not moving.

He crawled the several feet toward the body and the voice. The voice began again, "Andre?"

Ernst picked up the small mobile phone that laid beside the body.

In his best French, "This is Professor Ernst. Your Andre is unconscious on the floor."

"Where are you?"

Max Ernst reached to feel the pulsation in Andre's neck. "In the hallway leading to the recreation area. I believe this man is dead," he answered in a crackling voice. "Send a priest."

There was no answer.

The two assailants crouched outside the doors leading to the recreation area. The green canvas bag was open beside them. The taller man carried a handgun. He placed a clip in the gun and one in his rear trouser pant pocket.

The sound of the irregular impact of the racquetball could be heard with occasional verbal outbursts interjected. The taller man rose on his knees to peer through the glass portion of the upper half of the door. The younger man crouched on his hands and knees saying inquiring, "Did you kill that man?"

"Be quiet," was the answer. "Get your weapon ready. There is no one in the passage," he whispered. "We will go now, slowly, quietly." He slowly depressed the handle latch and leaned on the door. The door opened without a squeak or a quiver. "Stay down," he ordered as he crawled through the open door. The smaller man wiped his nose on his sleeve and wondered if his illustrious leader could feel his heart beat as hard as his was beating.

The staccato sound of the racquetball ceased as a voice was heard below in French. "Alert, Commandant. Code Yellow. There is infiltration. Andre is down, maybe dead." This was followed by a flurry of command type conversations below.

The taller assailant had reached the wall of the racket court on his knees and hands with his accomplice beside him. On hearing the conversation in French, which he did not understand, he quickly raised his head above the wall saying, "Over there," motioning his accomplice to his left. He raised his weapon over the edge trying to discern his primary target among the racquetball players racing to the back wall of the racquetball court as ordered. He rattled off a short burst. One player fell, sprawling forward leaving a smear of blood on the floor.

The shorter man raised his weapon. His squeaky excited voice exclaimed, "We will—"

Almost simultaneously, the door from the basketball court opened and the security guard, Dieter, appeared on one knee. A rapid series of bursts of gunfire flew at the assailants. The shorter man suddenly assumed a semi upright rigidity for a flashing moment and then crumpled to the floor. The taller man, in quick response, was prone on the floor, behind his fallen associate. In the process, he dispatched a fusillade of shots ending in the wall above Dieter's position. As Dieter retreated momentarily behind the door, the assailant inched closer to the fallen man, into the pool of blood forming about the man, to present a minimal target with weapon ready to the return the attack of the security guard, Dieter.

Single shots now came from the racquetball court warning that a second foray by the assailant in that direction would be met with resistance.

"One thing at a time," the tall man cursed under his breath. The door opened a foot. No gun or person presented. He let loose a short burst from the handgun and quickly replaced the clip. He was about to follow this with a second volley, then crash to the side of the door when a cloud appeared to cover the racquetball court. The appearance was a momentary distraction. Thoughts of gaining an advantage on the security guard were suspended. The appearance of the strange cloud meant he would have no opportunity to see his quarry. Random shooting would be of little value. The bright searing oblong light that appeared immediately before and above him interrupted the thought of a rapid retreat. The light was too bright to look at, too overwhelming to respond to. He covered his head with both arms crushed against the soft unmoving body, the moist warm blood against his face. A hand gently touched his shoulder. Such sudden complete coldness of his entire body he had never experienced before. The desire or ability to move disappeared. His fading brain heard the cloudy drawn-out words. "It is all right, commandant. It is quiet here now. Tend to Dr. Marcus' wound."

The tall man was now flaccid, seemingly asleep.

Sam Crawford had finally reached Sacred Heart Seminary. He had hovered at the Westin Hotel. He knew the agenda for the evening but had no sure idea where the racquetball match would take place. As the group left the service entry it had been by chance that he had heard the seminary mentioned. By the time he had reached his car, his quarry had a significant head start.

He stopped his car behind the black limousine. It was the same vehicle he had staked out at the hotel in his quest.

Retrieving his coat jacket from the car seat, he began walking rapidly toward the front door. He was not surprised when the driver intercepted him asking, "Can I be of service to you?"

Crawford recognized the courteous security method of interception. The shoulder brace firearm that distorted the left side of the security driver's jacket and the military type communication phone confirmed the impression.

The security driver had moved away from the limousines as he intercepted the reporter.

"I am here to visit," Crawford replied with his best innocent smile.

The agent persisted, "What is the purpose of your visit?"

He took his credentials out of his suit coat pocket and began to present his plausible story. "I'm a reporter for the *Press*," he began, "and am doing a story on the seminary." He held out his credentials.

"I will call and have you escorted," the agent began.

The semi-farcical affair was interrupted and concluded by a blurted message of urgency from the radio. The message in French, "Alert, Commandant. Code Yellow. There is infiltration. Andre is down, maybe dead."

Crawford did not understand the message but the urgency and character of the message was evident and the urgency and character were confirmed by the sound of gunfire as the message ended.

The security driver, dismissing Crawford as part of the threat, ordered Crawford to, "Stay right here," and ran toward the entrance.

His thoughts rattled through history. As John Paul had been wounded by the fanatic Agca and other attempts, known and unknown, had been thwarted, the religious fanaticism continued. Was this pope wounded or perhaps killed in this attempt? How many were there? Who were they? And why, this time?

With weapon out, the Swiss Guard bounded up the steps, into the school building with the reporter behind.

The few evening occupants of the academic building, alerted by the gunfire, were in the hallway as the two raced by.

On hearing Daniel's assertion, Dieter entered the passageway with his weapon at ready.

The cloud that had shrouded the racquetball court had dissipated.

Dieter ascertained that the taller man was immobile, rolled him to the side and affixed the handcuffs. As he sought to appraise the condition of Pope John Alexander and the participants, the rector appeared from the recreation room soon followed by the security guard and the puffing winded reporter.

"One is dead and the other in cuffs," Dieter called to the commandant.

"And Andre?" he responded, "How is he?"

"I believe he is dead," Professor Ernst reported.

John Alexander had removed his tee shirt and with it had cinched a tourniquet on the bleeding wound of the upper right arm of Marcus.

CHAPTER 26

The presidential suite occupied over one half of the top floor of the Westin Hotel. The conference room of this floor being used for this small impromptu meeting was fronted by a long picture window opening to a patio. The view was of the dynamic General Motors Headquarters Building, the original Renaissance Center, on one side and the Detroit River with Windsor as a backdrop and the low arching Ambassador Bridge as a frame to the south. The patio, a half step down with a masonry wall, sported an artificial green carpet flooring braced by aggregates of large low pots containing various shaped evergreens and interspersing rose trees and green plants. Three umbrellas covering seating table areas were present.

The opposite wall was a partial glass cased bookcase with sundry books, a miniature library.

Sam Crawford stood at one end. His red-blond hair was neatly combed. His seersucker suit, the brown one, was neatly pressed. He sipped his coffee, the strong bitter coffee, from the refreshments set on the serving table before him. The coffee was something to do. He looked into the mirror above the refreshments. His tie was neatly in place with the shirt buttons also in place. He observed the variety of fruit, large fresh strawberries, slices of orange and melon, the pastries, some chocolate covered, others inviting a visit of their secret ingredients.

He was not as concerned of the secret ingredients of the pastries as the unknown contents of the blue book decorated with flowers that sat before Monsignor Majee who was seated with his own cup of black coffee.

The blue book, the diary of the deceased housekeeper, Marie, the object of this meeting that had been successfully retrieved by the public relations man,

Peter Stone, and his Hungarian speaking associate, Annette. It sat there locked, as yet unopened. The two rescuers of the nefarious diary had not been invited to this unveiling. Sam didn't know why he was here but he waited with his associate, the religious editor, Charles Evans.

He recalled the conversation. "Monsignor Majee was impressed by the direct vision you had on recovering the diary."

"You seem to imply that the two PR's have been successful," he had replied.

Charles had gently twisted the end of his waxed mustache with his delicate fingers as he smiled and continued, "The letter you suggested really did the trick and, of course." He stopped to gently twist the opposite end of his mustache.

"Of course, what?"

"The likable Annette in her persuasive way, in Hungarian, induced the mother that it would be a holy thing, a holy requirement, that she would want to make the diary available to his holiness, her pope, her countryman."

"And how much did this cost? How much did they have to pay her?"

"She wouldn't take a holy dime, not one lira. After she retrieved the diary she handed it to Peter and wouldn't take a cent."

"Well, damn."

"Well, they had to pay Ricardo, the reporter for the *Gazetteer*. It seems Monsignor Majee had promised him a reward."

"How much?"

"One million lira."

"One million, damn. That's lira."

"Six hundred dollars. One million in lira. It sounds a lot."

"Why didn't Peter sell it to the *Informer*? Part of it? He knows what it's worth."

"Fifty-thousand? Six months pay to probably put his reputation at risk. Besides, the diary is still locked."

"No one's looked in it?"

"Not yet."

"Well, damnation."

"This afternoon. You're invited. The monsignor, you, me and the pope."

"The pope and me. Well, damnation, excuse me. Why me?"

"We, I, will have the exclusive for the story. Why you? Majee, the monsignor says the pope said something about liking you, your relationship with this Daniel."

Sam Crawford looked in the mirror at his associate. He checked his tie. He watched Evans deposit a small paper bag on the desk. He filled his cup again. He lifted his package of cigarettes from his jacket pocket and replaced them.

The door opened. A somber cleric entered the door alone. Pope John Alexander entered the room. He was dressed in plain clerical white.

Majee rose. "Mr. Charles Evans," he said pointing to the seated Evans, who rose, "and Mr. Sam Crawford."

"I am pleased," Pope John Alexander greeted. "Let us be seated. We will all speak English, American," he said with a slight smile that broke the somber atmosphere momentarily.

Sam, whose anticipation, whose nervousness, seemed to break at the greeting of the pope, asked, "Would you like a cup of coffee, your, ah, your excellency?"

"Please," confirmed John Alexander. "I understand you are Jewish, Mister Crawford. Don't let that come between us."

Crawford sat the coffee before Pope John Alexander.

"Sit. Sit. We sit together as friends and as children of one God." He nodded to Majee. "Open the book."

Crawford watched. Majee emptied the paper bag, just like a bag Crawford thought that he would buy penny candies in when he was a kid. He watched as Majee tried one key. The little suitcase key wiggled in the lock. The diary was light blue with darker blue flowers on the slightly padded cover. The flowers had been accentuated, outlined by dark black pen markings. The small gold lock did not give way to the key. A second key was wiggled in the lock by Majee. The spring lock could be heard as a small click indicated it had sprung open.

"Now, so everyone knows, understands, Janos, Monsignor Majee, will read the diary. It is obviously in Hungarian. As he and I have discussed, anything he reads that is private, of no relevance to, ah, the question, he will forget. Any passage that is relevant he will read to us, translated into English."

Charles Evans opened his notepad and placed it on the table. His throat was dry. He felt uncomfortable being privy to the private thoughts about someone who had betrayed the leader of the Catholic world who was seated at the same table. He left the table momentarily. He was himself a private man. He found it difficult to swallow like there was cotton in his mouth. He retrieved a diet Pepsi and a glass of ice from the refreshment table.

Sam Crawford placed his hand in his pocket to assure his tape recorder was there.

Pope John Alexander sipped the black pungent coffee. Then leaned forward hands holding his temples, elbows on the table.

Monsignor Majee flitted page by page through the diary. He paused. A faint blush began at his neck. He shook his head and uttered an, 'Eh'. He paged more slowly now and began to speak, "Wednesday, June, ah, no man I have ever known is both so strong and so wise. I can barely stand to look at him. I feel so weak."

John Alexander shook his head slowly in the negative.

Evans did not write.

Crawford felt his pocket to make sure he could feel the vibration of the tape recorder receiving.

Majee turned the pages, one by one. "Monday. My diary. There is no other man that I would want but I am so young and just a housemaid. Oh, my diary, there is no one else that I would want."

"No. No," John Alexander interrupted. "Only those things to the question."

Majee turned the next page, and the next, and the next, and the next as his eyes became a deep stare, his eyes enveloped the diary, his neck and cheek pinked. He sighed. He turned back the page.

He read slowly. "Wednesday. Dear diary. I have told my good friend, Annette, about how I feel about Daniel. She wanted to know why I call him that. I told her this was his real name."

He paused. Ran his finger down the page and back. "Diary. Annette told me she could have any man she wanted. She is very beautiful and probably has. She said she could probably have Daniel if she were me. Dear diary, I cried."

"Why is this relevant?" John Alexander asked. He picked up his cup of coffee and walked to the refreshment table.

Majee turned the page and looked up at John Alexander who now was refilling his cup of coffee.

John Alexander carried the coffee samovar to the table, filled the coffee cup of Sam Crawford. He returned the samovar and stood at the door of the patio.

Majee now looked back to the diary and continued. "Dear diary, Annette bet me fifty thousand lira that I couldn't have Daniel." He stopped. His face now flushed because he already knew the later entries in the diary.

John Alexander did not turn around as he said, "So, that's the fifty thousand lira in her letter. She felt guilty making such a wager."

"Not exactly," Majee countered. He continued, "Dear diary, this morning I have sinned. Daniel had taken a late shower and when I was bringing the clean laundry in, he was standing there, so strong, so tall, with only his bath towel in front of him. He stood there. He told me to leave but he stared at me and his lips moved as kisses. I took my blouse off as he stared at me. He turned and went into his room. I followed. There he lay on his bed asleep. Sound asleep. I looked at him. He was so beautiful. I don't understand. I put my blouse back on and began to leave. Then I though of the bet with Annette. His used underpants were there by the bed. I rolled them up and hid them in my purse."

John Alexander turned around with serious pursed lips. In Hungarian he said to Majee. "Marcus has told you why that might have happened?" as a rhetorical question.

"But, of course," Majee agreed. "A problem with your medication. There are only several more entries." He continued as in haste to get the distasteful purging over with, pausing. "Must these two be privy to this?"

"We will trust them and decide."

"Dear diary. Annette did not at first want to believe me and wanted to know about it. All about it. I told her the first part and then said that when he was exhausted he went to sleep on the bed. I got up, stole his underpants. She paid me the fifty thousand lira."

"Thirty dollars," Evans quipped.

Majee looked up at Evans. "You would trust this man?" and looked at John Alexander.

John Alexander smiled slightly and looked down at the floor. "There is more?"

"Dear diary. I told mama. She told me I should 'confess' to Daniel what I have done. I will try tomorrow and will quit my job."

John Alexander again was seated at the conference table. "That is all?"

Majee's finger ran down the page. "A few days later, the last entry. 'I will try to tell him tomorrow.'"

"The day before."

"Yes, the day before her death."

John Alexander sat silently before the tribunal. A tear leaked from each eye as he stared ahead. Each man could feel the pain that each tear etched upon his heart, upon his soul.

"She was a blessed girl, a young girl of threatened innocence. A repentant blessed girl," he said.

There was silence.

There was no reply possible to such a statement from the shepherd of the people, of all the people as he had emphasized.

"You might as well know the ending. It was all so sudden, a tragic twist, a tragic ending. She came to me saying she was sorry for what happened. I protested that I did not understand, exactly. She said that she had sinned, as she said 'sinned grievously,' and placed her arms on me and sobbed on my shoulder in innocence, in despair. I consoled her. I don't recall what I said but then I asked if she had been to confession. She backed away put her face in her hands sobbing, saying yes, and then she suddenly turned away. She stumbled over the footstool falling forward several steps off balance and fell through the window and screen. I grabbed at her. It was all so sudden. I could not hold on to her as her skirt slipped through my hands."

Tears were now streaming down his face. He placed his face in his hands and his body slowly shook.

Charles Evans had ceased jotting notes.

Sam Crawford had turned the tape recorder off.

"I was afraid of this diary," Majee said. "A friend psychologist has told me that many women lie, fantasize, to their diaries."

John Alexander now sat more composed as he wiped his face dry. He assumed a solemn attitude as his demonstration of despair waned. After all, if he was 'too much man', as some alleged, he was also very human.

"I don't think that there is a story there in any form, gentleman. Those who don't believe will disbelieve. Those who believe don't need to know. We deal in the tomorrow. We proceed with our message of the joy and hope of the living word of our God, of the salvation of the one who gave his life for us and is one in God."

Janos Majee pushed the lock shut on the diary and placed it in front of Pope John Alexander.

Charles Evans tore the sheets of notes from his note pad, folded them and pushed them across the table to Msgr. Majee.

Sam Crawford knew that he must not betray the trust that he had been given. He removed the small cartridge from the recorder. Anyway, there are bound to be other stories before this pope's visit is over, he thought.

CHAPTER 27

The evening was tepid. The sun seemed to hang endlessly in the western sky imparting it's last potion of solar rays to heat the steam rising from the side walk in front of the house with the new steps. Daniel was finishing a last coat of sealer to the steps to protect the finish. In a few moments the sun would be gone and the six degree fall in temperature would be cooling. He stood watching one of the marveled and revered miracles of God's handiwork. The sun disappeared at night and reappeared in the morning in every spot of the earth. And the planets coursed their charted path in a grand parade. Even the earliest people recognized this and marveled at the unknown hand that controlled it and paid homage to this maker. All this happened according to a giant plan controlled by clockwork that would stagger the imagination of the finest scientists to attempt to duplicate. And at the same time, the inconsistencies of weather with the rains and floods, the earthquakes, famine and drought caused man to question their faith. Even though mankind marveled at God's handiwork and had used God's gift to evolve scientific miracles and medical advances, mankind had been unable or unwilling to follow the precepts of God's word. Man had not progressed in his image. They had trampled on his commandments. Throughout the world man's challenge to human survival, not only in the flesh, but in the basic spirit of God's laws was at a peak. Man was in danger of a shriveled soul that would wash the majority of mankind off the earth. Man had little respect for nations, for his neighbor, for family, and even for himself. The majority of mankind with increasing frequency was breaking each commandment. Man's soul was in a state of disrepair. God could not be pleased with what he saw. The tears of God would flow in their silence. And in his day of return, how his heart would be shattered. But He new, of course, that sin had over taken this world that He had given to man. Sodom and Gomorra were only a speck of humanities' downfall compared to the depths that mankind had wrought upon itself this day contrary to the commandments of God and further failing to recognize His gift of salvation. The gift itself was even beset by failure to recognize the simple basic commandments so necessary to life in its own innate requirement to survive.

The black sedan that had stopped at the curb abruptly interrupted his ruminations. The car stopped with the motor idling and Daniel's glance could not make out the occupants because of the blue tinted glass. He picked up his paint can as the sun was nearly setting and it was time to prepare his evening meal.

He turned to leave when the rear car doors opened. Two men got out of the car and briskly approached the startled Daniel. He stopped as the men came close to him with one impeding his passage to the side walkway of the house.

The other man spoke firmly, "Our boss wants to see you now."

"Who is this boss who would like to see me and for what purpose? Are you from the police?"

With a laugh he answered. "Hear that, Tony? He wants to know if we're from the police." Turning back to Daniel he continued, "We really don't have to tell you anything. When the boss, Mister Bartolo, wants something he gets what he wants. But since he wants a favor from you, I'm gonna tell you he wants to see you because his old lady, his wife, is sick and the doctors aren't doing her any good. Since you've been doing mysterious things around town, he wants you to take a look in on her. He's sort of desperate and could be doing crazy things, so you oughta cooperate if you know what I mean."

Daniel listened patiently to the accosting man. It was impossible to command him to do anything to satisfy this boss person. Perhaps this was another situation as the Perkins boy. He knew that he could not deny these men if only as a brother to brother. It was apparent that their vision of the relationship was not exactly the same. They were commanding his services not seeking a response based on such values. "Let me take a moment to put my things aside and I will be glad to visit your Mrs. Bartolo."

"He wants you to come right now."

"I will put my things away first and perhaps you will assist me to place a board with the 'wet paint' sign before the steps." He proceeded to the walkway with the paint, brush and cloths only to have the impeding man grasp him by the arm. Daniel stopped. "Please," he said. "It has already been a long day. We will finish my chore first."

"The boss said to come now."

Daniel gently grasped the arm of the insistent protagonist. The man stared at him, closed his eyes, and slumped to the ground. The driver of the car emerged from the car with his hand affixed to the inside of his coat about to extract the handgun.

"What have you done to him?" the partner asked with a voice that betrayed a fear that he could not hide. "Is he still alive?"

"He is well. He will awaken suffering a coldness he cannot understand. You are both unmannered in seeking this favor as you state. I will put my things away now."

The partner ordered the driver, "No need for any force."

The driver withdrew his hand saying, "He might do us all in."

"I don't think so. Help Tony up. He seems to be coming around." By this time Daniel had disappeared to the back of the house.

"He's taking a dodge. Don't you think I should go after him?"

"He'll be back. You'se guys don't understand such people. How are you doing, Tony?" he asked of the shivering associate.

"What happened? I'm freezing. I got him in my hand and suddenly I'm out cold. I mean I'm freezing to death on the ground. I'm awake but I can't move. Nothing works. I'm gonna give that guy what for when he gets back, if he comes back."

"Just leave him alone. He'll put you on the ground again. Like the boss says, he's a mystery. Now let's get the board and 'wet paint' sign up in front of these steps so when he gets back we can get on with this."

"Well, I don't want him touching me again." He still grasped his body with his arms to provide some warmth.

"You can sit up front."

The house was of old brick, a Tudor three-story structure, ensconced in a wooded retreat within the enclosed gated estate. The gateway was not visible from the house hidden by the trees coursing down a winding tree arched drive. The sprawling structure sat silent in the dusk except for the beagle hound that pranced about the car as they departed the car.

"What kind of a watch dog are you?" The man at the front door of the house inquired of the hound that was paying close friendly attention to Daniel. "He doesn't take to strangers like that," he continued. "You must be Daniel. I hope my emissaries were not too harsh. They don't have too many manners. Of course, they're not used to your kind."

"Yes, I am Daniel. Bart and I seem to be good friends all ready. You are his master and John Bartolo."

"Yes. I'm John Bartolo. I am pleased that were willing to come. How did you know my dog's name?"

"It seemed to be his name," he replied as he approached the steps.

"Please come in," he invited as he offered his hand in greeting. John Bartolo was a small man but with a bearing and presence that betrayed his stature. His dark black hair clung to his scalp as you felt he would cling to a problem at hand until it was satisfactorily solved. His gray suit fit well and was double breasted such to cover the small paunch he had developed with forty eight years of heavy good living. The paunch rested on the unseen liver that was well scarred from the diet of scotch that relieved his attention to business. The hands that greeted Daniel were soft and gentle not betraying the mind that had carried the decision of life and death to enemies and disloyal associates.

The appearance was not deceptive to Daniel as he stood in the presence of a man he could tell was of immense evil. And such a man sought the gift of God's mercy.

John Bartolo ushered his guest with the lackey, Alfred, close behind into the house. "Something to drink?" he offered Daniel as he stood before recessed bar to pour himself a scotch.

"A grape juice or orange juice would be pleasant," he suggested.

"Of course. I might have expected you didn't drink the hard stuff."

"Oh, a glass of wine is not uncommon."

"It's about my wife," Bartolo began, interrupting Daniel as he handed him a glass of orange juice. "She's been ill with the fever for two months now. She's lost weight, keeps getting these strange lung infections that the doctors treat. She's been taking her medicine, the AZT and some new stuff, for four months now and she don't get better. Maybe you can do something for her. I'm about to go crazy over her. She's only forty-one and too young to die and that's the way it looks. Always been healthy. Played tennis, golf with the best. Never ran out of energy. Party all night and be ready to go. Now, she can barely lift a spoon let alone get out of bed by herself."

"Sometimes, God's will is difficult to accept."

"God's will?" Bartolo said with a rising voice of slight anger. "Look. I'm as good to the church as any one. I paid for the new stained glass windows behind the altar in the cathedral and who do you think pays the lease on the new Town Car the new archbishop drives? Anything he wants he just gotta ask me. He knows. Alfred even drives for him frequently."

"You are friends with the archbishop, Archbishop Gregory?"

"Me and him could be brothers. Best friend he's had since he came to town. Naw, this isn't God's will not with what I done for the church, even before Gregory, all the time, anything they need. Naw, this isn't God's will."

Daniel could feel the betrayal this man felt. After all, he had purchased all that he needed of God's will. Such was the vision of mankind so often. Such was the misguided vision. "You are a man of God? You worship God? You are a follower of God's commandments?" Daniel stated as a matter of fact. This man was not a man of God.

"I go every Easter. Never missed a christening."

"I see. You ask God for life in this world and do not follow God's way," he stated again.

"I do not ask anything for myself," he protested understanding what Daniel was saying. It had always nagged at his unspoken awareness that his life often came in conflict with the things he had learned as a child. But business was business. He had learned from his father and then from his uncle after his father's death on the street in Detroit that strength and the family rules were what counted and were how you kept the 'business' together. 'Every body else wanted a piece of your operation' his uncle had taught him and had taught him the family ways of controlling this world. The thought nagged again at him as he led Daniel up the stairs to Angela's bedroom or bedroom suite.

There in the dim light, the pale small woman lay propped up against soft pillows in expectation of Daniel's visit.

"You did come. You did come," she repeated as Daniel approached the bed.

Bartolo led Daniel to the bed and said, "This is Angela. Please, look into your heart and see to her."

"It is God who looks into the heart. It is God who knows what is in the heart of a person. What is in my heart is of little importance at this moment," Daniel said quietly as not to disturb the seriousness of the scene. "Yes, I am here, Angela, and you can be sure God is aware, which is more important than my presence here."

"Tell me what I should do," Bartolo asked. The tone in his voice was more a plea than a request.

"I am sure you are aware of God's way in life, of the commandments long ago brought to you. Life is to be built upon these laws in every way. You have known this all your life."

"I know. I know. I am lost. But, Angela. Angela is a child of God. She is not responsible for my misgivings."

"It is a way of great dismay. You of many talents, of many gifts of the God who you deny, who could be successful in giving to the world in so many ways have chosen to cross swords with God."

"It is too late for me," Bartolo confessed.

"It is never too late for those who see and understand. God would rather save one soul in the son's name than condemn." Daniel knelt before the bed of Angela. He reached out and clasped her hand in his. He could feel her weakness in the grasp for life that responded. At his side beside him on his knees was John Bartolo. He could feel his quaking body near.

One warm and sweaty hand of Bartolo reached out to the united hands. "Are we going to pray?" he asked. "Will he hear my voice?"

"He will hear each voice in it's own sincerity. He will hear Angela's whispers in her mind."

"Will you, will he, heal my Angela." Tears ran down the cheeks of John Bartolo. "You have saved others."

"It will be God's will. God's will is as it will be. God's gift and God's salvation is not only within this life. The glory of God may be found in the eternity." Daniel kneeled in silence to those around him. The silence was such that no one would interrupt the silence. They could not hear his inner being. 'I beseech you, my God, O Father of this world, father of the living God and the son of the father in spirit and being to look into the heart of this woman. Let thy will be done. Let the spirit of God's way come into this house. May their hearts feel the glory and the majesty of thy way.' The silence of the moment was broken as Daniel uttered, "So be it."

The face of Angela cast a smile at Daniel. Her hand grasped the hand of John Bartolo. Her voice was stronger in a distant way than expected. "Oh, John. It is so beautiful. It is more beautiful than I expected. So soft, so white and bright. I can see the way. I am coming."

"She's delirious," Bartolo declared.

She grasped John Bartolo's hand. "I am coming," she whispered. "Wait. Wait for me," her voice droned on and her hands fell limply within his.

Alarmed, Bartolo cried out, "Angela, Angela." With tears flowing upon the bed he leaned his body to embrace the now quiet Angela. "Why? Why?" he cried sobbing. "Why you, so pure, so sweet? Why not me? Why not me? I am the sinner in this house." He stood up facing Daniel. "Why have you done this? You know very well I am the sinner in this house."

"It is nothing I have done. What you have lost in this life, she has gained in God's. She shall surely know salvation. Will you?"

Bartolo turned to the door. Alfred stood awaiting him outside the doorway. "Alfred, whatever you and Max had planned for this evening, call it off. In fact, just cancel the whole job. We're not going to do things that way around here any more. Now, get me the archbishop. You and Tony go pick him up. No excuses, Angela needs him here right now."

"But it's a job for the archbishop. It's a setup scam on the pope. Max found out when he got the room number. Can you believe that? The archbishop scamming the pope," Alfred blurted.

"Not with us helping him. Who does he think he is? Get him here now," John Bartolo said in determined words. "Can you believe that?" he continued now facing Daniel.

Daniel stood silently by. He did not reply. He knew that this archbishop had strayed from his way.

Bartolo ignored him for the moment as he retreated to Angela's bedside. "Well, God took you away from me. I wasn't good enough for you. But God, how I loved you." He cried and again fell on his knees and across the bed to take her in his arms. The tears flowed as his voice croaked haltingly, "God knew how much I loved you and took you any way. Maybe you were just better than me. Well, you were better than me. Well, this archbishop is going to give you the best funeral anyone ever had." He stopped for a moment, stood up and faced Daniel. "Well, you couldn't save her."

"It was not my doing. God will lead her to a better place."

"That's what I'm asking. Is there any hope for me that I might see her again, you know, when I'm gone?

"Is it true what you said about his saving one soul like my miserable sinning soul rather than condemning?" he continued as tears ran down his cheeks.

"The lord will know what is in your heart and soul, truly. Pray to the lord that you might know the way, know the path to the peace you seek. Words that come from the heart, enter the heart. He will hear and he will know."

CHAPTER 28

The University of Michigan football stadium was the largest venue that Peter Stone could engage in the Detroit area. The stadium could seat 110,000 in the stands with 20,000 added to the field. The combined seating of the Silverdome, primarily a football venue, would only reach 90,000 compared to the total 130,000 of the university stadium. He had pushed every lever and pulled every string that the Abbott agency could possibly entangle to get permission to lease the facility. The availability of the stadium at the end of August was not the primary question. There were just too many people who didn't believe that a public university stadium was the place to hold a religious convocation, a Roman Catholic convocation.

His genius was in such a manipulation. Charles Evans was a cog in the manipulation. Evans description of an ecumenical prayer service led by the all-embracing Pope John Alexander had been a front-page series. He had reported the morning and afternoon meetings. Each morning meeting had been with a Christian sect, the Anglican, the Methodists, the Unitarians and others. Each afternoon meeting had been with a non-Christian forum, Hindu, Moslem, Jewish. Dialogue of individual leaders was part of his daily series. He had reported the dialogue with Islam, and in the next paragraph he quoted words of the local imam of the mosque in Dearborn.

Charles Evans was in his glory. He was the ultimate source. Peter Stone created the word of ecumenism in Charles Evans to be read and distributed to the world as choreographed by Stone.

The only genius that Peter Stone felt deficient in was choosing an open weather venue. Rain could mar the day. The Michigan football stadium compared to the enclosed Silverdome carried that risk.

The press had been mobilized. Stone knew well the saying, if 'it' didn't happen in New York or Washington, 'it' didn't happen. The word was from Peter Stone's group that if the media didn't field this gem into New York and Washington, the news as 'it' happened would reach them from London, Paris, Rome, Cairo, Bangkok and even the moon for this event was to be wired, rewired, condensed, canned, talk-showed, evening news promoted and internet transmitted. The world was the stage because of the magic of technology.

Sam Crawford had requisitioned the van from the newspaper to transport the three. Daniel appeared at the curbside of his house at the appointed time, ten-fifteen, to await the van. Edgar J.L., lunch bag in hand, stood there with him.

"Are you sure I can go with you?" Edgar inquired.

"You will be welcome," Daniel assured him.

"Holy cow," Evans evoked. "He's got that black kid with him."

Sam quipped, "Why, you almost swore, Charles."

"Well, how are we going to get the kid into the show?"

Sam slid the side door open. Daniel ushered Edgar J.L. into the van. As he closed the door, he greeted, "Good morning Sam and Mr. Evans. This will be a wonderful day."

"Morning, Daniel," Crawford returned.

"How are supposed to get the kid in?" inquired the agitated Evans.

"I'm sure a way will be provided," Daniel responded.

"I doubt it," Evans retorted.

Sam Crawford had set his sight on the trip to Ann Arbor. "Yes sir," he began, "this is going to be a great day," ignoring Evans protestation.

"It will take more than an hour to get there?" inquired Daniel.

"No problem. You sit back and leave the driving to me. Know the way like the back of my hand," he assured. "Why, this is just a practice run. Football season starts in two weeks. It'll be just like old times and we're going to have a great season. This quarterback, Benson, may be just a sophomore but if coach Harris had played him more last year, we would have gone to the Rose Bowl again instead of ending up third in the nation. We would have beat Ohio State like we will this year with this kid."

The silence evoked Sam to question, "What, no football fans here today. All religious, eh? Well, damn," he concluded.

"I bet you right, Mr. Crawford," Edgar J.L. spoke up. "And I bet he throw a lot of passes to Barry this year."

"Barry? Barry who?"

"You don't know Barry, Barry Wadkins? He be faster than A.Z., I bet. Spent his freshmen year in junior college, grades you know. Bet he start right off this year."

"What makes you think he'll be as good as A.Z.Carter. You're not old enough to know A.Z. He was the best."

"People say, Mr. Crawford. People say. He's from my high school."

"I still don't know how we're going to get you in when we get there, Edgar," Evans said preoccupied with the problem. "They don't have enough tickets for those who requested them."

"I will speak to Mr. Stone's people when we get there," Daniel stated.

"Then maybe we'll make that your job," Evans concluded with a soft smirk on his face. "How come the pope has taken a fancy to you, anyway? Asking, specifically, that you be invited, too."

"It would be a long story," Daniel replied.

"Well, we certainly have most of an hour to hear this story," Evans informed Daniel almost as a challenge.

Daniel didn't reply to the challenge seemingly presented by Evans.

"I thought so. There isn't much of a story."

"I don't think you would believe the story. You may be the religious editor but it would take more faith that I think you have," Sam taunted.

"You mean you believe the stuff you've written? I told Gilly to hold you down, that I knew more about these things than you."

"You weren't there. You wouldn't know the truth."

"I just print the facts, the living history."

"You're embarrassing our guest, Charles."

"It's all right, Sam Crawford," Daniel interjected. "I believe that my journey is ended today."

"What's that supposed to mean?" Evans inquired not understanding what it might mean.

"Just what he said, Charles. I hope that's not the case."

The van transporting the select 'media' group had coursed its way amidst the vast caravan advancing on Ann Arbor from all directions. The event was unremarkable to the involved aggregate of local, county, state and private police. It was a re-enactment of football Saturday at the University of Michigan except this was a Tuesday chosen to avoid a holy day of any religion across of time zones of the world.

They arrived as directed an hour before opening ceremonies. The parking lots already were filled to the brim with buses.

The buses were a sundry of vehicles varying from large greyhound transports, to small yellow school or parish buses. Buses badly in need of repair had made the journey. License plates and banners told the story. Not only buses from Michigan but vehicles from other states, Indiana, Kansas, California, from Ontario, Manitoba and Mexico would have their own stories to tell.

Perhaps the god of genius, unspoken of the successful public relations specialists, brought the favor of a partially cloudy sun laden day to Peter Stone. Without pause to thank the calendar or other entity for such a day he watched as the day unfolded.

Crawford had maneuvered the van into a familiar parking spot. "There are more people milling around here than any football game. There, that's the Abbott public relations van parked by gate five," Sam indicated to Daniel.

"I'll be just a moment," Daniel informed the group. "Please wait for me."

Several minutes later Daniel exited the van.

"You got the ticket?" Sam inquired of Daniel and casting a knowing smile toward Charles Evans.

"Indeed," handing the ticket to Edgar J.L.

"Well, I'll be damned," Evans blurted who settled back in his seat while twirling his wax mustache end in a measure of disdain.

"Well, damnation," Crawford said with a laugh. "You can swear, Charles."

"Never believed for a moment," Evans in condescending confession conceded, "that you would be able to get a ticket."

"Things are meant to be," Daniel explained simply as they passed through the gate receiving directions to the aisle of access to their seating.

"What did the ticket taker say?" Charles asked.

"He said aisle eight. He said only people with green tickets would use aisle eight like green tickets were special. That's to the left toward the fifty yard line."

As they entered the stadium, they were a minuscule portion of the nearly filled football stadium. Few empty seats could be identified in the stands. A bloc of red decorated cleric fronted a black and brown-garbed bloc. "Forty-five minutes before show time," Sam noted, "and almost a full house."

"Never saw so many priests in red sashes," Evans noted as they climbed the aisle opening only to then descend toward the field area.

"Like that, Charles, red caps, red sashes, bishops, archbishops, cardinals," as he pointed to the quadrangle of partially filled seats to the right and adjacent to the partially canopied stage area erected over the track on the fifty yard line at the west side of the football field. "Over eight hundred, a field of red, all the right hand of Pope John Alexander."

Sam Crawford led the way. They approached the canopied area and veered to the right.

"This can't be the way. All the red is this way."

"Trust me. Look at your program. These are rows A, area four, seats 37 to 40. That's where we're heading."

"We must be on the other side."

"Nope. Look over there. That's his guest side, the ecumenical side. See, all sorts there, Orthodox, others in various religious garb, even some women."

"Yes." exclaimed Charles," Rabbis, all sorts of collars. Why there's the Moslem imam and Swami Bhdara."

"You know all those people?"

"Personally," Evans avowed exuding the pride of his professional expanse. "Also most of them are recognized on page six of the program."

"Well, these are our seats," Sam said. "The first seats of the box. First row."

"Must be. Hello, Elbert. You been here long? Got many photos yet? How come we rate first row seats? This is Daniel and his friend Edgar J.L., Elbert."

Elbert rested his camera on his rotund abdomen, looked at Daniel, and asked, "This the fella you been writing about, eh, Sam?"

Daniel nodded his head in recognition of Evans' introduction.

Edgar J.L. stepped forward to greet Elbert. Elbert ignored him, raised his camera, made a few adjustments and took a photo of Daniel. "I don't know why we rate first row seats, Sam, but I don't have to wrestle with the media group over there," he directed with a broad smile pointing to the opposite corner of the platform area. Dozens of media were localized there, photographers, people with microphones aimed at the stage, while to one side of them in front was a bank of television cameras. A solitary television camera was on an elevated stand. "That's Peter Stone's pool camera, it's hooked into a bank of cameras placed inside and outside the stadium. Annette is inside the truck monitoring and controlling the feed with the producer. It's the only camera with direct sound from the platform."

The choir, in their gold tunics, occupied a block in the stands behind the podium. Eight hundred voices had been gathered under the baton of Mischa Zatkof. They were gathered in groups of four or eight from any and every religious faith. Alto, bass, tenor, soprano molded their fervor and individuality into a giant religious musical epoch. Magically energetically Zatkof had whacked three dozen batons to pieces before his speaker on his music stand cajoling the eager participants to the discipline that finally brought a smile to his frenzied furrowed face. The evening and early morning practices had resulted in eight presentations that would be repeated as necessary to fill out the prelude and the ceremony. The amalgamated chorus seated above the podium electronically filled the stadium with a musical religious rendition that well set the mood for this moment. Technicians had positioned and repositioned their variety of microphones that the chorus would funnel with clarity to the pickup of the pool television.

"Where are the two local cleric reporters?"

"Word is they won't be in the seats," Elbert informed. "And Stone and his aide will be a while, too much to do."

"It's only thirty minutes before things begin," the reporter announced. "This could be a hotter day," he continued. "The clouds help a lot." He ran his thumb beneath his limp collar and undid the shirt button. He was tempted to take the blue seersucker jacket off.

Another helicopter had roared over the stadium with its advertisement banner trailing behind.

The platform only a few feet away was draped in broad stripes of yellow and white. There were six chairs on the dais. The central chair was elevated a single step above the others. The chairs were beneath an oblong bright yellow canopy to protect from the blaze of the noonday sun.

Eight gray suited men already were standing alertly at intervals surrounding the platform. The one in the immediate front was active with the communication radio. He rose momentarily and took a few steps toward the red mottled seats. He stopped until he attracted the attention of single person, then bowed slightly from the waist and nodded his head and smiled in recognition. Many red-capped guests waved back to the greeting as did Sam Crawford. Only Daniel stood up and mirrored the recognition with a slight bow and nodded greeting.

"Who is that?" inquired Evans.

"That is the commandant of the Swiss Guard," Sam Crawford replied.

Daniel remained silent once again seated.

Commandant Raymond was now pacing back and forth in front of the platform in continuous radio communication. He walked to each corner security guard speaking in French.

Only Daniel could understand his angry announcement, "Another one of his spontaneous foolish impulses. He wants to greet the people entering from the end zone under the goal posts. The plan had been for him to be transported to the podium. Instead of coming from out behind the podium, he's coming from the end of the stadium, walking," he was telling the other plain clothes guards.

Raymond's reason for discomfort was soon discerned as a roar from the crowd and attention of the stadium was directed to the north end of the stadium. Raymond and the congregation watched the television screens as Pope John Alexander led a small procession of bishops down the center aisle of the field. Raymond could count the sixty yards he would travel by the beats of his heart relieved only by the phalanx of gray suited security guards that surrounded John Alexander and enforced the restraining rope line that he had insisted be erected to delineate the seating from the passageways of the stadium floor seating. He watched as John Alexander slowly made his way carrying the cross of St. Stephen at intervals of six or seven yards, then stopping to turn and bless the crowd to each side. Conductor Zatkof urged his choir into a symphony of reception in competition to the continuous progression of applause and cries of adulation from the congregation. Raymond was continuously in communication. The entire stadium was standing. Raymond checked his watch. It had taken thirteen minutes for his ward to reach the fifty yard line and turn toward the podium. He breathed a momentary sigh of relief. The journey was nearly over. The final twenty yards to the podium were a tedious four minutes as John Alexander stopped at intervals, greeted and blessed the crowd. John Alexander smiled as he stopped before the podium and winked at commandant Raymond. Raymond smiled, bowed to his ward pope and saluted. John Alexander turned to the right and blessed the crowd. He turned to his left and blessed the reds and bowed gently in that direction with eyes fixed on one person. Daniel, standing again as everyone else, bowed slightly in acknowledgment. The pope ascended the podium followed by the bishops and archbishops who would attend him on the podium. Conductor Zatkof led his combined ecumenical chorus as the penetrating alto voice of the Jewish woman cantor. She offered a rendition from Psalm 118, 'Blessed is he who comes in his name' to begin the formal proceedings. The applause receded as Pope John Alexander was seated with his podium consorts. The chorus became the dominant feature as the crowd settled in their seats in anticipation.

John Alexander, pope less than a year, sat in the giant gilded chair that someone thought was appropriate for the vicar apostle of the Roman Catholic

Church. It had been designed especially for this event that would be seen by millions throughout the world in person by video in theaters and arenas nearby, in areas and theaters throughout the world, in home television, transmitted by internet, with delayed representations to those fast asleep or at work. Even in those parts of the world usually fast asleep, many rose in the night to be part of this historic event.

The mobilization of the vast world of communications, of the vast array of satellites encircling the earth, challenging heaven's airways was no accident.

The directions of John Alexander had been to leave no part of the earth bare to the word, the living word, which would be presented. The love and hope embodied in the spirit would be able to be heard in every living corner. It was all written out. He would speak of violence, violence among landowners and nations, among segments of nations, of classes of society, of religious violence. Violence is not the way of the spirit. He would speak of violence in society, man against man in the street, man against the defenseless unborn, the agony that this caused God, the God of all men, the violence of man against the condemned criminal.

He would speak of justice, social justice where love of the family was the backbone of a just society, where love for the brother in need was recognized and the gift of God's dignity supplied by sharing one's possessions.

He would then speak of the love and hope.

Rabbi Edward Teller had gathered his seminar class on world religions to view the much promoted media presentation of Pope John Alexander's ecumenical congregation. They gathered before the large television set in the commons room. Rabbi Teller was an advocate of information. He had often said that the more information one has the more confident one can be of their own position in life and more understanding of other people and their position. He pointed out this to the class. "You will see that this leader of the Catholic people has continued the crusade of his predecessor in the call for unity among the various factions or sects of the Christian world. At the same time he has continued the tradition of increased dialogue among the various religions of the world, as we are studying, so that we may better understand and appreciate one another. As I have said before, hundreds of millions of people of the world do not believe as we do. As you know, they are as sincere in their beliefs as we. We have discussed the major religions of the world and some of the reasons why so many religions exist with primary concentrations in various parts of the world. One of the reasons I believe this educational experience is important is that within this country we are experiencing a large increase in the various religions principally within our metropolitan areas. These people will be part of your everyday life, if not personally, in your business or professional activities."

"Will there not conflict among the fervent of various religions as has been occurring around the world?" one student asked.

"Fortunately, as you know this country is built upon the respect and tolerance of all individuals for each person's individual views, including religious preference. Of course, the process is not perfect and individual animosities do rear their ugly head. Look," he digressed, "they are viewing the people there. There are leaders of many religions. There. There are several rabbis. I cannot make out who they are on the screen but I know that Rabbi Miller is there. There. They have passed several priests of the eastern rite. You remember our discussions of the orthodox churches." The screen redirected to the podium. "It appears they are preparing to begin the proceedings. It was a privilege to have our cantor singing. I will have to write to Rabbi Miller."

"One chair on the platform is empty," Evans noted.

"If you read the program Archbishop Gregory is supposed to read scripture. I don't see him up there," Crawford observed.

"No, he isn't there," Evans agreed. "That's Cardinals Vittorio and Conolly to his right. I don't know the archbishop to his left."

Daniel Adams sat quietly. He now knew that this was the acro moment of this visit. The intertwining of people and of events during the past several weeks would culminate in the next moments. A reason for these events would now become clear. The meeting of the individuals, the simple and the complex events of the players, would lead to the propulsion of the messenger, Daniel Adams, into the midst of an event that would challenge and confirm the belief of all who bore witness to the moment.

The chorus abruptly ceased, not musically, but abruptly because it signaled an end to the prelude. The silence heralded the onset of this meeting of flesh and souls.

Pope John Alexander began with the introduction. Seated in the grand throne chair that he silently had disavowed as too splendant he read from the prepared script. He read in a slow calculated set of phrases such that each thought could remain a landmark to the listener. "My friends, here and around the world, we meet in the glory of God. We meet in the glory of the God of man before Abraham. We meet in the glory of the God of Abraham and of David. We celebrate the hope and joy of the salvation of Christ our Lord.

"As we proceed from history and to tomorrow to oblige the laws of Moses as ordained by Yahweh, I greet all the Christian followers and all the Catholic faithful professed as your shepherd.

"We search for a common answer to mankind's relationship on earth rooted in the principles of our common pursuits of justice not only within our Christian teaching but to reach a mutual understanding with our non-Christian brothers." He lowered the text signaling the end of his introduction. He would have more to say later. He looked out surveying the vast assembly. They rose in thunderous applause and waved their banners reflecting their enthusiasm.

"Powerful. Powerful words," Charles Evans proclaimed. "The true shepherd of the people," he added.

Archbishop Paul Gregory was at the moment not a man of ecclesiastic inclinations. In fact, he was watching the proceedings on television at the funeral home of Angela Bartolo. His status bordered on rage as he repeated for the now uncountable time, "You can't do this to me. I'm the archbishop. I'm supposed to be there on the podium with Pope John Alexander. I am to read scripture."

John Bartolo explained again as he had at each other moment of protestation, "You are lucky to be here all in one piece. When Alfred explained last night what you had planned for the pope last night, I found out just what kind of a person you were. I have decided your penance for such a dastardly deed. You will be here as long as I decide you'll be and pray for my Angela. An archbishop must have some legitimate purpose. It damned well isn't to play dirty tricks on the pope so it might as well be what you were intended for so you just keep praying for my Angela. You're just lucky you even get to see the pope's service on television."

"You will suffer at the lord's hand for this."

"The lord has greater things to chastise me over."

"The police will be all over you for this. This is kidnapping you know?"

"Don't bother me with your prattle. Your job is to be on your knees praying for my Angela. Now pray. You can read your scripture right here."

The funeral director again interrupted the proceedings with the delivery of more flowers. "More flowers," he indicated as he and an assistant carried multiple flower arrangements to add to those already present. "At this rate," he continued, "this will be the largest funeral ever here." He spoke to the archbishop with admiration, "And we have never had the clergy so involved in a funeral, especially an archbishop."

John Bartolo spoke up to Paul Gregory, "See? My Angela is loved by everyone and she is a truly holy woman."

The choir responded in a prolonged liturgical refrain featuring the alto and bass sections.

Excited conversations appeared to be exchanged on the platform.

"They're trying to decide who will do the scripture reading," Sam Crawford ventured. "The program indicates Gregory, the host Archbishop Gregory, would read but he isn't here."

A bishop rose. He looked out to the crowd and to the entryway to the rear and side of the podium in expectation of the missing archbishop. With some hesitation he began the short walk to the lectern.

There was a flutter of commotion at the base of the podium. Daniel Adams had left his seat and had advanced toward the steps at the center of the podium. Commandant Raymond had taken a step forward to intercept him. His hand was positioned inside his gray suit coat.

Words were spoken from the podium. Raymond looked back to see Pope John Alexander wave his hand indicating him to move away, to allow Daniel to proceed.

The bishop stopped his preparations at the lectern in confusion to watch Daniel ascend the four steps up onto the platform.

There were words of complaint from the reds behind. Murmuring spread through the congregation. Someone shouted, 'Get him off the altar'. Charles Evans exclaimed to Crawford, "What does he think he's doing?"

Sam had the smile of knowing triumph on his face. "You are watching destiny in living color, Charles."

"He must be crazy, out of his mind."

"Pope John Alexander might be too. He's told his security not to interfere with this apparent intruder, Daniel Adams."

The pool television announcer narrating the proceedings took his cue from the producer. "This is truly extraordinary. A spectator has ascended onto the podium. There has been no interference by the security. You must know that security is extremely cautious and concerned about the safety of the pope so this is a remarkable occurrence. It appears that Pope John Alexander has indicated to the security to allow this man passage. As already described, the head of security, the commandant of the Vatican Guard, secures the central steps and has stepped aside to allow this man's approach.

"As you can see this is a slightly build man perhaps in his forties, dressed in simple informal clothing, white cotton or denim trousers and a white collarless long sleeve shirt seemingly quite inappropriate for this spectacular occasion. He has a short beard. He is now slowly approaching the pope."

Daniel had approached Pope John Alexander who received his uninvited guest, almost as if expected. The bond between the two, Pope John Alexander, primate of the Christian world, and Daniel, the messenger eternal, allowed this momentous occurrence to proceed. John Alexander knew deep within that this was no accident. The world would speak in protest or watch in amazement at the unfolding events. Two people knew of the mystical tie that traversed the understanding of men that bound these two men together. The first, Sam Crawford, surmised and believed that Daniel and John Alexander were bound by the hand of fate, a destiny, and if asked he would identify that hand as the long hand of God, the God that he had ignored, even disavowed. The second, Commandant Raymond, recognized that his ward, the pope, revered this man for some historical mysterious reason and trusted him. He had seen the cloud form during the racquetball court assault and knew that Daniel had been associated with the immobilization of the assailant. He didn't fully understand how all this had happened but he was quick to show the same deference demonstrated by John Alexander.

Edgar J.L. proclaimed quietly to Crawford, "He be a holy man."

"You may be right, but please be quiet."

John Alexander nodded, smiled and with his blessing said, "Proceed, my friend," and presented his hand toward the lectern.

Cardinal Vittorio expressed his displeasure to the pope, "Your Holiness, this is preposterous."

"It is done. It is done."

Daniel walked slowly to the lectern. The large bible sat on the lectern. The bishop had accompanied him to the lectern at the urging of John Alexander with the whispered instructions to assist in opening the book to the proper place, if necessary. Daniel looked out to the assembly and adjusted the microphone.

The assembly had ceased the rumble and murmuring. Even the reds now sat in anticipatory silence. The stranger in white stood in preparation. As he turned in each direction to survey them, each person was sure that he had greeted them personally, that their eyes had met his eyes and that his smile was meant for each of them individually.

The bishop slipped a finger below the green ribbon, opened the book to the previously identified passage and returned to his seat.

Daniel raised his hand, once again recognizing the congregation slowly from his left to his far right. His words spread as a blanket of comfort and seemingly embraced each spectator individually, "Peace be with you."

Each spectator felt a bond toward this stranger who was now identified as a friend.

There was a widespread scattered response, as usual, "And peace be with you." Each individual felt they had personally, individually, exchanged greetings with this enchanting stranger, now friend.

He continued.

"*A reading from the fourth letter from the teacher, Clement, to the congregation at Alexandria.*"

There was a stirring on the podium.

The archbishop adjacent to Cardinal Vittorio protested, "I opened to the proper reading."

Cardinal Vittorio threw his hands up. "There is no such thing in our bible. This is preposterous."

Pope John Alexander waved his hand in quietude. "Let us listen," he prompted, he instructed.

In Brooklyn, Rabbi Teller sat with associate rabbis and students. "Who is this Clement?" he was asked.

"We will know. We will know. We will listen and we will know which Clement he refers to. There were several Clements in early Christian history. This is very strange, unbelievable. This is no ordinary man that speaks. We will listen."

The television commentator observed, "This continues to be extraordinary and mysterious. The stranger has begun a reading that is different than that indicated in the program. Do you know this passage, Monsignor Taylor?" he asked of his official clerical adviser.

"No, I don't. We are witnessing something either very extraordinary, as you say, or a tragedy."

"Our theological consultant is as mystified as we are."

Archbishop Gregory had stopped praying as the remarkable events unfolded. His outrage of his detainment by John Bartolo was now replaced by a new out burst. "The heretic. That man is the devil himself. They must get him out of there," he shouted. "Get him out. Get him out," he shouted.

The funeral director with his aides and Bartolo were quickly upon the archbishop. The director whispered, "This is a place of worship, your eminence."

Bartolo was less kind. He grabbed the archbishop by the scruff of the collar and while dragging him from the room declared, "Shut the hell up in front of my Angela. You are acting like the devil yourself." As he deposited him on the floor in a service room adjacent to the viewing room he added, "That man you call a heretic is a holy man. Where do your evil thoughts come from? I don't think I even want you to be praying for my Angela. You just stay here until I decide what to do with you."

Archbishop Gregory rose unsteadily from the floor. "You can't get away with this."

Bartolo left the room.

Alfred stood silently to one side as a silent praetorian guard with his arms folded before him watching the irate cleric.

Daniel continued.

"I write to you again from my exile in Cappadocia. Great humility attends my message for I know how you suffer under the legions of Septimus Severus.

"It is for this reason that I relate an extraordinary experience of faith and finding in the salvation of the bountiful love of the living church of the Body of Christ. It is with joy that this witness is brought to you, that it may reinforce your refuge."

Daniel stopped for a moment. He stood in a silent world before one hundred thirty thousand entranced pairs of eyes. Untold millions watched the drama unfold in their homes, meeting places, department stores and places of worship on television or internet.

Rabbi Teller informed his students. "Those are the words that he speaks of Clement, a gentile Christian, of the second century. He had been exiled from Alexandria fleeing to Cappadocia because of his conflict as a Christian with the occupying Roman forces. He was a teacher of Christian doctrine at the end of the first century. I have heard of Clement's first and second letters to the Alexandrians but none others. It is important to study history in addition to our own writings and history." He paused for a moment and continued, "This man who speaks is a mystery however. He is not a cleric and he is more than a teacher, a rabbi, even. He commands the attention of the Pope of Rome and the people."

Daniel continued the reading.
The student, Elias, and I were returning from a prayer meeting at the home of an elder.
A great cloud appeared at the base of the mountain. An angel shone forth from the cloud and held it's hands up saying, "Wait and hear the word of the Lord."
Elias, a devout student, and I fell to the ground and I clasped my hands before my eyes.
"It is he. He has come in judgment," proclaimed Elias.
The angel responded, "Fear not. Judgment is not today."
I looked up as a new voice spoke to us from the cloud. "O Israel, my people, why have you forsaken me?
"You turn away from the commandments.
"You tempt the darkness to destroy you.
"I have given to you a new temple, a new land, of salvation, O Israel, a new land with its temple within your hearts and souls, until I come again.
"Before my return, in your darkest hours, when the righteous despair at the greatness of the transgressions of the world, I will send you a messenger. He will lead you back to the commandments."

The personage of Daniel became cloaked in a white tunic that reached to the floor and glowed whiter than the daylight as he thrust his hands to the sky and he continued to read the words of Clement,
"Behold," the angel said, "As the Lord made the earth and the heavens, his power is great.
"Day will become night."
And then only the brightness of the angel did light the shadows of the day as the sun became clothed in the cloud and darkness was all around. I felt the strength of God about me in the darkness. Elias moaned with his eyes still shielded by the clothing, "I am not worthy."

The world about the stadium and congregation beheld a sudden change. As if there were an eclipse without the moon. The sky darkened. The sun faded. Darkness filled the stadium. Darkness filled the world. The moon failed to appear. The heavens shown only the brilliance of the stars.

The coldness of the dark began to envelope the congregation. This was as frightening as the darkness.

Shrieks and prayers, distasteful epitaphs were shouted from multiple areas of the congregation. "Hell and damnation." "This is the end." "It's judgment day." Crying, moaning, and shrieks filled the new night with the presence of fear. Individuals could be noted fleeing the arena as shadows in the darkness. The voice of Daniel penetrated. The fear of the congregation became transfixed on the figure that now glowed brightly white in the darkness.

The words of Clement continued,

The cold of the darkness slowed my thoughts and I fell to the ground asleep.

There did I see and hear my Savior. Though his lips did not move.

"*My child, you of the righteous, you, as you follow my son, shall know my kingdom as a temple within your heart.*

"*Be not tempted by the path of darkness. Place the commandments within your heart.*"

Rabbi Teller stood before his gathered group, as darkness filled the room. He raised his hands in supplication. "Listen to the words of the prophet Joel and Amos. Heed the word of the Lord. Bring forth the commandments that we might live." Tears streamed down his face. "How have we failed you? O, my Lord. We, your chosen, have suffered in the darkness. How have we failed you?"

He sat down in the darkness with his head in his hands still watching the television screen with luminescent figure of Daniel, the mysterious Daniel there. He quietly asked above the tears, "What is this temple within our heart? Have we been searching in error?"

As quickly as the stars had become the light of the new night the stars of darkness faded to the brilliance of the returning sun. The forum again was cast into day. The world was a new day. The warmth of the sun returned. The moon on the other side of the world hallowed the light as the sun's messenger.

Daniel's voice still penetrated the congregation and held the world in contemplation.

"*How shall I know?" I asked. "Oh, my lord.*"

The angel touched my shoulder. "You will know. The messenger of God shall fill your spirit with the truth of love and hope. You will know and see the transfiguration."

I awoke as Elias did. The day was again light and we were once again warm.

Elias once again was fearful that the end had come. I told him of the vision and the message that he had not experienced.

Oh, brothers of Alexandria, this is the word of the Lord. He again gives us refuge in his son. He again promises us the new temple, the new nation, within our hearts and souls.

As I have said before, brothers! We must think of Jesus Christ as we do of God, as the judge of the living and the dead.

These words of God tell of those who transgress and that in the time of that darkness of transgression and sin in the world he will send a messenger to lead them to the path from that darkness.

Even the unbelievers shall see his glory again that they may find this path before his coming.

These are his words. Praise.

The brightness of the personage of Daniel glowed in the daylight.

The earthly fixation of Daniel became a vision as the gleaming white cloud that was Daniel spread from the podium and effused into the congregation as a stream of light.

The figure of Daniel passed in recognition before each and every one of the congregation. Each individual came face to face with the gleaming white personage of Daniel.

Edgar J.L. clutched the arm of Sam Crawford. "Amen, oh, precious Jesus," he whispered afraid to raise his voice. Tears streamed down Sam Crawford's face.

Rabbi Miller, face to face, raised his hand as to ward off the light. The vision of Daniel passed through the body of Rabbi Miller. He shuddered at the chill of the revelation.

Swami Bhdara stretched out his hands to embrace the encounter, whispering. "Enter my soul, with love." The vision of Daniel passed through the body of the guru. His body flailed at the recognition and he slumped to the ground.

Edgar J.L. fell upon his knees to face the flowing whiteness of love and hope. He folded his hands in prayer. The vision of Daniel passed through. Tears flowed from Edgar J.L. He rose up as his body in shrieking prayer uttered, "Amen. Hallelujah."

Sam Crawford placed his hands to his eyes. The vision of Daniel passed through. He fell to his knees. His mind felt the chill and spoke to his soul. "Oh, my God."

Rabbi Teller watched the scene. "The stadium is filled with His holy being. This speaker is indeed a messenger of God. He is no ordinary man."

He watched as the glow that filled the stadium receded.

The ethereal whiteness of the personage Daniel slowly faded. The man, Daniel, again in his white trousers and collarless shirt, stood before the lectern. The congregation remained in awe of the experience. Some sat with their hands to their face, as though touching themselves to assure of their own awareness. Others stood searching their neighbors for explanation and understanding. Others kneeled in profession or confession. Several who had fled the stadium in fear now returned. No one could take his eyes from the speaker.

Daniel raised his hands again to the sky. His voice penetrated the new stillness. "This is the word of God, in unity with his Son, the Living Word of Jesus Christ."

Avid responses from the congregation of "Amen," "Thanks be to God." The bewildered director Mischa Zatkof led his ensemble of eight hundred voices in the programmed scheduled selection. The sounds resonated throughout the assembly.

Daniel raised his hands and his eyes once again met each and every person who looked upon him. The pool camera zoomed in upon his face. Each person around the world at home, gathered in their meeting places, in department stores everywhere, who had been entranced by this unexpected extraordinary experience looked into the eyes of Daniel, saw, and knew that they had personally received the message of joy and hope that he delivered.

"Peace be with you," he concluded.

The one hundred and thirty thousand in attendance and the millions around the world watched the final scene unfold.

Daniel turned and slowly walked toward Pope John Alexander. He stopped a step before him. As if in expectation, Pope John Alexander stepped forward and raised his hands to the sky to join those of Daniel. Visibly, slowly, that all might see, if not understand, Daniel continued his journey and in one step the magic, the mystery, became fulfilled before the watching world. Daniel stepped into the presence and being of Pope John Alexander and was gone. And was gone. Daniel and Pope John Alexander now appeared as one.

Words of adulation, amazement, despair filtered from the assembly.

Pope John Alexander stepped forward, making the sign of the cross to the people in a low tone that fused with the congregation and began. "Let us pray."

The television announcer who in abject concentration on the unfolding seen had ignored the prompting of his producer now seemed to awaken from some sort of trance as he had truly been entranced by the scene before him. "This is the most amazing occurrence I have ever been associated with in all my eighteen years of broadcasting. We have just experienced an extraordinary exposition of a religious event for which I have no adequate explanation. From the audience came a man, a nondescript man, who led a religious event that has never occurred before. His message, in some way, called upon God to cast the world into darkness. Oh my, I just cannot go on. The majesty of what just happened is beyond imagination. Oh my. Monsignor, can you explain, can you tell us what has happened here? Oh my. I am sorry. The monsignor is praying. I cannot disturb him. I will now send this broadcast back to the station."

Rabbi Teller turned to his students. "You have just witnessed the union of the messenger of God with the pope. Pope John Alexander is truly a messenger of God. May the world accept the truth of this message. The kingdom of God is not a place, not a land. It is a temple within our hearts. Let us go forth to reaffirm God's commandments."

0-595-30731-0

Printed in the United States
16149LVS00002B/297